Lost and Found
at
Sun Market

Michael
James
Preston

To all the named and unnamed folks throughout the years that shared their joys and pains with me, and who allowed me into their lives.
And, always, to my wife and children, with my deepest love and gratitude.

Acknowledgements

My deepest thanks to Karen Lone Hill for her feedback and information regarding Oglala Lakota traditions and the Pine Ridge Reservation. Any errors related to the people or place are strictly and entirely mine.

And my gratitude, as always, to Wendy Lady, a wonderful editor and even better person.

PROLOGUE

Shit.

Lila had just started counting the thin wad of bills she had grabbed from the bottom of the silverware drawer when she heard murmuring voices outside the trailer. Snot was dripping from her nose, but she forced herself not to snuffle and wiped her face with the back of her army surplus jacket, then shoved the money into her pack.

She knew she should leave immediately but found herself back in the living room, squatting next to the body of her foster-mother who stared sightlessly ahead; the congealed and drying blood around the bullet hole in her forehead gave the impression of a third, malevolent eye. Lila swallowed bile as she looked at the husk of the woman who had raised her, anger and grief warring inside her. She reached out tentatively, her hand trembling, and closed Mama Elise's eyes, then gave a small gasp when they slowly opened again.

The mumbled voices were now coming from just outside, and Lila pivoted in panic as the door handle jiggled. From long experience, she knew that regardless of reality, she would be blamed for what had happened here.

Lila looked back at the body of the only person who had ever shown her compassion and took a deep breath as she tried to steady herself. Her fingers brushed gently across the dead woman's cheek and whispered words she had rarely used when her foster-mother was alive.

I love you, Mama.

As the door handle rattled again and the voices took on a frustrated, angry tone, she picked up the backpack and headed for the small bathroom. Climbing up onto the toilet, she began yanking on the small high window above it that faced the back of the trailer, but years of multiple coats of paint kept it sealed. The voices outside stopped, and she waited, silently, hoping whoever it was had given up.

She hit her head on the mold spotted ceiling when the pounding started, which was soon followed by the sound of metal and wood breaking.

Lila reached down and grabbed her pack and used it to smash through the window, pushing it through onto the hard packed dirt outside. She swung her leg up onto the frame as she pulled the rest of her body up and through the small, jagged opening, letting out a sharp cry as glass dug into her calf.

There was a dark stain on her jeans surrounding a large shard of glass protruding through her pants. Cursing, she pulled the glass out, grunting at the searing pain. The voices were now inside the trailer and yelling.

She had taken a bus to get to Pine Ridge, as she always did on her weekly visits, but waiting for the next bus back to Rapid City, even assuming she could make it the two miles to the station with her hurt leg and without being seen, didn't strike her as a particularly good idea.

The area around Mama Elise's trailer was mostly bare ground with scrub growth and trailers interspersed with a few worn, small houses. She squinted at Leonard Stern's mobile home two doors down. His old motor scooter leaned against the side of a large wooden spool that Leonard used as an outside table. Lila limped over and saw the key sitting in the ignition.

With effort, Lila mounted the scooter, biting her lip as she swung her damaged leg over the seat, and reached for the key.

"Hey, that's her! Come back here!"

The voices weren't familiar, but the tone was. Lila turned the key, thanked the spirit of Mama Elise as the little engine sputtered to life, and cranked the handle accelerator all the way. The moped started slow, and she wondered if whoever had been at the trailer would soon grip her shoulder after a leisurely stroll to catch her, but her new ride bucked its way through gears, and she was quickly zig-zagging around the neighboring trailers at forty. She made her way toward the main road that would lead off Pine Ridge Reservation as the voices faded beneath the sound of her ride.

She knew she couldn't go back to her tiny studio apartment in Rapid City. That would be too obvious. As she turned out onto Grass Creek Road, she decided heading east would be best. Her entire life was between Pine Ridge and northwest to Rapid City, so anyone who knew her would probably look in that direction first. But there was another reason as well.

Until recently, Mama Elise had been tight-lipped about how Lila ended up at Pine Ridge, changing the subject or simply refusing to discuss it when Lila brought it up. Lila had gotten to the point of not asking anymore, but to her surprise, her foster-mother raised the topic recently during one of Lila's visits.

Lila had been born in Maine.

Mama Elise had been very short on details, but as Lila guided the scooter out on Route 18, heading east, she wondered if Mama's death might somehow be related to whatever had resulted in Lila, a young white girl, living at Pine Ridge Reservation.

She looked down at her throbbing leg. The dark stain on her pants legs had stopped spreading, at least, but she would have to stop at some point and bandage it. For the moment, though, she wanted to put as many miles as she could between her and whoever had broken into the trailer. Whether or not they had anything to do with Mama Elise's murder, she had no desire to deal with them.

Or anyone. She wiped her blurring eyes as she continued down the road. Lila wasn't sure she would be able to figure out what had happened or if there was a connection to her birthplace in Maine, but she could at least try.

She owed Mama Elise that.

Chapter One

The leaves, what Frank liked to think of as fall leftovers, crinkled as he stepped through their wide-scattered skeletons. April teased, as it tended to do this deep in New England, today giving a hint of warmth to the few buds that had poked through the ground around the periphery of the Sun Market & Trailer Park lot.

Two weathered picnic tables stood beside the tree that Frank approached. Their slight list was a testament to the parsimonious nature of Egan Lothe, owner of the Market. Their location was an indication of how long Frank had been part of the Market 'family.' Even the slight shade the trees offered on the hottest days of summer was better than the baking, sandy exposed ground that most of the vendor spots occupied around the dusty open field.

Not, Frank thought, that Egan would have offered the spot if he hadn't been pushed. Long unspoken history between them still tended to drive any dealings between the two men. But Market tradition was that the few choice spots on the lot were assigned based on vendor longevity, and Frank had been around longer than most. So long, in fact, that many other old-timers had questioned and complained to Lothe on Frank's behalf when the occasional shaded spot became available. He hadn't asked them to, as he knew Lothe wouldn't budge. And Lothe hadn't. Other than a grunt and change in topic, the vendor delegates received no response. But when this table's previous tenant had moved on, Frank's unofficial advocates simply started moving his wares to the now vacant space. Lothe said nothing, continuing to ignore things as he tended to do.

Frank dropped the duffle slung over his shoulder onto the edge of one table and unzipped it. As he began emptying its contents, he heard his name.

"Frank! Hey, Frank!"

Forrie Laperse waved from his table two lanes over. Frank waved back and looked around at the sparsely populated tables around the lot.

Just the Stallers here this early in the season, thought Frank, pulling an ashtray, collapsible flagpole, banner, and bag of "Crunchy O-Rings" from the duffle. The origins of the name *Stallers* were lost in the mists of Park lore, and some Stallers took exception to the name, but it was unlikely to change. Frank thought it was a pretty good description of most at the Market, including himself.

He cut off the musings. That mental path was more than well-trodden, and he didn't want to bring the day down before it had even started.

Frank attached the banner to the flagpole and slid the pole into the bracket mounted on the side of one table. Black musical notes on a green background fluttered lazily in the slight breeze.

Next, the ashtray on one side of the table, the bag of O-Rings next to it.

Everything in its place, as his mother always said.

He walked back to his beater truck and opened the tailgate. Eyeing the contents of the bed, Frank grabbed a couple of suitcase-shaped boxes and hauled them back to his spot. On subsequent trips, he added a cymbal with a stand, a ribbed wooden cylinder, a clarinet, and a guitar. With everything laid out on the now crowded table, he pulled two harmonicas from his fatigue jacket and laid them up front.

The instruments were obviously used and worn, but all were clean, playable, and tuned.

And priced accordingly. Frank believed in providing honest value. Which, Frank thought as he looked at his current wares, probably had something to do with his limited income. Unlike a few others at the Market, Forrie Laperse among them. Forrie was honest with the other Stallers, Frank would admit, but gods help anyone who fell for one of his "one of a kind" deals.

Frank shook his head and smiled as he pulled the stub of a cigarillo from his breast pocket, stuck it in his mouth under his faded blonde mustache, lit it, and inhaled deeply. He remembered one time last year when Forrie was offering a...

"Hey there!" a tuneful voice shouted from somewhere below his shoulder blades. Arms encircled his waist. Even if he hadn't seen the slender, tan arms ensconced with bangles, Frank would have known who it was from the voice and underlying scent of sandalwood.

"Sloe, where did you come from?" Frank turned around, holding onto the hands as he did.

Brown eyes looked up over a foot into his green ones. Grinning, the woman replied.

"Well, Mom always said it was at the Ashland fourth of July party but…"

Frank's eyes crinkled as he put his finger over her mouth. "None of your shenanigans, Ginny Jean Blunt."

The woman made to bite his finger, which he quickly withdrew, and reached out, hugging Frank again. "It's good to see you, Frank."

Hugging her back, he sensed a bit more behind the hug than just the usual Market opening day greeting from his friend and goddaughter.

After another moment's embrace, he pushed her gently to arm's length and said, "Sloe, what's going on? What's happened?"

Sloe's eyes got brighter. The smile stayed in place, but the edges quivered as she spoke. "Frank, it's Welp. He, he's…." she stopped.

"He's what, girl? Spit it out."

"Welp wants to leave the Market!"

Damn.

Sloe and her husband, Welp, had been at the Market even longer than Frank. Sloe, in fact, had been born here, back when Egan Sr. had still been running things. Jessie Blunt was eight months along with Sloe when she interrupted the man dickering with her for a set of floral teacups.

Five dollars, and that's….

Excuse me, Jessie had said, and with one arm swept the top of her table clear, carefully half-climbed, half-rolled onto it, and breathed in and out in quick puffs.

Thirty minutes later, Ginny Jean 'Sloe' Blunt was taking in her first meal at her mother's breast.

Sloe had the teacups too, Frank knew, given to her by Jessie as a wedding present, just a few weeks before ALS had finally worn Jessie's indomitable strength down to nothing.

Frank gave Sloe a squeeze and asked, "Why does Welp want to leave?"

"He says we...he... is wasting his life here." Sniffles. "He says it's like having your life slowly sucked away through a straw, a little at a time. Pretty soon we'll just be empty glasses."

Sloe blinked. "But this is my *home*. I know what it is, and what it isn't. But it's still home." Unspoken except in her eyes was the question, *Do you understand?*

Frank did understand and nodded.

"Yeah," He looked toward the back of the lot where a fence separated the Market from the Park. His trailer wasn't visible from here, but he knew it was there. It wasn't much, but it was his. The Park might have started out as nothing more than a temporary refuge, but at this point, it was his home, too.

"Yeah, I do understand," he repeated, and squeezed her hand. "Do you want me to talk to him?"

"Oh, thank you, Frank! I knew you would help." Her smile had stopped quivering, and the eyes weren't quite as bright as they had been.

He squeezed her hand again. "Ok, I'll come by tonight, around eight. Time enough, I think, before things get into full swing."

Sloe nodded her thanks and stood on her toes to kiss his cheek.

"Now, go get set up." Frank glanced over at the customer parking lot. "It's half an hour to opening and folks are starting to line up."

Her moccasins silently came together in an exaggerated attempt at standing at attention, gave him what appeared to be either an open-handed salute or a sign she had a migraine, whirled around and bounced toward her set up at the fence-line.

Frank watched her skip away and thought of Sloe's mother. Solid was the word he always associated with Jessie. Solid in body, solid in mind, solid in her commitment to taking care of her baby girl, as Jessie had thought of Sloe to the day she died.

For a moment, he had the mental image of Jessie before she was confined to a wheelchair. Mischievous smile, freckles that had come down to her daughter, a breeze that followed her quick movements...he shook his head with a sad smile and returned to checking his wares. There was still the question of which instrument to use for the kick-off ceremony.

Opening day traditions had changed over the years. When Frank first arrived, Egan Sr. had simply unlocked a padlock on the sliding gate, pulled back the fence, and stepped out of the way of any early shoppers. A few years later, the younger Egan, back from college, had, with a stiff back and barely concealed grimace, accompanied his father to the gate, but the routine had remained the same. Then, the season following Sr.'s death from a massive heart attack, opening day started late. At eight-thirty am, half an hour past standard opening time, Egan Jr. was nowhere to be found. The vendors were getting anxious and chattering amongst themselves, trying to decide if they should nominate someone to find the newly minted owner or perhaps force the gate open, which was now secured with an electronic keypad.

Standing at the periphery of the gathered group, Frank hadn't taken part in the conversations, content to see how things played out. But when he saw the would-be customers stirring, and a few turning to leave, he walked over to the fence. Harvey Kettle, a Staller whose specialty was used plumbing parts, noticed and cut off the other vendors chattering. He pointed at Frank, and their attention turned to him.

Not mindful of the audience, Frank stood staring down at the keypad. His hand came out from his pocket and hovered over the pad. A few seconds later, he poked at it, hitting a sequence of six digits.

The gate whirred and slid open.

A moment of silence from the vendors as customers began entering the Market, then cheers.

It was a busy, condensed day, so Frank's gate magic didn't come up until after closing time. Of the two annual after hours Market events, one marking the start of the season in the spring, the other the last day in the fall, the Opening Day Blow-Off was the more mellow. It was a matter of degree, however, the primary difference being the spring gathering resulted in fewer puddles of recycled drinks spotting the open field next to the Market, and only one or two Stallers waking up the next morning in an unfamiliar bed.

Somewhere around midnight, just after Frank and a few other Staller musicians had finished a rousing rendition of King of the Road, not all at quite the same time, a voice rang out. Frank saw it was Harvey, who had been celebrating the sale of five boxes of assorted elbow fittings to a would-be plumbing entrepreneur. Harvey popped up from spooning the keg and shouted,

"Hey! Hey, y'all! That was freakin' amazing!"

Frank's eyebrows rose in surprise. Roger Miller was probably spinning in his grave after that last note...or notes... of King of the Road.

But Harvey wasn't referring to the music.

"I mean, Frank opening that goddamn gate. We should have him be the official gate-open-guy...open-gate-guy...open..." Starting to wobble, Harvey tapered off as he landed back against his cuddle-keg.

Then, "Screw Egan Lothe!" The Staller just managed to shout it before heaving into the brush behind the keg.

The rest of the vendors took up the cry, some from prone positions.

"Screw Egan Lothe!"

Fists in the air, the chant continued as Frank looked around the crowd, raising an eyebrow.

"Well, now."

Sloe stepped up next to him. "How *did* you know the code, anyway?"

"Common ground," he replied cryptically.

She cocked her head at him, but then turned to the crowd and raised her hand.

"A vote!" she shouted. "All in favor of Frank being the official Opening Day Gatekeeper say 'aye'!"

The lot reverberated with roars of approval.

She looked around. "Opposed?"

The only sound was Harvey's continued purging of fourteen cups of Coors Light.

Sloe turned to Frank and pulled his arm up from his side, beaming.

"Sold!"

Frank shook his head again, thinking back to that ridiculous 'vote', several years in the rearview mirror now. He looked down at the various instruments laid across his table, then walked to his truck and grabbed a long, slender case from the back. Clarinet wasn't necessarily what could be considered standard for a gate opening ceremony, but who the hell knew what was? Besides, damn it, he still resented how he had been railroaded into the role, so would do things his own way. Anyway, he planned on bringing the instrument to Hilford at the end of the summer for the Maine town's Bagel Bonanza festival, so it was a good idea to get a feel for it in advance.

Moistening the reed, he blew a few experimental notes. *Not bad.*

After running up and down a couple of scales, he tucked the clarinet under his arm and headed over to the gate. In the days following that original drunken vote, various Stallers had pitched in to build the small, raised platform he now faced, over to the side and on the Market side of the public gate. Subtle was not a word that anyone would associate with the homemade stage. Frank couldn't even see the wooden underlying structure through the donated decorations. Flyers from various vendors, colorful scarves, an American flag, and, Harvey's addition, half a dozen old cast-iron pipes standing on end at the back of the platform, acting as a backdrop.

Frank peered at the pipes. There was something new hanging from them. He reached out and touched the fluttering white circles.

Doilies.

Marty Florchet, the newest addition to the Park and Market family, specialized in handmade doilies and other small pieces of sewn items whose purpose was a mystery to Frank.

Not sewn, crocheted.

When Frank first met Marty and used the word sew in relation to the various shaped pieces of linen, he had received a twenty-minute explanation of the difference between sewing, crocheting, knitting, and he didn't know what else. His head still hurt when he thought about it.

Aside from Marty's fixation on useless pieces of cloth, though, Frank liked her. She fit right in. Good thing, too, since she had moved into Ruford's old trailer, right next to his.

A shout ended his musings.

"Frank! it's almost time!"

Turning away from the highly decorated pipes, he scanned the Market. Two tables over from his he spotted Sloe, standing expectantly next to the scattering of toys that formed a semi-circle around her own shaded spot.

I don't see Welp. Not a good sign, especially on Opening Day.

Turning to scan the crowd gathered outside the gate, he nodded with satisfaction at the number of potential customers waiting for the Market to open. In addition to the extra-anxious ones right outside the gate, there were more lined up at a small hotdog stand just outside the entrance. Water bottles and soda cans were displayed across the raised counter. Amanda Fleming was serving up drinks as her furry companion, Velcro, sat beside her, watching each transaction. Only once in Frank's memory had someone tried to short pay for a drink. An apology was quick in coming for the "mistake" of handing the sightless woman a one-dollar bill instead of a five when Amanda's canine accountant began barking furiously, straining against his short leash.

How the hell does he do it? Frank asked himself for the hundredth time, as did all the Stallers.

Mysterious are the ways of dogs. And people.

Maybe one day he would understand dogs. He had given up trying to understand people.

"Frank!"

Time to go.

As he brought the clarinet to his lips, the rest of the Stallers stood watching. Frank had never repeated the same song on Opening Day. The first year he had gone with a trombone version of Entry of the Gladiators, the classic circus song everyone knew by ear if not by name. There was discussion throughout the day that it had been a message of some sort to Egan, who skipped the opening. The following year he played Blue Monk, a classic jazz piece, on the flute. There was puzzlement over Frank's choice until Frances, a dealer in 'antique' kitchenware, had remembered that a recently deceased Staller, Louis, had studied for the priesthood in his younger years. The Park owner did show up that year, but not until well into the afternoon, walking through the maze of tables, nodding brusquely at the vendors before returning to his home across the road, disparagingly referred to as Lothe Manor by Park residents.

Year three was a synthesizer powered by an extension cord run to the Market's Snack Shack and a blazing version of Van Halen's 'Jump.' No puzzlement with that one. The son of Frieda Wilkins, a Staller who sold sports memorabilia, had left for boot camp a few weeks before and planned on joining the 82nd Airborne. Egan once again came through later in the day, not speaking to anyone, just making his presence known, then departed.

So, all Staller eyes were on Frank as he took a breath and...

Laughter from the older vendors, joined by the younger ones when they were told the name of the song by their associates. A recent run-in between Egan and a now-departed short-timer's pet capuchin was still fodder for jokes at Lothe's expense. 'Hey, Hey, We're the Monkeys' left no doubt in anyone's mind regarding the subject of Frank's selection.

As the last notes drifted up into the cloudless sky, side bets were made on how soon Egan would make an appearance.

Frank stepped down from the platform, punched in the code to the gate, and stepped back as the first of the day's customers began hurrying through and sidled up to tables.

Another season at Sun Market had begun.

Chapter Two

Lila could see tendrils of smoke eking their way up from the scooter's engine. They didn't seem to be in a hurry, any more than the scooter itself was. Almost two thousand miles was more than she had a right to expect out of the poor beast. If it was picking now to give up its combustion ghost, who was she to complain?

"Damn it," she muttered, complaining anyway.

The very used scooter had started the trip from South Dakota all right, but within a day had begun misfiring every few minutes, although it had chuttered along reasonably well aside from that. The last few days the misfires had been coming closer together with an occasional stuttering hiccup thrown in. But since this morning, Lila had known the chipped up little green machine was approaching its final gasp. The hiccups had segued on to belches accompanied by mini seizures. Now, as the smoke wafted upward, she felt the entire machine starting to shudder, and her previous forty-five mile an hour cruising speed dropped to under thirty, then a bare twenty. She pulled onto the shoulder of the county road, turned off the ignition, and pushed it over to a tree a few yards off the road, limping as she walked. Lacking a kickstand, she leaned the bike against the maple.

Lila stood for a moment, looking at the scooter.

"Let's rest a bit, shall we?" She gave the overheated machine a gentle pat and sat down on the grass next to it, stretching out her left leg and pulling off her pack. She knew talking to the scooter was silly, but it had gotten her, and it, this far. A quick rummage through her pack produced a bottle of water and her pack of cigarettes.

Double shit, she thought. *Down to three.*

Up to last month Mama Elise would have verbally tanned her hide if she knew Lila was smoking, but these days, Mama Elise wasn't doing much tanning or anything else.

She pulled one out, smoothed the wrinkles, and lit it, taking a deep drag, then looked at her phone GPS, estimating how many miles she had traveled so far today. She realized it didn't matter when she tried to adjust her leg and felt a shooting pain in her calf. Regardless of distance, between her leg and the little green bike's death rattle, she needed to rest.

Wisely, she had put on loose-fitting yoga pants when she broke camp in upstate NY that morning. Even so, rolling up the blousy material past her calf was painful as hell. And the day's heat was getting to her, too.

Damn it.

The redness had inched its way past the edge of the bandage and was spreading toward her knee.

Definitely done for today.

She looked at the phone map again, checking for the nearest town.

Hopefully 'Bridgett, New Hampshire' has a walk-in medical clinic.

Her money was also running low, not that it had been much to begin with, even augmented by the little bit she had managed to grab from her Mama Elise's hidey hole.

For a moment she was back in the closed-up trailer, a sickly sweet smell hitting her when she first walked in. She had looked around in confusion, then saw Mama Elise sprawled in her ratty recliner, dried blood around the hole in her head. Lila didn't know how long she had stood there, motionless, trying to process the sight, before dropping to her knees, sobbing. Then, as she held the wrinkled, cold hand, trying to make sense of things, it dawned on her that based on history, she would probably get blamed or somehow implicated with her foster-mother's death, and had started looking for Mama's hidden stash before hearing people outside the trailer trying to get in.

A continuous *ding-ding* sound brought her back to the present with a start. An oversized man with a beard was walking along the side of the road, pushing an undersized bicycle. He smiled as he came even with her spot under the tree and she quickly pulled her pants leg down and pulled herself up, using the bike for leverage.

"Howdy!"

"Hi," her response was more cautious than his wide-open greeting. It had been a long road from Rapid City, and she had learned not all smiling, bell ringing, bike-pushing guys were nice ones. Hell, she had known that since the age of five.

He pulled the bike over, propped it up on its kickstand and stood looking at her. His size was in direct, almost comical, contrast to his T-shirt that spelled out *Wheely Good Bikes*, and the faded pink two-wheeler, its ratty handlebar tassels fluttering in the light breeze.

She tamped down her immediate thought that he looked harmless, and slid her hand into her pack, feeling around for the travel-sized can of RAID that stood in place of mace.

As she did, Lila realized she was staring. The man didn't seem phased, however.

"Visiting or passing through?" he asked.

"Passing through." A pause, then, "How do you know I'm not from around here?" She realized it was a stupid question the moment it came out of her mouth since her license plate said South Dakota.

But he didn't mention the plate.

"You don't look like you're from around here."

Lila stood straighter, trying not to wince at the dull ache in her leg.

"What does *that* mean?" she asked, surprised. She realized it came out sounding annoyed, but didn't really care. Her hand was still around the can, bag dangling from her shoulder.

The man seemed to sense he had touched a nerve.

"Whoa, I didn't mean to insult you," he said, and raised his hands. He made no move to approach her, but continued studying her face from his position next to the pink bicycle. "Hmm, well, it's just that you have a look of...elsewhere, I guess."

She had no idea how to take that as he looked from her hiking boots up to her short helmet-hair. "I mean, it's not like you have a bubble over your head with the word 'stranger' in it." His eyes moved to her face. "It's just..." He shrugged, apparently either not sure what to add or not wanting to delve any deeper.

She looked back at his open expression, appreciating both possible reasons, and made a decision, letting the can of bug spray go.

"Fair enough," she said and stepped forward. "I'm Lila."

The bearded man approached slowly, as though she were a deer that might bolt at any moment. When she didn't, he held out his hand.

"Good to meet you, Lila. I'm Welp."

Welp's morning had started routinely. Sloe was up before him, and he could smell coffee as he made his way groggily toward the kitchen from the bedroom. Pausing to look down the length of their home, he saw furnishings mostly left over from Sloe's mother, Jessie Blunt, along with an oversized lime green recliner traded from another Staller last year. Above it hung a print with a winter scene of trees and birds Sloe had painted at a Wine and Painting date night. At least, he thought, they were supposed to be birds. The trees did resemble some sort of green growth, but the birds looked a lot more like swooping demon cats.

Demon cats were also what he felt clawing at his insides when he thought about another season at the Market.

His wife entered the trailer as he was adding cream to his cup and picturing claws ripping through his colon. Jumbled toys were sticking up from the box she carried. Her T-shirt read "Classic Fun." Wheely Good Bikes was Welp's business, although by nature they worked together on both. Puns were his thing, not Sloe's.

"Hi, sweetie," she said, putting the box down on the kitchen table. "Better drink up. We have to finish getting set up."

The demon cats started break dancing in his stomach.

Sloe sorted through the box's contents, not noticing his pained look. She pulled out a somewhat stained Cabbage Patch doll and examined it with a practiced eye.

"Hmm...not too bad." Turning it over, she said, "Not an original release, but mid-eighties, I think." Sloe looked up and smiled at Welp. "We should be able to get at least thirty or forty dollars for it, with any luck."

Welp tried a smile on for size and gave up after a few seconds.

"Sloe," he said, "I really..."

She interrupted him, knowing what was going to come next. "Welp, please. I don't want to talk about it again. The Market is home and that's that." She continued pawing through the box, not looking at him.

He knew she didn't want to talk about it. He didn't, either, if for no other reason than his jumbled thoughts never came out the way he needed them to. Anytime he tried, she somehow thought it was about her. And it wasn't, damn it. It was about him and what he wanted. Needed.

The problem was he didn't really know what he needed. Except Sloe. That was a definite and immutable fact, now and forever.

Why couldn't he explain? He was still trying to think of what to say and how to say it in a way that wouldn't piss her off again when his cell phone rang.

Unknown caller, but a local number.

"Wheely Good Bikes," he answered.

After a few seconds of listening, he said, "Sure, sounds interesting. I'll be there around nine or so, if that works for you. We'll see if we can make a deal."

He hit the red button and turned to his wife.

"Kid's bike. Woman looking to sell. Lady's down off County Line Road."

"Welp, it's opening day." She looked up at him, sounding frustrated. "And even if it wasn't, we need the van for inventory," Sloe said.

"You have everything about set for opening anyway," he replied defensively. "And it's only about a mile, so I'll walk. If I buy the bike, I'll push it back."

It was Sloe's turn to not say anything. Her eyes were on a slow simmer as she looked at him, then she turned back to her sorting.

"Fine," she said, and he knew it wasn't. But he needed space to think and decompress.

As Welp took a last sip of his coffee and opened the trailer door, he called back to her, "I'll be back in a couple of hours."

Sloe can handle everything, he thought, defending himself to himself, as he walked toward the Park entrance.

The air smelled like spring, with a whiff of the summer to come, as he stepped out onto Phelp's Road. Tips, the term Stallers used for Market customers, rarely saw this side of the Market and Park. The big wooden gate between the two sides was shut during Market hours. A quarter mile down Phelps and the road T-d into County Line Road. Turning right would bring him out to Franklin, which fronted the Market.

Welp turned left, away from town and toward the waiting bicycle.

An hour later, he was making his way back with the slightly wobbly bike. It hadn't taken more than a brief glance to see the bicycle wasn't worth much, but he thought, *What the hell, I did make the walk.* Following a cup of some of horrendous brown sludge that may or may not have been coffee and a diatribe from the woman regarding everything from her lazy husband to her belief that a recent change in flavor of Velveeta was part of a secret government program to drug and control honest, hardworking Americans who still believed in God, honor, and the Second Amendment, Welp was on his way back to the Park, thanking whatever powers that be for Sloe.

As he made his way down the curving road, he checked the time on his phone.

Good, the gate should be open by now.

When he looked up, he saw the small female figure and green moped at the side of the road.

"Is my scooter going to be ok there?" Lila glanced over her shoulder at her sad, comatose motorbike as they moved down the pitted pavement. She was trying not to limp. Welp seemed about as harmless as an oversized hamster, but in Lila's experience, showing weakness was asking someone to take advantage of you.

"Not much traffic on this road, except for locals," Welp replied. "Between that and the sign, I think it will be fine until we can come back for it."

Welp had scrawled "Don't Touch! Welp" on a page Lila supplied from her notebook and had wedged its edge under the seat.

"Um...ok," the young woman said, dubiously.

He looked at her and chuckled. "It's a small town. And most folks around here know me, at least by name."

"So, you're like, a local tough guy?" Lila's question looked up at him, re-evaluating her preliminary belief about his harmlessness and wondering if she should take the can out of her pack again. His six foot plus height combined with his beefy build alone would be very intimidating; she pictured him throwing a chair, or person, across a sawdust strewn bar and took a small, hopefully unnoticeable, step away from him.

Welp burst out laughing and stopped pushing the bike.

"Nothing like that." He started walking again. "But you grow up in a little town in the middle of East Bumfuck and you're either related to or know everyone else."

Lila watched his face as he said this.

"I guess," she finally said, wanting to fill the silent space. "Rapid City isn't Manhattan, but it isn't a small town either. Pine Ridge was even smaller. I knew a lot of people, but they were mostly either from school, work, or lived in my neighborhood."

Welp nodded. "Makes sense. Never been out that way."

There was only an occasional passing car as they walked, and once a motorcycle whose rider shouted *Welp!* as he roared by.

A bit to Lila's surprise, the silence turned comfortable, like going for a walk with an old friend.

Right, she thought wryly. *Of course, I'm still not sure he isn't a serial killer.*

She peered at him out of the corner of her eyes. An image of a giant hamster armed with a chain saw popped into her head.

Lila had to stifle a laugh.

She must not have swallowed it entirely, as Welp gave a questioning gaze. Lila shook her head to dismiss the unspoken question.

He didn't pursue it, but it prompted him to continue their conversation.

"Speaking of travel, it's a long ride from South Dakota. Once we come back for that broken beast and get it squared away, where are you headed?" A hesitation. "If you don't mind me asking."

Lila mentally sighed. She didn't mind talking about where she was headed. She just didn't plan on talking about where, or what, she had come from.

"Maine, for a bit at least." She left it at that and hoped he would as well.

Welp did, simply nodding. After a moment, he looked down and asked. "Your leg okay?"

Damn.

Lila had tried not to limp as they made their way down the road, but it had been difficult. She had hoped it wasn't noticeable.

So much for hoping.

"Yeah," she said. "I had a bit of an accident leaving Rapid City. It'll be fine." It was hurting more, and she was worried it might be infected, but she wasn't about to share that.

Welp didn't comment.

By the time they turned onto Phelps Road, Lila had given up trying to hide the limp and was feeling hotter than the hazy sunshine warranted. When Welp pointed to a bright yellow sign with neon pink lettering spelling out 'Sun Market and Trailer Park' a hundred yards or so ahead, there were drips of sweat rolling down her face.

As they entered the gate, Welp said, "Let me drop this off at my place and we'll go check in with my wife at the Market."

Lila nodded and opened her mouth to reply when she collapsed...

...and woke screaming, eyes still closed. They had found her, come to drag her back. And she couldn't, wouldn't, go back, now that Mama Elise was gone.

She felt hands on her head and someone holding her arms down. Kicking out, she heard an *oof* followed by a crash.

"Lila!"

The voice sounded somewhat familiar. But of course, it would sound familiar. As she had told the big hamster guy, everyone at Pine Ridge knew everyone else.

"Lila!" The voice was louder and almost begging. "Please, stop! Your leg, it needs to be dealt with!"

Her leg?

Her eyes flew open and saw a big furry face hovering just above hers. She blinked. It was hamster guy.

Welp. His name is Welp.

Whipping her head around, she didn't recognize the room or anyone else in it. There was a middle-aged man with muttonchop sideburns pulling himself off the floor at her feet, a table tipped over behind him. Holding her arms was a petite woman with large dark eyes, anger flashing in them. Lila tried to free herself, but as small as the woman was, the grip she had on Lila's wrists was like frozen steel.

Deep breaths, girl, Lila tried to calm herself. *Deep breaths.*

More coherent now, she stopped struggling and looked around again. The group of people, even the tiny angry woman, seemed to be concerned about something.

Me? Well, they were all staring at her so, probably. *But why... wait, my leg.*

She tried to sit up, but Welp laid his hands gently on her shoulders and said, "Easy, Lila. He's almost done. You're going to be fine."

Realizing she didn't have a choice, and at least somewhat reassured by Welp's calming voice, she laid back but put her chin on her chest, trying to peer down at her leg. They were both exposed and someone had removed her pants and replaced them with a pair of neon pink shorts. And what was that embroidery on the front? Was that...

A freaking heart? Where am I, at a twisted S and M high school slumber party?

She laughed a little and Welp, and the woman looked at her curiously. The man at her feet ignored her, continuing to examine her leg.

"Never mind," Lila said, and put her head back down. Staring up into Welp's quizzical face, she asked, "So, am I being held hostage, or what?"

She meant to say it in a joking manner, but it came out with a petulant, fearful tone.

Mutton Chops answered, not looking up from her leg.

"No hostages around here, kid." She hated being called that. Twenty-four wasn't a kid, and certainly not with her history.

Mutton Chops fiddled with something on her leg and Lila realized she hadn't felt anything in that area since waking up. "There, done." The man stepped back and looked up at her fully for the first time.

Lila felt the Welp's hands as well as the dark-eyed woman's lifting away from her. She sat up.

"What the hell happened?" she asked, scanning the small crowd around her.

"That leg has a nasty infection," Mutton Chops told her grimly. "You're lucky you didn't pass out while driving that scooter Welp told us about." He squeezed sanitizer onto his hands. "It had started to spread and was as like as not to kill you if it wasn't treated."

Her calf had a neat bandage around it, the underlying ugly redness extending just past the edges of the tape.

Mutton Chops finished putting his supplies into a small duffel. "I gave you an antibiotic which you'll need to keep taking for the next two weeks." He pointed to a pile of small metallic envelopes on the kitchen counter.

"Thank you, um…"

"Mike. Mike DeTony."

"Thank you, Dr. DeTony."

The small woman spoke for the first time, a dry chuckle in her tone.

"Oh, he's not a doctor, honey."

Lila looked with confusion from the woman back to the man, who nodded. "Nope, I'm not," he said. "Just an EMT with a bunch of samples."

The petite woman snorted. "*Just* an EMT. Right."

Lila looked questioningly at her.

"He helped deliver me," the woman told her.

"And there are days I question the wisdom of that, Sloe." He turned back to Lila. "Keep your weight off it for a couple of days and I'll stop by tomorrow to check the dressing." He nodded to Welp. "See you in a bit." He pulled the duffel up over his shoulder, dipped his head to the rest of the group and opened a latched door. Over his shoulder, Lila noticed it was dark outside.

How long was I out?

She took in a bit more of her surroundings. Based on the narrowness of the room and how each seemed to lead to another, she guessed she was in a trailer. Across from her was a worn recliner with some sort of painting above it.

Modern art, she thought, not able to make out what it was.

"Hey."

Lila turned to the tiny woman.

"Now that you're not dying, do you think you could get off my coffee table and maybe move to a chair?"

Welp said, "Now Sloe, go easy on her."

Lila tried to sit up but wasn't sure she would make it when Welp's hands slid under her arms.

"Nice and easy, Lila," Welp said. "Between the infection and the antibiotic, you might be woozy for a bit. Let me help you."

The woman watched for a moment, frowning, then took one of Lila's arms and helped steady her as Lila gently swung her legs over the edge of the table. She still couldn't fully feel her calf, but there was a slight tingling, so she assumed Mike DeTony had used a numbing cream or something similar.

With Welp and...*Slow, was it? Must be his wife...* With Welp and Sloe's help, she did a one-legged hop across the small room to a dining chair pushed back from the re-inverted table.

Getting her butt planted again was a relief. Lila's head was fuzzy, bordering on spinney, by the time they made it across the few feet to the chair.

Sloe brought a glass of water from the sink and put it in front of her. The flashing in Sloe's eyes was still there, but there was more concern there now.

"Here, Mike said lots of fluids."

"Thank you, Sloe." Lila sipped at the water.

The silence that followed wasn't quite at the level of comfortableness she had felt earlier walking with Welp, but it wasn't totally awkward either, to her surprise. But there was definitely an air of 'what the heck comes next?' which, in Lila's experience, meant someone was bound to speak up soon.

"Well."

Lila stifled a chuckle. Welp won the prize, having broken the quiet.

"Well, indeed," followed Sloe.

Silence again, so Lila figured it must be her turn.

"Well...shit."

A pause, then Sloe burst out laughing, her eyes dancing now, and Lila thought the smile looked much more natural on her than did her previous angry expression.

"Can't argue with that, honey," Sloe said. She pulled another chair over and turned it around to sit backwards, facing Lila.

"Welp tells me you're on your way to Maine." She cocked her head to one side, waiting.

Lila nodded vaguely. "Initially, at least. Something I need to check into there." Lila shifted her leg a bit and winced. "Looks like I'll be a bit delayed, though, between my scooter and this," she said.

"By the way," she looked up, "who did I piss off?"

A puzzled look from Sloe, who looked up at Welp. He shook his head in confusion, and they both looked at Lila quizzically.

"I really wasn't angry at you and the coffee table," Sloe half-apologized. "Just tense and worried. Aside from that, why do you think you pissed someone off?"

Lila pointed down to the terrycloth shorts she was wearing.

Sloe glanced at the heart-decorated shorts, apparently confused. She was wearing fuzzy pajama pants with a Hello Kitty imprint and a T-shirt with a dragonfly large enough to that, if it came to life, could have swallowed a cat.

"They're mine," Sloe said. "Mike had to cut your pants off to examine your leg, so I grabbed those out of the back of my dresser." She looked a bit concerned. "Aren't they comfortable?"

Lila looked at Sloe's earnest expression, hesitated, then said, "Thank you," not wanting to anger the woman again.

Sloe smiled again. "You're welcome! I have a matching top too, if you want it."

"Um…no, thank you. I'll stick with my T-shirt," Lila said.

Sloe looked at Lila's shirt. It was what Sloe's mother would have called shit brown, with a logo for Castle River Casino in white letters across the front.

"Ok," Sloe said. It was quite apparent the two women had very different views on fashion. "You can keep the shorts, though."

"I don't—" Lila started to say, but Sloe interrupted.

"Remember? Mike had to cut your pants off."

"Oh. Yeah," Lila responded.

She looked around for her backpack and saw it lying on the floor next to the door Mike DeTony had exited through. There was another pair of yoga pants in it she planned on changing into as soon as she found a motel room.

Speaking of which…

"I really appreciate everything you've done." She pushed herself up from the chair and immediately felt wobbly; she managed to stand by leaning on the chair back and slowly began limping toward her pack.

"Welp, I'll come back tomorrow, and we can go get the scooter together, if you're still willing." The wobbliness increased as she slung the pack over her shoulder. "Can either of you tell me where the nearest…"

She was almost at the door when the wave of dizziness hit her, and she started to go down. Her arms windmilled as she tried to catch herself and the door opened, a mustached man stepping inside. She clawed at his shirt and saw the surprise on his face, but his hands grabbed her outstretched ones and kept her from falling.

Her hazel eyes met his faded blue ones. From behind her, Sloe chuckled.

"Frank, meet Lila."

Chapter Three

Settled back down onto the chair, Lila watched Frank's face as Welp and Sloe brought him up to speed. He showed no emotion as they spoke, just nodded when they finished.

"I wondered why you left Willie in charge this afternoon," Frank commented, laying his jacket across the chair opposite Lila.

"He didn't give the store away, I hope," Sloe said, handing Frank a bottle and held up another toward Lila, who nodded; Sloe popped the top off another bottle and put it in front of her.

Aah.

The first sip hit her empty stomach with a rush, and she had to force herself not to gulp it down. She missed part of Frank's response to Sloe.

"...made sure he stuck with your rule, Sloe. Two dickers then done," he finished.

"It was Jessie's rule, but it's a good one. Thanks, Frank," Welp chimed in. He was sipping what appeared to be iced tea. "So, what brings you over? Pre-party drink?" His smiled faded when Frank and Sloe looked at each other. Confusion followed by understanding came into Welp's eyes and he exclaimed, "Damn it, I do not need an intervention!"

The flashing was back in Sloe's eyes. Lila, who already felt bad for putting the couple out, now felt like an interloper in a family crisis. She looked at Welp, trying to figure out if it was coke or maybe pills. He was too clean for it to be meth, unless it was a recent addiction.

"Hey," she said. The other three paused and looked at her.

"I don't want to get in the middle of anything."

Sloe's face indicated it was too late for that, but she shook her head, and her response seemed to be heartfelt.

"No problem, Lila. You're welcome to stay."

"Thanks, Sloe. But if you point me toward a local motel or something, a cheap one, I'll get out of your hair. I really should ..."

"No."

Lila looked over at Frank.

"If Mike DeTony said you need to stay off that leg for a few days, you can be damn sure you better stay off it. He isn't one to coddle anyone."

"But..." Lila started again.

Sloe put her hand on Lila's shoulder. "Lila, it's fine, really. You aren't intruding. And even the cockroaches try to avoid the Bridgett Motor Lodge. You can stay here," At Lila's surprised look, Sloe added. "Really, isn't a problem."

"Sure, we can make up the couch and--" Welp jumped in, but Frank interjected again.

"No," he said again. He looked at Sloe and Welp. "I think everyone could use a bit of privacy right now. I have an air mattress you can use."

Lila hesitated. She was running low on money and knew she should follow the doctor's...EMT's...advice, but...

"Do you have a spare room?" Frank seemed okay, but you could never tell.

Welp said, "I was going to ask about that too, Frank. Did you finally clear out your second bedroom?"

Frank's eyes twinkled.

"Nope."

Welp paused, then said, "Yurt serious?"

Sloe groaned. Lila was totally lost.

Turning back to her, Frank said, "You'll have your own space, Lila. No double-bunking, I promise."

Before she could respond, she heard what sounded like muffled explosions from outside.

"The fireworks have started," said Frank, glancing toward the door. "I need to get ready." To Sloe and Welp, he said, "Can you help her over to the festivities? I can get her settled in later."

"Unless you're too tired," he added to Lila and left through the latch door without waiting for an answer.

Lila was getting whiplash from the back and forth and frustrated with commentary she couldn't quite follow. She felt more like an outsider than ever.

"Too tired for what?" She directed this at the remaining two people. "What the hell was he talking about?" Her frustration was showing, but she didn't care.

Sloe didn't appear to be fazed, although Welp winced a bit at her tone. Sloe turned to the refrigerator, pulled out another bottle of beer, opened it, and took a swig before responding.

"Oddbow," she said, a raised the bottle in salute.

Welp dug a pair of crutches out of a closet and the couple helped Lila hobble down the outside steps as she asked them what an *oddbow* was. They explained it stood for 'Opening Day Blow Out.' Lila saw more trailers lining the way on both sides as they made their way down the gravel street that ran in front of Welp and Sloe's, but she was hard pressed to see much else in the dusky evening. There were dim entry lights outside many of the trailers they passed, but not enough to illuminate much except worn siding, scraggly patches of grass with occasional carefully maintained small flower patches outside some.

I come almost two thousand miles and it's like I'm still back at Pine Ridge.

The roadway ended at a wall of bushes, topping Welp's height by several feet. He stepped through an opening a few feet wide, followed by Sloe, then Lila, who was still trying to get the hang of the crutches. There was a glow up ahead, and Lila heard voices as they exited the shrubbery. Ahead of them was an open field with a large bonfire burning in the center. People milled around, mostly adults with a sprinkling of children. Over to the side, she saw a small stage. Frank, along with a few others, shuffled around on it, plugging cables in to various cabinets and setting up microphones.

"Frank's a musician?" Lila's interest was mixed with surprise. He hadn't struck her as a musician. The ones she knew were generally a bit on the grimy side, and too good-looking for their own, or her, good.

"Yep," Sloe replied, stopping at an empty spot close to the stage, but off to one side. Welp popped open the camp chair he had brought, made a show of dusting off the seat, and waved Lila into it.

"Best seat in the house," he said. Lila saw him smile for the first time since the attempted trailer intervention.

She was glad to sit, her leg throbbing now that whatever numbing agent Mike DeTony had used had worn off. Scanning the crowd, she felt guilty again about the trouble these people were going to on her account. There were a few picnic tables around the clearing, but the chair Welp had carried appeared to be the only one.

Wait. There was another, over by a cluster of kegs. A man leaned back in it, watching her, and waved a red cup at her in greeting. Lila didn't have a clue who he was but raised her hand out of politeness and waved back. Before she could put her hand back down, Sloe slapped a can into it.

"Here, we left your beer back at the trailer." The soft-sided bag Sloe had carried over from the trailer was open on the ground and Lila saw a handful more bottles and cans in it.

Lila didn't take a drink. One beer was enough for her, with the wounded leg and strangers all around. No matter how nice they seemed.

Sloe added. "It's soda. Grape, to be specific. I didn't think you would want to indulge too much with the day you've had." She smiled at Lila. "I have an orange, if you'd prefer that."

Not everyone is an asshole, she reminded herself. *Cut them some slack.*

Lila smiled back and forced herself to relax more than she had since leaving Pine Ridge.

"Trust me, I'd love to indulge all the way to the bottom of that keg over there," she said, which garnered her a chuckle from Sloe. "But you're right. Best not to push things right now." She raised the can and Sloe clinked her bottle against it. Lila was certain the other woman was not drinking grape soda.

"Yo, Sloe!" A voice from across the field. It belonged to the keg-minder who was waving rather wildly toward them.

A sigh from Sloe, then an exasperated shout, "Harvey, I got tired of that by the time I was nine, goddamn it!"

A quick turn to Lila. "Hang tight. I'll be back after I see what he needs. Other than a kick in the..."

Her voice faded as she walked away.

Chuckling, Lila looked around, scoping out the scattered crowd. It was like one of the church socials she had been dragged to as a kid. Even the keg wasn't out of place, as the non-denominational one Mama Elise had attended was pretty liberal. The only difference was this one was taking place under slivered moonlight instead of during the day.

Her eyes kept going back to the stage where Frank and the other musicians were getting set up.

Wonder what he plays?

She had an answer shortly. The group on stage, one woman and two other men, took places in front of microphones. Before stepping to the empty mic at the front of the stage, Frank pulled a clarinet out of a case.

He took a breath and blew a long, high note that cut through the chattering going on around the field. Voices died down and everyone turned toward the stage.

"Good evening," he said, voice echoing a bit from small speakers. The scattered response he received from the onlookers consisted mostly of comments that they couldn't hear him. He turned and said something to a woman sitting at a sound board. She turned a few dials and gave Frank a thumbs up.

Turning to the crowd again, he re-started.

"Good evening!"

It appeared to be a ritual as the crowd shouted, "Hi Frank!" and laughed.

"Welcome to another Oddbow!"

The shouts were louder this time, with cheers mixed in.

Frank had a half-smile on his face. Lila still wasn't sure what to make of him. Actually, she wasn't sure what to make of any of the people she had met here so far. Or the place itself.

Is it some sort of cult? She wondered. She thought about it and laughed. *Church of eternal double-wides. Hah!*

Frank was still talking.

"It's a tradition to do a request for the first song of the night," he said. "So, what will it be?"

"What the fuck?"

The voice had come from the back of the clearing. Lila doubted it was the name of a song. She looked around and saw puzzlement all around, confirming her suspicion.

Another voice, this one slightly closer.

"Egan?"

What's an eegin? Lila wondered as a swell of murmurs swirled around her. The confusion seemed to be outweighed by shock in those around her.

Out of the corner of her eye, she saw Frank's face harden as he gazed outward into the darkness. He didn't move from his spot on the stage and, even in the flickering light, Lila could see his jaw tighten. It looked like he was chewing on the edge of his mustache.

The people toward the edge of the bushes stepped back, almost recoiling.

A man stepped through the crowd. In other circumstances, Lila would have considered him attractive, in a mature way. Younger than Frank by at least a few years, whom she guessed to be in his early forties, and lithe, even if he was currently walking like he had a stick up his ass. But as she studied his face, the ice-cold look in his eyes overshadowed those thoughts. She had seen that look often enough at Pine Ridge, and it generally didn't bode well for anyone on the receiving end.

The 'anyone' in this case was Frank. The man approached the stage, and she turned in her chair to watch the proceedings, wincing as her leg twisted.

She didn't really know any of the people around her, but the ones she had met so far, including Frank, had shown her more kindness and compassion than most she had known for far longer. More importantly, Mama Elise had raised her with a firm understanding that you paid your debts, so she had more than a passing interest in what the newcomer's beef was. And felt frustrated that if the shit hit the fan, her damn leg would likely prevent her from helping.

There was an empty beer bottle a few feet away, and she leaned over to grab it, almost toppling out of her chair as she stretched for it.

Give me a reason, she thought as she looked at the man. He would have stood out in the crowd even if everyone around him wasn't giving him copious amounts of space, essentially creating an open circle ten feet around him. His pinstriped suit and shiny shoes, along with his slicked back hair, were in stark contrast compared to the more-than-casual-ness of the crowd.

Frank put the clarinet down on a chair and walked to the front of the stage, meeting the suit as he stopped in front of it.

The man glared up at Frank.

Frank dropped down from the stage to face the newcomer. They traded stares for a moment, then Frank said, "Hello Egan. Joining the Oddbow this year?" He pulled the stub of a thin cigar from his shirt pocket, followed by a stick match, struck the match on the side of the stage, and lit it. He tipped his head up and blew smoke into the evening sky, looking back at the other man with a half-smile.

Egan snorted. Lila noticed he was clutching a piece of paper as he raised it and shook it at Frank.

"Five years, Frank. It's been five fucking years." The words grated from his mouth.

Frank's response was quiet, "Tomorrow, Egan. It will be five years tomorrow."

"I know it's fucking tomorrow. Do you think I would forget?"

Frank said nothing, but she could see his jaw clench, then unclench.

Softly, almost gently, he said, "No, Egan. I don't think you'll ever forget. Any more than I will."

If Frank thought his response would diffuse Egan's attitude, he was wrong. Crumpling the paper in his hand, Egan threw it at the stage; it bounced back and lay at Frank's feet.

"This was delivered by that lawyer twat, Jerry McMurphy, this afternoon. You remember him too, I'm sure?"

Frank didn't move to pick up the paper.

"Of course. What is it?"

"A letter...from her!"

Lila turned at a gasp just behind her. Sloe had apparently come back from her chat with the keg guy and was standing just behind her, hands on the back of Lila's chair.

"Who..." Lila began, but Sloe paid no attention, her eyes glued to Egan and Frank.

Lila cut herself off, leaving it for later, and refocused on the men.

Frank had also given a start at Egan's statement. He bent down and picked up the paper, carefully smoothing it against his leg before bringing it up to read in the dim light.

Based on Egan's comments and the apparent sensitive nature of bringing *her* up, Lila thought she was prepared for any reaction Frank might come out with. She wasn't, however, expecting him to laugh.

"Oh, my God," he said and looked over at Sloe, who hurried to the front of the stage, stepping around Egan as though encountering a pile of dog droppings.

Frank handed the mysterious paper to Sloe, grinning as he did.

Sloe read it and the grin quickly spread to her face. She looked back up at Frank, and the smile quivered. Her eyes filled with tears as she burst out crying.

"Mama!"

Frank swept her into a hug.

"Kush, kush," he murmured. "I know, Ginny Jean, I know." His hand stroked her back as he spoke.

Egan looked on with a strange expression. "Sloe." Egan stepped forward hesitatingly, reaching a hand toward her.

The flash Lila had seen earlier was nothing compared to the nova that appeared in Sloe's eyes as she swung toward Egan. Lila hoped for Egan's sake that Sloe wasn't hiding a gun under that firefly shirt.

"Don't you *ever* call me that, you greedy, shit-eating, horse-fucking bastard!"

"Ginny..." Egan stepped back with a lurch.

"Get out of here. Now! This is for Stallers, you piece of grubbing slime snot!"

With that, she turned and walked over to Welp, who had been watching silently along with the rest of the crowd. He put his arm around her, and the couple moved toward the hedges.

The entire group around the field observed their progress in silence until they were out of sight through the opening.

Frank turned back to Egan, who continued to stare after Sloe and Welp.

"Egan, I'm sorry. She always did have her own ways. But you really should–"

Lothe turned without a word and headed toward a gate across the field, a black road shimmering in the moonlight just past it. The crowd parted in front of him, clearing his path.

Frank watched for a moment, shook his head, dropped the remaining nub of the thin cigar and ground it under his foot, and swung back up onto the stage. He turned to the other musicians, who nodded in response. He walked to the woman sitting at the keyboard on the side of the platform and whispered to her. Lila had seen but not really looked at the keyboardist before. She was stunning, her dark skin setting off improbable blue eyes with a grace of movement Lila envied as she pushed back the piano stool and stood.

Lila watched as she walked to the front of the stage and sat at its edge. The other band members followed her lead, put their own instruments aside and joined her, making a line of dangling legs across the small stage.

Frank sat at the keyboard and cleared his throat. "The first song is by special request."

His fingers moved smoothly across the keys. Lila listened to a somewhat familiar melody roll out of the sound system, impressed. Clarinet, and now this.

Lila glanced over toward the gate where Egan was just ducking under it. He stood abruptly on the other side and froze as the notes wafted across the clearing.

Frank's baritone voice overlaid the melody of the keyboard. Lila felt there was a hint of whisky in the singing. Other than the rustling of clothing, the field was quiet. Frank's eyes were closed as he sang.

Jessie paints you pictures, About how it's gonna be... Everyone's eyes were on the stage, but Lila turned back toward Egan, standing stock-still at the gate. He jerked, turned, and walked stiffly across the dark road.

The song continued and as Frank sang the last line of the song, there was a dustiness in his voice.

Oh, Jessie you can always sell any dream to me...

The notes trailed off. The keyboardist turned from her perch, her dark curls swinging, and looked at Frank. He nodded to her, and she and the other musicians got up from their spots and resumed their positions, picking up their instruments as Frank moved to center stage and picked up his clarinet.

Frank cleared his throat again, looked around the clearing, his eyes not lighting on anyone, and grumbled out, "Let's party. One, two, three..."

Lila had never heard Beyoncé performed on clarinet. It worked, though, and she shook her head and began singing along.

Chapter Four

Lila watched with fascination as Frank switched instruments
every couple of songs, moving from the clarinet to electric
guitar then to stand-up bass. On the last song of the set, he
stood to the side of the stage shaking a tambourine as the
keyboardist belted out Gypsies, Tramps, and Thieves, doing
one hell of Cher impression. And she should know. Mama
Elsie had been a Cher fanatic and Lila had grown up knowing
the words to every damn one of her songs. Lila was certain that
was part of her always-present feeling of being slightly out of
kilter with her peer group.

Sloe and Welp returned just before that final number. Lila
wasn't sure what to say when they approached her chair, so
simply smiled at both. It was a good choice, as they smiled
in return and Sloe reached out and gave her hand a squeeze.
Then Sloe was gone again, but this time preceded by a squeal
of delight as the Cher song started and the tiny woman joined
half a dozen other women and girls who whirling and twirling
around the bonfire, dancing with an abandon Lila wished she
could allow herself, even when her leg was whole.

The set over, the musicians put their instruments aside
and Frank announced a break. Sloe and the other dancers

disbanded, and she came back, sweat beaded on her face. She looked happy.

"Thanks." Sloe said, taking a bottle of beer from Welp's hand. She gulped it for a few seconds and handed it back to him. Welp peered into it, shaking it back and forth, and sighed.

"I'll go get refills from Harvey," he said sadly. "Lila?"

Lila shook her head and held up the can of orange soda that had replaced the empty grape one.

"Right," he said and headed over toward the keg.

After a moment, Sloe said, "Well."

Lila responded, "You know, a lot of our conversations seem to start with that."

She received a gentle chuckle in response.

"Sloe, can I ask you what…"

"He's my uncle." She spit, then added, "Technically."

"Egan is your uncle?" Lila was shocked.

"Egan Lothe, owner of the Sun Market and Trailer Park, yes. Also, brother of Jessie Blunt, formerly Lothe." She looked into Lila's eyes. "My mother."

After a moment, Lila said, "Well."

Sloe's eyes crinkled, and both women laughed.

"See? Handy word, isn't it?" asked Sloe.

"Oh, definitely," Lila agreed. "I'm adding it to my standard conversation openers from here on out." She paused. "Can I ask you something else?"

There was wariness in Sloe's eyes now, but she nodded. The pain of the earlier run-in with Egan was still bubbling under the surface and Lila could tell she really didn't want to get deeper into things.

"Grubbing slime snot? Couldn't you do better than that? I mean, come on! I'm happy to help you with your swearing in return for you not charging me royalties for the use of 'well.'"

The women were still laughing when Welp came back with the beer.

Frank joined them a few minutes later after walking a circuit around the clearing, stopping to briefly chat with the various small groups along the way. Everyone seemed to know everyone else, Lila thought, then felt an unexpected pang of homesickness. Pine Ridge had been like that. But she reminded herself that with Mama Elise gone, Pine Ridge was no longer home, if it had ever been. She pushed aside the feeling and tried to just enjoy the easy camaraderie of the group, even if it was secondhand. But then something else occurred to her.

"Frank?" she asked as they stood around her chair chatting. She could have asked Sloe or Welp, but she had noticed that wherever Frank was, people seemed to defer to him, and she had picked up the same habit.

"Yes?"

"Sloe mentioned the Sun Market and Trailer Park. What's the Market part?"

"It's a flea market," he replied, then pointed back toward the hedge through which they had come. "Park," he said, then turned and pointed across the field they were in at another hedge on the opposite side. "Market." Looking toward it, Lila could just make out an opening in it as well that presumably led to the flea market.

"Got it," she said, nodding. "So, everyone here is a…" she tried to remember the word Sloe had used earlier, "a Staller? Vendors?"

Welp was the one who responded. "Staller," he said agreeably, but with a touch of something Lila couldn't identify. "Everyone who rents space at the Market is a vendor, but Stallers are the old-timers who also live at the Park."

"Hey, who are you calling old?" Sloe spoke up, hands on her hips.

Welp held up his hands protectively. "Long-timers, I meant long-timers!" Then, shaking his head, he muttered, "Hen-pecked" to general laughter.

Lila thought the couple may be having problems, but it was obvious they loved each other.

She squinted, trying to make sure she was clear on things. She always liked to know the lay of the land. It had kept her out of trouble more than once. Or at least not as much trouble as she might have gotten into.

"So, all the Stallers live at the Park." "Does everyone who lives at the Park work as a Staller?"

"Not everyone, but most," Welp replied, apparently getting her need to better understand her current environment and the people she had fallen in with.

Sloe took Welp's hand and pulled him. "Come on, Mister Pecked. I want to thank Willie for helping out today." They nodded at Lila and Frank and aimed themselves toward a group that included adults, a few children, and one gawky looking teenager.

Frank and Lila faced each other. After a moment, Frank said, "Well."

Lila laughed. Frank looked confused. "Something I said?"

Catching her breath, Lila said, "I'm sorry, Frank. Just something Sloe and I were talking about earlier."

He still looked puzzled, so she changed the subject. "The band is really good."

"Thanks. It's just a throw-together thing. Depending on who shows up and is sober enough, the group varies. I think we do pretty well." He grimaced just a tad. "Had a bit of an issue in that Dixie Chicks' number, but I guess no one would have noticed except us."

"You mean that slip-up going into the first chorus? Yeah, that bass note drop didn't really work." She grinned at him.

His look took on a measuring tone.

"You play?"

"Some," she replied, already regretting teasing him, then added, not quite truthfully, "High school and messed around for a while after." She had been in a bar band until her unplanned journey eastward from South Dakota.

Lila didn't understand his wince when she said this, but it only lasted a second and Frank said, "Good. You're drafted for the second set."

"Wait, what? No!"

"Oh yes, missy." His faded blue eyes became stern. He pulled out another cigarillo and lit it. She was hit with an urge, watching him draw deeply on it. A lazy waft of smoke followed, floating up through his mustache. The last cigarette she had had was just before meeting Welp, and her last two were back in her pack at Sloe and Welp's trailer. She held out her hand.

He raised his eyebrows but then handed it to her and she took a deep drag...and coughed. He laughed. "Sorry, but it does have a kick." But then the stern look was back, "You shouldn't smoke."

The absurdity of the statement as he took the cigarillo back wasn't lost on her, but she heard it often enough from older smokers. She just nodded and gave a standard quip in response.

"I'm trying to quit. I figure something else will kill me young."

The earlier twitch he had given when she mentioned playing in high school was nothing compared to the one he did now and, although it was difficult to tell in the scattered bonfire light, she thought he turned pale. She didn't know what had set him off, but quickly tried to change the subject.

"Frank, about performing. My leg..."

He blinked and seemed to come back to himself. Then, totally ignoring her comment, said, "What do you play?"

"Um...guitar, and some sax."

Frank looked down at her in her chair.

"I don't have a sax at the moment, so that's out. Guitar? Hmm...do you sing?"

"Uh...yeah."

"Perfect." He turned. "Marina!" The keyboardist looked over from her conversation with two adults and a kid a few yards away. "Track down a straight back chair, please. No arms."

He turned back to Lila. "You're hired."

Before she could respond, he turned and headed back to the stage.

Damn it.

A few minutes later, she was being escorted toward the stage, and Frank, Welp, and a teenager, Willie, who she assumed was the Market fill-in for Welp and Sloe she had heard about earlier, lifted her up onto it. Muttering under her breath, Lila glared at Frank and Marina. Neither seemed the least bit bothered by the dirty look. In fact, Marina appeared to be enjoying it, telling Lila it was nice to see Frank wasn't prejudiced in his shanghaiing of defenseless women.

"Wait, you aren't a professional musician?" Lila said, sitting on the stool provided by Willy.

Marina handed her an acoustic guitar and said, "I'm a dietician, although I did minor in music. Moved into the Park a few years ago and started selling vitamins at the Market on weekends. I made the mistake of telling Frank that I was looking for a spinet piano, and the next thing you know I'm playing Oddbow and the Blow-Off. He even brought me with him on one of his walkabouts last year."

"Walkabout? What's that?" Lila asked. Unconsciously, she started plucking the strings on the wooden instrument, her other hand making minor adjustments with the tuning pegs.

Having finished running a lead chord from the guitar into an amp, Frank said, "Enough of that, you pill pusher." That garnered him a tongue being stuck out at him by Marina, along with a raspberry blown in his direction. He ignored it and told Lila, "It's time." Then he cocked his head at her. "Mezzo-soprano?"

Lila had the impression it was a test, as well as a straight question.

"Yep. Don't throw any contralto keys my way, otherwise we'll both be embarrassed."

His eyes crinkled and his half-smile was back.

"Okay. We generally keep things loose. Someone starts a tune, takes lead vocals, and everyone else joins in as best they can." His mouth curled up in a full-on smile. "First time, lady's choice."

Lila's eyes widened, but she nodded. "Okay."

Marina returned to her keyboard with a pat on Lila's shoulder as she passed. Frank grabbed an electric guitar from a stand and slipped its strap over his shoulder. She saw the two other musicians, both men, that she hadn't had time to meet yet move into position, one sliding behind the drum set, the other picking up an electric bass.

She looked out at the field. The chatting that had filled the air died down, and everyone looked up at the stage expectantly. The number of eyes trained on her was disconcerting.

She didn't need to be told that everyone here, all Stallers, most likely already knew who she was. That's just how it worked in places like the Park. She knew they were curious about her musical abilities.

Wondering if I'm going to fuck up, actually.

That realization didn't help the butterflies in her stomach.

Shit, she thought and exhaled. She had spent enough time on stage that her nerves shouldn't be acting up. But she normally wasn't front and center. More a sideline player, adding her voice to harmonies. Max, the lead singer of the

Flashbungs back in Rapid City, had pushed her to take some solos, but she had always managed to avoid it.

Now, though…

Just do it, girl.

Lila knew she had a good voice. And Christ, she thought, looking out again at the faces, it's just a bunch of half-drunk flea market vendors.

She noodled across the guitar frets, playing snippets and chords, telling herself that it wasn't a big deal. Her fingers settled into a repeating pattern, and she suddenly knew what the song would be.

As she worked her way through an instrumental verse and chorus to notify the other players what song it was, she adjusted the volume on the front of the guitar. Looking over at Frank, she expected to see him ready to take the first verse, which was normally sung by a male.

Instead, he looked like someone had kicked him in the stomach.

She did another instrumental round, wondering if she would have to take the opening vocals, but then with evident effort, his face smoothed and he began playing and stepped up to his microphone. The bass player and drummer joined in, as did Marina, but Lila noticed the keyboardist seemed concerned, and kept glancing between Lila and Frank.

Still looking a bit peaked, Frank completed a run on his guitar, far beyond anything Lila was capable of, and began singing.

I spent twenty years trying to get out of this place, I was looking for something I couldn't replace… He finished the first verse, handing vocals over to her with a nod, then joined back in for the chorus, along with Marina. Lila's leg continued to ache, but as they played, and as their three-part harmony on the chorus blended seamlessly as though they had been playing together for years, the pain faded into the equivalent of background noise.

Who says you can't go home?

There's only one place they call me one of their own...

Another verse and a final chorus; Frank's fingers ran up and down the neck of his guitar as Marina's traveled across her keyboard, Lila playing rhythm. She wished she could stand, this being a perfect opportunity to do an old-fashioned rock and roll ending, jumping up and bringing her guitar down to end the song.

Frank apparently had similar thoughts, although his feet never left the stage. He turned to face the band, lifted the neck of his guitar over his head and brought it down. All the musicians came to a stop within half a second of each other.

Pretty freaking solid, Lila said to herself, smiling out at the applauding spectators, a small trickle of sweat sliding down her temple.

Frank and Marina stepped over to Lila's chair and put hands under each of her arms, helping her stand. The bass player and drummer joined them at the front of the stage, and they all took a bow. As the applause finally tapered off, she turned to sit again, but the hands holding her up didn't loosen, and the others on stage all pointed toward her. The clapping started again, accompanied by shouts.

"Woot, woot! Yeah, Lila!"

She looked down to the front row and saw Sloe and Welp, Welp's deep voice bellowing her name. Sloe was beaming, waving a flickering lighter over her head.

Lila felt blood rush to her cheeks. She looked at Frank, who refused to catch her eye, although she could see the corner of his mustached lip curl up. Marina was grinning at her from her other side.

"Oh, stop looking like you just found out your puppy died. You deserve it. You're damn good, Lila," the keyboardist said, and for a moment Lila worried Marina was going to ruffle her hair, but she only chuckled.

Lila looked back for a moment, sighed, and said in her best five-year-old, petulant voice, "Fine."

Marina shook her head and laughed again.

As the second round of applause finally ended, Frank handed Lila off to Marina and Willie, who had jumped up onto the stage. He grinned at her as he and Marina helped her move over toward the side of the stage. As Marina handed the guitar back to Lila, she said, "Heard you were staying at Frank's. How about I walk you over after the set? The drinking gets serious then and," she looked down at Lila's leg, "I don't think you're up for an extended party." She then added, reassuring Lila that it wasn't an inconvenience, "I have to get up early so don't plan on hanging out, anyway."

"Sounds good." She thought it might give her a chance to ask some more questions about the Market and Park.

Marina nodded and hurried back to her keyboard. The bass player, who Lila had heard referred to as Perty, stepped up to the mic Lila had vacated and raised it to his height.

"Hey now, Perty has an original to share!" Frank waved his hand to quiet the crowd.

Perty looked younger than Lila and very embarrassed at being the center of attention. She sent positive thoughts to him, knowing too well what he was feeling. He nodded somberly at the crowd, looked down at his hands, and started laying down a bluesy riff.

After a couple of bars, Lila nodded, and jumped in, back in her happy place, as the other musicians also picked up the rhythm and joined in.

Leg aside, it was the best night she had had in a long time.

The second set ran longer than the first, mostly because the keg-sitter, Harvey Kettle as Lila later learned, and another guy named Forrie, had gotten into an argument over which was better, Roadhouse or Die Hard.

"Jesus, Harvey! Willis would have kicked Swayze's ass any day of the week. I mean, Ghost? That's all I've got to say."

"It just shews...shows his range as an actor, Forrie. You'd never see Willis doing that pottery scene, would you?" Harvey was taking the disagreement seriously enough that he had pushed himself up from his lawn chair. The effort required was substantial, as were his attempts to speak clearly following his many samplings, strictly for quality control purposes of course, from each of the four now empty kegs laying nearby plus the current one that was down to its last dregs.

"Exactly, you addle-brained ass," Forrie exclaimed explosively, grabbing Harvey's shoulder to keep from tipping over. The two men teetered together for a moment before leaning against each other and pulling themselves upright.

The band had paused. They, along with everyone else, watched and waited for whatever would happen next.

Which was catastrophe.

From what Lila could see from her vantage point on the stage, Forrie didn't mean to knock the keg over. He had simply kicked out in frustration, but the metal barrel was close to being empty and toppled over.

Harvey looked horrified for a moment, then roared as he launched himself into Forrie. A ring of bystanders quickly surrounded the two, and shouts of *Fight, fight!* wafted through the night air. The physical side of the argument was quickly doused, however. Mike DeTony, the mutton chopped medic who had patched Lila's leg and who topped both men by a few inches, waded through the spectators and grabbed Forrie as Welp stepped up and grabbed Harvey.

"Knock it off!" Mike yelled. "I have no intention of driving to Lebanon to get your fool heads sewn up, and I'm in no mood to do it myself." He lifted Forrie by the coat collar while Welp held Harvey in a headlock.

He looked back and forth at the two drunken fighters. "Besides, last I knew, neither of you two idiots had health insurance." After a moment, Forrie shook his head, but Harvey continued to pull at Welp's grip. It was, Lila reflected, looking at Welp's massive frame, like watching an antelope trying to escape a tiger's mouth, and as likely to be successful. She remembered him laughing at her comment about him being the local tough guy. He apparently would play the part if forced to. But he didn't look like he was enjoying it; it made her like him even more.

Mike got in Harvey's face. "Well, Harvey? Did you sell a truck-load full of pipes and suddenly decide to donate to Blue Cross?"

Harvey scowled but stopped trying to pull away from Welp's grip on his arms. He shook his head slowly.

"Fine. Then both of you, knock it off. Harvey, I'm sure Forrie didn't mean to knock over the keg, right, Forrie?" He seemed to be daring Forrie to disagree.

Forrie said, "Of course not." He looked mortified at the thought of intentionally wasting beer.

"And Harvey, you just reacted out of instinct, right? Like a mother hen coming to the defense of her baby chick."

Lila wasn't the only one to laugh at that.

"Yeah," Harvey said, relaxing in Welp's grasp. "Yeah, I guess that's right."

Mike beamed.

"There we go, then. Welp, you can let Harvey go." Harvey stretched his arms as Welp's grip released him.

The EMT stepped to the keg and set it back upright.

"No harm, no foul." He grabbed a plastic cup from a beer-side table and primed the pump on the keg. "It's just about kicked, anyway. Harvey? Perhaps you and Forrie could grab another from the Snack Shack cooler?"

He didn't wait for them to respond, simply turned and walked toward the stage.

Lila could just hear Forrie and Harvey beginning their argument again as they headed through the shrubs. Mike was standing just in front of the platform and raised his cup to Frank on stage. "Back to you, Maestro."

As the band began playing again, Lila just caught Mike's final comment as he walked away, back toward the bonfire.

"Damn fools. Anyone knows Swayze would have kicked Willis's ass."

Chapter Five

By the end of the second set, Lila was more certain than ever that Frank had been a professional musician and a damn good one. His performance was just too polished. She was also curious as *hell* as to how he ended up at the Sun Market and Park.

Then, with chagrin, she caught herself.

He's probably wondering the same thing about me.

She thought about the gash in her leg, the cross-country scooter ride, Mama Elise...

Life happens.

Handing the guitar to Willie, who blushed, she stood carefully, using the nearby crutches to keep the weight off her bad leg. She looked around for stairs, then remembered there weren't any.

A plan was coming together in her mind that involved a combination of butt sliding and one-legged balancing when Willie came back with Welp.

She grumbled as they told her to sit back down so they could carry her, but the grumbles were for show; she was quite relieved.

"Thanks, guys," she said as the chair legs gently touched the ground. Willie mumbled something, cheeks an even brighter red than they had been, and walked off quickly.

Welp chuckled. "Puppy love."

Lila gave an exasperated sigh. "Great, just what I need," Lila said, getting to her feet once more. She shook her head.

"Marina tells me she is going to take you over to Frank's place," Welp said. At Lila's nod, he added, "She's good people."

"She seems it," Lila responded. A question popped into her head as she continued to connect all the pieces of the Market, Park, and people.

"Is Marina a 'Staller,' Welp? Has she been here long enough?" She paused. "What are the rules?" Then, hesitatingly, "Is there some sort of initiation?"

A few people looked around at Welp's roar of laughter but, seeing there was no additional entertainment immediately pending, turned back to their own conversations.

"Sorry, but initiation?" He spread his arms out. "We aren't a cult, you know."

Church of the double-wides...

She smiled back.

"Well, you said long-timers who live here are Stallers. I just was wondering how you decide vendor versus Staller other than living at the Park. Is there a time limit?"

He looked at her. "Are you looking to join the club?"

"What?" She felt her cheeks flush. "Uh, no."

He paused before responding. "It's an interesting question, Lila. And not something I've actually thought about. I doubt anyone else has either." He paused and cocked his head slightly.

"Except maybe Frank. Never know what is going through his head." He frowned. "It's a frame of mind, I think. I guess at some point, people just more or less settle in and start thinking of themselves as Stallers and everyone else does as well. No grand plan or anything." He looked at her. "Not sure that makes sense."

"It does, yeah," she said. She was technically no more Native American than Welp, she guessed, but that didn't matter. From the age of five, she had lived with Mama Elise on the Pine Ridge Reservation. She was, in her mind, Lakota, plain and simple. And God help anyone who argued the point with her, including the Council.

At that point, Marina appeared.

"Ready?"

There was a 'whoop' from a picnic table near the keg and Lila looked over to see two women engaged in an arm-wrestling match, a small group cheering them on. The number of families with children had lessened significantly, the remaining adults getting more boisterous by the minute.

"Definitely," Lila responded.

She thanked Welp and told him she would see him the next day. Marina kept the pace easy to match Lila's slow progress on the crutches; the two women exchanged small talk until they arrived in front of a faded yellow trailer in the back of the Park. Marina pointed down the gravel roadway, past where they had turned off the Park entryway.

"Sloe and Welp's place is down at the end." Extending her finger just across the way from Frank's, she said. "And that's my place."

A small pergola was standing just outside Marina's door, flowers climbing the sides and spilling over the top. There were a few colorful wind streamers tacked up to the posts, and a small metal bistro set under it. Frank's, on the other hand, was about as personal as a canned photo in a picture frame at Walmart.

Lila turned back to the trailer that would be her temporary home. It wasn't small as far as trailers went, but still...

"Frank mentioned a private room..." She trailed off.

Marina ushered her past the trailer as Marina said, "I don't know if I'd call it a room, technically."

They walked to the other side of the trailer and Lila saw, squatting up against the outside wall, what looked like a small...

"A Teepee!" Lila almost squealed with delight. There had been a few of them around Mama Elise's house in Red Shirt. Mostly for tourist shows, but it still gave Lila a flush of warmth.

"Technically, it's a yurt," replied Marina, and smiled at the other woman's obvious joy.

That explained Welp's comment when Frank offered her lodging.

"Yurt not kidding," said Lila. Marina sighed.

"I see you've been spending time with Welp," she said, shaking her head.

Lila grinned and said, "This is great."

She hobbled up to it and used a crutch to push up the canvas covering the doorway. Inside was, as promised, an air mattress along with a battery-powered lantern hanging from a center hook, and with a small heater with an extension cord running from it to under the edge of the yurt wall closest to the trailer. Next to that were two collapsible camp chairs and a small table.

From behind her, Marina said, "Frank uses it on his walkabouts. I bunked in here when I joined him on a trip as well. Works at least as good as a tent, and certainly looks cooler."

Lila ducked and shuffled through the entry, cursing the crutches and her leg. Marina stepped in behind her.

They both plopped down into the chairs and Lila said, "You mentioned walkabout before. What's that about?"

Marina leaned back in the chair. Her cheeks puffed out as she blew out her breath.

"Hmm. Where to start." She leaned forward, arms on her legs. "Look, did you see Frank's reaction when you started that first song?"

"Oh, yeah. It was weird. Like I had hit him. And similar reactions earlier when I mentioned playing in the high school band and probably dying young."

The other woman studied her, then seemed to change the subject. "You know he isn't from around here?"

Lila nodded her head. "I know he's been around long enough to be a Staller. But...he doesn't seem to quite fit the profile of someone who was born here."

That earned a sharp glance from Marina.

"And what profile would that be?"

Her tone wasn't lost on Lila. She shook her head.

"Look, I grew up in a single-wide on a Lakota reservation. I'm not throwing shit. It's just that he seems like he ended up here, as opposed to being from here."

Marina leaned back again, still studying Lila's face. After a moment, she nodded in return. "Fair enough. And you're right. He did end up here, fifteen years or so ago. He's originally from the Midwest. From what Sloe has told me, he spent the first few weeks after he arrived burning through Mike DeTony's whiskey stock."

"Mike keeps a supply of whiskey?" Lila was surprised. Mike hadn't looked the type.

Marina laughed. "He and his husband have a liquor store and tobacco shop a couple of miles from here. Most of us have regular jobs, separate from the Market."

Lila felt a bit foolish. She should have thought of that. Making a full-time living doing a flea market would be tough.

Lila nodded. "And when Frank arrived, he had a drinking problem." Lila thought for a moment. "He was drinking tonight. Does he..."

Marina interjected. "I think it's more accurate to say he had a problem and for a while tried to solve it with drinking."

Lila understood that. She had seen it far too often growing up.

"So, what was the problem?"

"That, my dear," Marina said, "is Frank's story to tell. If he wants to." She cocked her head. "But there is no harm in asking. Might be a good thing." Marina stood and stretched, and said, "Long day and tomorrow is a regular job day for me, which means I have to be up extra early to drive into Lebanon." She faced Lila and held her arms out.

Lila looked uncomfortable.

Marina sighed and stepped toward her, putting her arms around her. "Girl," she said as she hugged Lila's stiff body, "you're safe here." She stepped back a pace, still holding Lila's shoulders, and looked her in the eyes. "I don't know what your story is…" before Lila could respond, Marina went on, "…and I'm not asking. Just know this - Market and Park folks, particularly Stallers, may be a bit peculiar, but we take care of our own."

Lila looked back at her for a moment, then gently pulled away and turned. She felt her eyes filling up and didn't want the other woman to see.

Still not looking at Marina, she said, "You don't know me." She had intended it to sound dismissive, but it came out filled with sadness.

Marina's response was quiet and gentle. "No, not yet. But Welp brought you here. He might tell the worst jokes this side of the Mississippi, but he reads people well." A chuckle, then, "Besides, that voice of yours tells me the rest I need to know."

Startled, Lila turned back to her, wiping her eyes. "Wait, what? What does it tell you?"

Marina had a sad smile.

"That you've got pain, Lila. Deep. And a lot of it." Then her mouth quirked. "A lot of folks around here are familiar with that, for one reason or another. It's why many came, and in particular why many stayed."

Lila felt like an onion being peeled back and said in a defensive tone. "What about you?" regretting it as soon as she said it. Part of her resented Marina's comment, but the keyboardist had been nothing but kind. And her last statement seemed to come from a personal place.

The gentleness was back in Marina's eyes as she replied, "Maybe we can trade stories. But another day." She turned to leave. "Get some rest."

Something came back to Lila. "Wait, you still didn't tell me what a walkabout is."

Pushing aside the doorway flap, Marina said over her shoulder, "I'm sure you'll be finding out directly from the horse's patoot soon enough."

Lila's mind didn't want to switch off after the other woman left. She pulled out a worn Rand McNally atlas and lay down next to it, scanning the roads into Maine. Her finger was still tracing routes when her eyes closed.

It had been an interesting day, Frank thought as he made his way back to his place. The party was still roaring, but he was tired and knew he would be asleep shortly after making it into bed. Egan's appearance at the Oddbow with the letter had been a double whammy, emotionally.

Damn, Jessie, you are a stubborn woman. Even in death.

He shook his head.

Never mind. He would think about the letter, and Egan, tomorrow. Right now, he wanted to strip and climb into bed. But first, he had to check on his houseguest.

The lantern was shining through the wall of the yurt, and he called Lila's name softly, but there was no response, so he lifted the door covering and peered in. She was passed out with a map spread underneath her head, her injured leg sticking out awkwardly over the edge of the air mattress. He hesitated, not wanting to intrude or wake her, but then stepped inside and gently slid her leg onto the mattress and pulled the crumpled blanket at her feet up over her.

He looked down at Lila. She looked peaceful.

Or at peace.

Awake, her eyes reminded him a bit of Sloe, fierceness laying just under the surface. But there was a deep wariness that Sloe didn't have. He wondered about her background and what had brought her this far from South Dakota. He suspected it wasn't good, whatever it was. And it had damaged her.

He snorted quietly. He was the last one to talk about damaged goods.

As he continued looking down at her, he realized why she seemed familiar when she first fell into him, trying to stumble out of Sloe and Welp's trailer.

She reminded him of...

What was her name? Rebecca. Rebecca Morrissey, that was it. Sat second seat flute, right behind...

He cut off the train of thought. But then came an image of Jessie in her wheelchair, a few months before she died, her body having almost totally betrayed her by that point, scowling at him. He had gone to check on her and Sloe before heading to the Road Kill Cook-Off in West Virginia. Jessie's voice rang clearly through his mind, although her words had been heavily slurred with some not even understandable, her voice having been one of the first things affected by the disease, eating away her body and life. But he had understood her sharp tone and message.

"Damn it, Frank. When are you going to be done carrying that cross around? Much longer and you won't even know how to put it down." She had sucked on the mouthpiece of the ventilator before continuing.

"You can't spend the rest of your life atoning for something that wasn't your fault."

He had tried to speak, but she cut him off. She could only move her head slightly, but Frank could sense the violence behind the tiny shake. The one finger that retained any voluntary muscle movement also twitched up and down.

"Let me finish, goddamn it. You're a good man. And Sloe and I would be a hell of a lot worse off if you hadn't shown up. But that doesn't mean you aren't still being a self-flagellating idiot!" More sucking on the tube that was now all that kept her alive. It took her a few minutes to catch her breath after the exertion.

"Stop it. Just...stop. Do your little trips, what other Stallers are calling 'walkabouts', but if you do, do them for you. Not to make up for..."

Tears slid down her cheeks as she lost her breath, and Frank squatted down, pulling out a bandana. Frank knew that bouts of uncontrollable crying or laughing were one of the more eccentric symptoms of the ALS, commonly called Lou Gehrig's disease, that had been slowly killing his best friend. He suspected Jessie's current tears, however, were a combination of frustration at what she called her 'traitorous body' and him.

She also hated having to rely on others to do things for her, which at this stage included everything involved in her staying alive. As he dabbed the tears on her cheeks, he felt guilty for making her upset.

She glared at him as she caught her breath and spoke again.

"You're doing it again."

"What?"

"Feeling guilty. About me." He worried she was going to get worked up again and start gasping, but her gaze softened, and Frank saw the old twinkle, subdued and wrapped in pain, but there, nevertheless.

"Will you at least consider that you're not the second coming and don't have to take on everybody's sins?"

The side of his mouth came up, and he stroked her cheek with a finger.

"I promise."

By most measures, it wasn't a "good" memory, but he smiled anyway, thinking of his friend. He blinked and saw he was still standing over the blow-up mattress. He bent and smoothed the blanket covering Lila, then turned to leave. Stooping under the door cover, he heard Lila's murmured, "Thanks, Mama," and paused, looking back for a moment as she rolled over in her sleep.

He closed the flap behind him.

Chapter Six

The Market wasn't open on Mondays, which was just as well for the Stallers that had overindulged during Oddbow, at least the ones that didn't have day jobs. Frank had stayed sober, mostly, but was still glad to not have to be anywhere this morning. He was an early riser by nature and a gentle glow was just penetrating the overcast horizon when he stepped out of his trailer. It was supposed to clear later in the day, but in the meantime, he was content to sit at the worn picnic table in the dirt and gravel rectangle running the length of his trailer and extending over to the wall of the adjoining plot about fifteen feet away. His yurt was technically on Marty Florchet's plot on the other side of his trailer, but she had given him permission to leave it up indefinitely since she spent no time outdoors except on Market days.

His trailer was second to last in the back row of the Park, furthest from the Market. The gravel roadway leading out the gate to Phelp's Road was two doors down in one direction, Marty's place next door in the other. The newcomer doily-maker had not decorated her trailer or plot with lace, for which Frank was grateful, but had asked for his help to carefully position several garden gnomes on her roof. She referred to the resulting set up, complete with a small cement hedgehog perched on a faux stump surrounded by the gnomes as a 'woodland diorama.' Frank thought it looked more like a twisted pagan Disney manger scene in miniature. But what did he know?

She wasn't alone in adding a personal touch to her place. Most of the Park residents had taken the time to add color and whimsy around their premises, distracting the eye from the faded and sometimes rusty metal tubes they lived in. Small garden patches, flowerpots, and decks decorated most of the trailers around the Park.

Frank's, on the other hand, was essentially the same as when he first moved in. The additional fading of the original trailer's yellow color to a dirty off-white and the picnic table were the only differences from fifteen years ago.

He was finishing his first cup and mulling over the contents of Jessie's letter when Lila came around the corner, swinging along on the crutches.

"Good morning," he greeted her.

A yawn then, "Mornin" He saw she had changed out of Sloe's shorts and was wearing a pair of yoga pants with a black T-shirt with *Slayer* spelled out in blood-red letters, a skeleton soldier and two people on puppet strings below the morbidly cheerful word.

He nodded at the shirt. "Not my favorite, but good at what they do."

She looked down, pulling the shirt out a bit to examine the logo. Apparently, she hadn't paid attention when putting it on.

"Not mine either, but it works."

She looked back up and sniffed the air. "Any chance…"

"Sure," he said. "Come on in." He stood and proceeded up the stairs to the door, holding it open for her to follow.

He made his way to the coffeepot, turning to let her know he needed to put on another pot, and saw she was standing just inside the doorway, scoping things out.

There wasn't much to see, he thought as he pulled out the coffee canister. A few instruments in cases and on stands scattered around the living room, with more in the spare bedroom. A couple of pictures on the walls, prints he had picked up on his travels.

"Make yourself at home," he said, rejoining her in the living room. She was still standing by the door. She didn't move.

He walked to the couch and sat down.

"Look, you can't have it both ways," he said.

Lila squinted at him.

"I get it, stranger in a strange land. And the Market and Park are stranger than most. But in for a penny, in for a cup of coffee, right?"

Thinking of the conversation with Marina the previous evening, she gave a chagrined smile and sat down in the chair next to the sofa.

Settling herself in, she said to him, "Not as strange as some things I've seen."

"I'm sure," he said, and waited.

Rather than expand on that, Lila asked, "What's a walkabout?"

He shook his head and put his cup on the coffee table. "Damn, Marina."

"What, is it a secret?"

He guffawed and said, "No. It's Marina's idea of a joke."

Lila cocked an eyebrow at him in question.

"A walkabout is, or was, a rite of passage for native Australians where they would go off into the countryside on their own. It was a spiritual and sort-of cleansing thing for them."

"Like a sweat lodge," Lila said, nodding.

He nodded. "In some ways, yes, as I understand things. At least as far as the purification angle goes."

He stood up and headed back into the kitchen, coffee cup in hand. As he topped his off from the fresh batch and poured Lila a mug, he said, "I do some traveling around, both off-season from the Market and some when it's closed during the week. Marina teases me and says it's my version of a walkabout." He held up a container of half and half to which she shook her head.

"I see." Lila moved to pull herself up on the crutches, but Frank waved her back and brought in the cups, putting hers down on the table in front of her.

"Is it?" she asked, cupping the mug and blowing on the steaming contents.

He nodded slowly and said, "In a way, I guess it is." He reached over and pulled an acoustic guitar from its stand. His fingers moved effortlessly up and down the frets, his other hand quietly picking notes.

Lila was familiar with the lingering silence following his comment. She did it often enough herself. It meant *I'm not going to discuss it further*.

So instead of asking what she really wanted to know, she asked, "Where do you go?"

"Different places. Small towns, mostly, having festivals of one sort or another."

He could see she was not quite following, so he added, "I perform."

Understanding lit her face.

"Oh! That sounds, um, interesting."

Frank's mustached twitched. "It is. Get to meet some interesting people, see different parts of the country. Not something I would have thought of doing on my own, but, well, it is interesting."

She let the comment hang and asked, "Do you get paid?"

He nodded. "Yes, but not much. Just a small stipend. But folks who run the festivals always provide some flat ground, at least, for the yurt. And all food and most refreshments are found."

Lila didn't have much of a poker face, Frank thought. *Strange* is what he read on it.

Well, I suppose it is.

The idea of inviting her to his next outing came to him during last night's performance. But the only person he had ever taken along on one before was Marina. And that had been a special case.

Jessie's voice echoed in his head again.

Stop being so stubborn, Frank!

He thought to himself that if Jessie kept squatting in his head, he might have to start charging rent.

He also thought it was a case of 'pot, meet kettle.' But he supposed the voice was right.

If only Lila didn't remind him of that girl from school.

"How would you like to tag along?" He asked quickly, before he could talk himself out of it.

"On your walkabout?" Lila seemed surprised.

"Sure," he said.

Lila didn't have time to respond. The door to the trailer opened and Marina walked in carrying a steaming casserole pan that set Lila's stomach growling so loudly both Marina and Frank looked at her.

"I'll take that as an indication you'd like a piece of strudel," Marina said, setting the pan down on the coffee table.

Frank thought about trying to work up an annoyed glare at her sudden appearance in the trailer, but he could feel his own stomach rumbling at the smell of the fresh baked goods. He reached over to break off a piece of the strudel once Marina had placed it on the table.

Marina warned, "It's only been out of the oven five minutes. You'll burn yourself."

He sniffed his contempt of the warning and pulled a piece loose. He then spent the next several seconds bouncing the pastry between his hands as the women chuckled. Finally deciding he wouldn't scald himself into muteness, he stuffed it into his mouth.

Around the mouthful, he said, "Don't you have work today?"

"You're welcome," she replied.

"What? Oh, thanks." He finished swallowing, thought of going for a second piece, and decided to wait. The tips of his fingers still hurt.

"And I do." Marina walked to the kitchen, took a mug off a cup-tree and poured herself a cup of coffee. "But I've seen you cook, when you even remember people need to eat, and thought I would save Lila from the heartburn."

"Hey!" he responded indignantly. He did not, however, argue the point.

Marina ignored him and told Lila. "He's a good guy, but I swear he can screw up boiling water."

Frank grumbled at that. He knew how to cook, damn it. Some, at least. Frozen meals and takeout were just so much easier when it was just you.

"Anyway," she said, "I'm going to be late if I don't get on the road and I'm only working half a day as it is, but wanted to see if he invited you yet."

Frank's grumbles turned into a scowl as he sat forward on the couch. "And what the hell makes you think I'm going to invite her?"

"He did, just before you came in," Lila replied, almost on top of that, causing him to sit back into the cushions, mumbling under his breath. He scowled again, seeing Lila's apparent enjoyment of his discomfort.

Damn women, he thought.

With a sigh, he admitted he had, then added, "You accosted us with strudel," he reached out and tore off another piece, "before she could answer, though. She might not even want to go. Not everyone is as crazy as you, Marina."

"Don't be silly, Frank. Of course she's going." Bright eyes turned back to Lila. "Right?"

It was Frank's turn, happily, to see someone squirm a bit as he watched Lila struggle to answer.

"Um, well, I am on my way to Maine."

"Not for at least a few days with that leg," Marina pointed out. "Besides, I heard your scooter needs major surgery."

Then she turned to Frank. "Aren't you heading out later today for a quick trip?" The way she said it, she seemed to know the answer already.

"Yes," he confirmed, seeing the trap and stretching out the word. "Duck Tape festival in Ohio. It's about a fifteen-hour drive," he said. Then, knowing the trap had sprung, he sighed and looked at Lila. "If your leg is up to it, we could take turns driving, otherwise I can handle it easy enough. The festival starts tomorrow. We'd be back by the end of the week."

He felt a touch of nervousness now that he had broken down and asked her to go. He had gotten good at keeping people at arm's length, but the fact was, he did hope she would go.

Seeing her hesitation, he added, "Welp will know by then if your scooter can be fixed."

Lila seemed to consider. "Well, I'm not getting back on the road for at least a few days, so I guess...sure, why not?"

Marina beamed.

"Great. So, we'll leave mid-afternoon then, when I get back from Lebanon."

"Wait, what?" Frank sat up, staring at Marina.

"I'm going too, Frank. My stuff is packed. I just need you to load the keyboard into your truck."

He managed a solid glare this time. "I don't remember inviting you on this trip."

"Don't be silly. See you this afternoon," Marina said. She winked at Lila and walked out of the trailer.

He glared at the closed door, then at the still grinning Lila.

Damn women.

Chapter Seven

As soon as Marina was out the door, Lila began peppering Frank with questions. He throttled his annoyance as he refilled their coffee cups and did his best to answer with good humor. He had invited her, after all, and it wasn't her fault that Marina invited herself. But the questions seemed to go on forever, and he found himself getting a bit short.

It's actually a Duct Tape festival but they call it the Duck Tape Festival. No, I don't know why except everyone mispronounces it, anyway...

There's a parade on the last day, Friday. Before that, there will be at least a couple of stage sets that we will join in on...

Don't worry about an instrument. You mentioned tenor sax this morning. We'll make a stop on the way to pick up one. I know a guy...

No, he isn't in the musical mafia, Jesus! He runs a music store and is an old friend, for God's sake!

She giggled at his mini outburst, apparently taking it in stride.

Well, if we're going to be spending the next few days together, she might as well know I'm not the best when it comes to closeness.

The questions finally ended, and he got things packed up. He wedged Lila's backpack between the keyboard case and the large canvas bag containing the yurt in the back of his truck. Various other instrument cases plus his duffel and the sparkly purple suitcase Marina had left next to the truck completed the load. As he finished tying everything down, the nutritionist pulled into her driveway and walked over, her dark hair bouncing as she came across to the truck. She gave him a smile, and he returned it, unable to stay annoyed.

"A little longer than expected, sorry."

"No problem," he said. "Everything else is packed."

"Great!" Marina glanced in the back of the truck, then over to Lila, who was sitting in one of the lawn chairs next to the trailer. "Lila, ready to roll?"

Lila pulled herself up on the crutches and said in a crisp voice, "Yes, ma'am!"

Frank smirked, "Ok, cadet. But I need a few minutes before we hit the road." He handed a key to Marina. "Mind making sure things are locked up while I check in with Sloe?"

Marina nodded her agreement, and he headed down the gravel roadway, passing the other trailers between his and Sloe and Welp's.

Ted Grota's trailer next door was dark and quiet, as it usually was during the week, except for the wind chime hanging on the pole next to one of a dozen bird feeders that filled the small plot; Ted worked in town at the IGA and wouldn't be home until past dark. Across the pathway intersection, he waved to Mike DeTony's husband, Larry, replacing some lattice around the bottom of their place. Larry took the late afternoon and evening shift, managing the couple's liquor and tobacco stores in Bridgett, so was off until later in the afternoon. Frank continued on, passing the currently empty trailer next to theirs, then stopped briefly in front of Amanda Fleming's place to scratch Velcro's ears, who was lazing in the sun. He could hear Amanda through the screen door, shuffling around and cackling to herself about something. The next, and last, trailer was his destination.

The only difference between Sloe and Welp's, formerly Jessie's, plot and most others was a white picket fence running around the perimeter, a climbing rose covering the arbored entry way. Welp had a pink bike propped upside down on a picnic table just inside the fence and was adjusting the chain as Frank walked under the rosebuds. Welp spotted him coming through and put down the wrench he was holding.

"Hey, Frank." Even with the cloud cover, the morning was warming up, and he wore a pair of cargo shorts and t-shirt. He wiped some trickling sweat from his forehead.

"Hi, Welp. Came to check in before heading to the Duck Festival."

The bigger man nodded. "Much appreciated. Sloe is inside, sorting through some toys she picked up at a moving sale."

Frank nodded back and started for the little covered stairway into the trailer.

"Frank."

He turned around.

"Look, I know Sloe asked you to talk to me, but...there isn't any point." He picked up the wrench again and nervously spun it around by the hole in its handle. "I mean, it won't change anything. Sloe is happy here. I'm not. That's what it comes down to."

Frank chewed on the corner of his mustache, not replying right away. He had known Welp since the younger man was fifteen and had moved in with his uncle and cousin following the death of his parents in a motorcycle crash. The uncle and cousin had departed the Park shortly after Welp's eighteenth birthday, at which point he had taken over the trailer until his marriage to Sloe, his former trailer now Amanda Fleming's.

He started Wheely Good Bikes that first summer and by the time he was on his own, he made just enough to pay for the trailer and necessities. His goal, stated often enough prior to Sloe, was to save enough to "get the Hell out of Dodge." Life, and love, had changed that.

"I don't like getting into the middle of other people's crap, Welp. You know that."

The wrench stopped spinning and Welp nodded slowly, then prompted, "But..."

"But," Frank said, uncomfortably, "you're both good people. I don't want to see either of you hurt. And you're both–"

Welp cut in, letting Frank off the hook from having to articulate it.

"Family," he said, and Frank nodded, gratefully. The bearded man, who topped Frank by multiple inches, put the wrench down and walked over to Frank.

"I know, Frank." His voice, normally a tad too loud for normal conversations, was uncharacteristically quiet. "What you did for not only Sloe and Jessie, but for me." Frank opened his mouth, but Welp continued. "Look, you may not realize it, but I doubt I would have made it through the first year if you hadn't been here."

He stared at Welp.

"No, really," Welp said. "I was one hurting, fucked up teenager." He looked back at Welp, shocked, and Welp asked, "Do you know how many times I thought about killing myself when I first moved in with Uncle Derek?"

Frank blinked. He knew Welp had been in a lot of pain, which is why he had tried to reach out to the teenager, but he hadn't known the depth of that pain.

Their first meeting had been a couple of weeks after Welp moved to the Park when he saw him sitting on the ground next to Derek Voncrough's trailer, throwing a pocketknife over and over into the dirt.

"Hi, I'm Frank. I live a few doors down. You Derek's nephew?"

"Fuck off." Welp continued to throw the knife, pull it out, throw again, not even looking up. That had been the extent of their communication the first few weeks, more or less repeated every few days when Frank walked by the trailer again.

Frank shook his head at the memory as Welp continued. "Yeah, I thought about it a lot. Even got to the point of writing a note."

Welp squeezed his eyes shut for a moment, then looked back at Frank.

"But then you showed up with that mountain bike."

Frank remembered. He could have simply left the kid alone; it really wasn't any of his business. But he found himself going out of his way to walk past Derek's trailer. The teenager's face kept gnawing at him. Derek wasn't a bad guy, but he had just lost his sister, Welp's mother, and had his own load to deal including taking care of his son who was a couple of years older than Welp and was in and out of halfway houses for addicts. So, Frank had walked down, day after day, trying to draw the teenager out. *Fuck off* was all he ever managed to get out of the grieving teen. Then, one day, he saw Welp leave his designated patch of dirt to help another Park resident, a nine-year-old named Marco Gillette, with his bike. The chain had popped off as he rode by. Welp had it back on in less than a minute and Marco was soon going too fast again around the curve onto the main Park driveway.

The following day was Friday, a Market day, and Frank had hit up every customer and browser that stopped at his table, asking if they had a bike that needed fixing. A woman looking for a trumpet for her son mentioned an old mountain bike she had that they were looking to donate. It was in rough shape and might not be worth fixing, but she was happy to give it to Frank if he would knock ten percent off the price of the trumpet.

He ended up selling the horn for below what he paid, and the woman came back about an hour later with the banged-up bike in her SUV. One wheel was visibly bent, the chain was missing, and one of the wires connecting the gear changer on the handle was hanging loose.

That evening after the Market closed, Frank dragged the bike down to Derek's. He had seen Derek head out on his weekly visit to the halfway house after closing up his Market stall, but Welp wasn't with him.

Welp wasn't outside the trailer, so he popped the kickstand, taking a couple of swipes with his foot to loosen the rusted metal and left it outside Derek's trailer.

He didn't see Welp the next day, Saturday. Sunday morning, however, Welp accompanied his uncle as he set up baseball and other sports memorabilia on his table. He was wheeling the bicycle along, but Frank had to look twice to verify it was the same bike. It had been cleaned, sanded, had a new topcoat of paint, sported a chain, and the gear wires were attached. It still looked like a used bike, but a gently used trade-in instead of something ready for the dump.

Two hours after opening, Welp had sold it for twenty-five dollars. The following week, crowded into Derek's space, was a small folding table covered with used bike parts, a sign hanging from it proclaiming "Wheely Good Bikes and Repair – Will Trade!" Welp's sullenness slowly faded and by the end of the season, he had made a few friends around the Park, including Sloe. Although Jessie's trailer was next door to his uncle's, they hadn't really spoken. But then Welp stopped at Frank's stall to chat, a regular occurrence that had started the week after his first bike sale, and Sloe was there helping Frank set up. As she turned from Frank's truck with an armful of cases, she slipped and started to fall. Welp grabbed her by the shoulders and kept her from falling, although the long slender case she had been carrying slipped from her grasp and fell to the ground.

She brushed her bright yellow summer dress and said, "Thanks."

Welp bent and picked up the fallen case. He handed it to her and said with exaggerated seriousness, "No problem. Next time, try to stay out of treble."

Sloe had been reaching for the instrument when he spoke. She froze.

"Really?" She gave Welp a mild version of the glare inherited from her mother, but her eyes crinkled slightly as she said it.

Welp put the plastic case into her still outstretched hand. "Don't hate me because I'm flutiful."

Sloe's mouth opened and closed like a beached fish. She looked over at Frank, who simply shook his head, although his mustache twitched. Welp turned, gave Frank a wink, and headed over to his table.

Back in the present, Frank said, "Welp, I—"

"No, Frank, it's okay." Welp wiped his eyes one more time, then took a deep breath. "But look, the Park is..."

"Sucking your soul away through a tiny straw?" Frank prompted.

That elicited a smile from the big man. "Nice line, isn't it? Can't take credit for it. Read it in a book by some guy named Jacobs. But yeah, it is."

Frank said, "It is rather poetic, in a depressing as hell sort of way." He put his hand on Welp's shoulder. "Look, whatever Sloe thinks, I'm definitely not some sort of relationship expert."

Welp snorted, but Frank ignored it.

"She loves you, Welp. And you love her, I know that. I don't know what the answer is. All I'll say is just keep talking. *With* each other, not *at*. Okay?"

Welp looked at him and for a moment Frank saw that kid again, sitting in the dirt, throwing the knife over and over.

"Ok, Frank. I will."

He squeezed Welp's shoulder before letting go. "Good. Now, let me give my respects to the lady in question and then get on the road." He headed toward the trailer door, calling back over his shoulder. "Don't want to miss opening ceremonies."

Sloe was indeed sorting through boxes when Frank entered. A pile on the floor next to the dining table had bits and pieces of toys that apparently couldn't be salvaged. On the table next to the current box was a stack of old board games. Sloe looked up and smiled at him.

"That time?" she asked.

"Yep. I have two stowaways this run, as well."

Sloe chuckled. "Marina and Lila aren't stowaways, Frank, if you know they're going."

He scowled. "You knew Marina was planning on tagging along?"

"Of course. Who do you think packed for her while she was getting ready for work this morning?" Sloe said brightly.

"Mmph."

Sloe came around and gave him one of her patented Sloe-hugs and he felt himself relaxing into it as she said, "Don't *mmph* me, Frank Pullman."

Another one started to come out of him, but he caught himself. He leaned down and kissed the top of Sloe's head. "You going to be all right until I get back?"

She pushed away from him a bit and looked up; half her mouth pulled up in a smile.

"I think I'll survive until Friday."

"I mean you and…"

She cut him off.

"I know just what you mean, Mr. Pullman," she said fiercely, but pulled him back into the hug. "Thank you, Frank. Yes, we'll be fine."

He returned the hug. Then disengaged, somewhat reluctantly, and said, "Time to go."

He was halfway to the door when Sloe asked, "What about Egan?"

Frank stopped and turned back to face her. His smirk was in full force.

"I think things can wait until I get back, don't you?"

She nodded. "But can Egan?"

That gave him pause, but he shrugged and went out the door.

Lila and Marina were in the cab of his truck, Lila leaning her head out the open window, fiddling with her bangs in the side mirror. Sliding into the driver's seat, he commented, "A bit cozy."

"Just no Mexican food this time," came Marina's pert reply.

Lila guffawed and Frank let out an exaggerated sigh. "Damn women." He put the truck into reverse, and they rolled back over the gravel.

In one of those oddities of the modern age and travel, it was actually quicker to take the interstate most of the way to Olmsville, Ohio, even though it was a longer distance than driving county and local roads. Frank, however, avoided major highways and cities whenever possible, which meant they would spend a few additional hours on the road than was technically necessary.

He didn't care, though. He enjoyed the trips and the quietness of tooling along country lanes.

"Marina!" Lila exclaimed, laughter filling the cab.

Usually.

Marina was sharing her substantial repertoire of dirty jokes and stories with the South Dakotan. While he had heard most of them before, they were new to Lila, who was finding each subsequent tale more hilarious than the last.

"Ladies!" he finally said loudly, with no effect at all. A few minutes later, following a story about a pickpocket, a ferret, and an improbable and unfortunate set of events, he almost swerved off the road as Lila's most recent outburst of laughter startled him into yanking the wheel to the right.

He checked the rearview mirror, thankful there weren't any other cars on the current stretch of road.

He growled, "Do I have to turn this truck around?"

Both women tried to staunch their giggles and took on an air of mock seriousness, staring quietly straight out the windshield. That lasted about ten seconds before Lila quietly said, "But how did the ferret get in there to begin with?"

The truck rocked with laughter again.

It's going to be a long drive, he sighed.

They stopped for dinner at a roadside diner that billed itself as having *The Best Pie in The Tri-State Area!*, which they all agreed it didn't, then walked out into the cool dusk to start the next portion of the drive. As Marina and he pooled money for the bill, Lila had tried to pay for her own burger, but he had absently waved away the offered cash and she frowned. Frank said he knew her savings must be anemic and if she had to pay for any replacement scooter parts, would most likely be used up. He was certain Welp would do the work for free, but might not be able to use salvaged parts.

Frank asked Marina to trade off for the next portion of the trip, thinking he might be able to grab a nap. Lila jumped in to offer to take a turn, but he told her no, saying he wanted her leg to get a bit more time to heal and maybe she could do a stint on the return trip.

It was then that Lila started cursing.

Frank looked at her in bewilderment.

"What?"

She glared at him. "I am NOT a total invalid. I'm also not a charity case and pay my own way, goddamn it."

He stepped toward her, but she swung away and limped off through the dusty parking lot.

"What the hell?" He turned to Marina and asked, "What should I do?"

"Apologize," she said flatly.

"What?"

She gave an exasperated sigh. "Apologize, Frank."

"What the hell am I apologizing for? I was just trying to help," he said with exasperation.

"Exactly. She isn't used to that. Or at least accepting help." She reached out and touched his arm, adding gently, "Sound familiar?"

"Christ on a stick," he managed.

"Yep. Now go apologize and let's get going. I'm still looking forward to that chicken fried steak for breakfast in Olmsville that you promised me."

He looked across the lot. Lila was sitting on a large rock just off into the tall, unmown grass, facing away from them.

He approached her slowly.

"Lila?"

He heard a sniff, but no words.

"Lila...I'm sorry."

She didn't turn around.

He stopped just next to the rock, looking at her back. Not knowing how to start, he picked up a pebble and chucked it onto the empty road.

"Listen, I really am sorry. For your leg, your scooter, your general situation." She turned around, watching him. "I, um, well, you're not a charity case. It's just...I want to help." He saw a flash in her eyes. "Not that you can't take care of yourself," he added quickly. "But...sometimes everybody can use a hand from a friend. And we are friends."

He looked questioningly at her. "Right?"

After a moment, she gave a brusque nod, and she wiped her jacket sleeve across her face. She hopped off the rock and walked back toward the truck. She said, "Let's go."

Chapter Eight

Two hundred miles further down the road and even the earlier sparse traffic had disappeared. Lila made an effort to put aside the hurt that had welled up earlier. In her head, she knew Frank, and Marina and Welp and everyone else, were only trying to help. But except for Mama Elise, there had been strings attached to any kindness she had been shown in the past. And even in Mama Elise's case, it had taken a long time for Lila to trust her.

Frank had dozed off, his head leaning against the passenger window. Lila and Marina had been chatting about non-things, weather, the festival ahead, a funny story about Forrie Laperse selling bogus vintage records to a naïve tourist.

As their shared chuckles tapered off following it, the conversation waned until Marina asked nonchalantly, "So what is it?"

Lila looked over at her.

"I'm trying to figure it out. You're not a druggy. I run into enough of them at the hospital. You definitely don't give the vibe of a prostitute on the run from her pimp."

Lila just looked back.

Marina turned her head a bit and raised her chin toward Frank, whose mustache bristles moved gently as he breathed in and out.

"You asked me what brought Frank to the Park. It's still his story to tell, but I will say this. He was running. From pain and guilt. I think that's why he spends so much time trying to take care of other people, trying to...." She shook her head and then she gave a sad smile. "Anyway, the fact that he invited you and didn't squawk, too much at least, at me coming tells me he has turned a corner. Finally." Then she turned her head more fully to face Lila for a moment. "I see some of the same thing in you. Running from whatever the hell happened to you back in South Dakota."

The silence that followed had a coolness that might very well slip into a freeze, Lila thought, if she didn't say something. She wanted to, but long habit, and scars, made her hesitate. As she struggled with her emotions, trying to decide what, if anything, she would say, Marina spoke again.

"I had an abortion."

Lila looked at her in shock.

Marina's dark face was a mask as she spoke, but Lila saw her eyes had taken on a shine. "You might have noticed I don't fit the classic New England English Stock pattern." Her lips quirked, her natural humor showing for a moment. "My parents are from Senegal. They immigrated separately, settled in Massachusetts, met and got married. Then came me." The mask was back. "It wasn't easy for them. They were both well educated in Senegal, but had to start over when they got here. Then the expense, and stress, of having a baby." Then she added, "And even worse, I think, no more after me."

Her hand came up and wiped her face.

"You would think my father would have blamed my mother, coming from a country where women are still second class. But it was my mother that couldn't handle it. She left when I was twelve. Most of what I remember of her is being blamed for everything, including her not being able to have more children."

Marina's pain was palpable now and Lila reached out and put her hand on the other woman's leg, not wanting to interrupt. She could tell that this wasn't a story Marina had shared with many except, she was sure, Frank.

"She told me I *broke* her." Marina pursed her lips as she took a few deep breaths. "Even then I knew it wasn't true, but…"

Lila finally spoke, almost whispering, "But she was your mother."

Marina nodded, ignoring the tears that now trickled down her cheeks.

"And in my heart, I blamed myself." She snuffed loudly, which caused Frank to let out a snore-snort. He immediately settled back into his slumber and Marina said in a quieter voice.

"My teenage years were not pretty ones, especially for my father. I said and did things I still regret. We're back on speaking terms, but I don't know if I'll ever be able to make it up to him." Another snuff. "Anyway, I got my shit together in my early twenties and started a belated college career."

She paused, as if considering her next words.

"I was still a virgin at that point." Marina seemed to sense Lila's surprise. "Yep, the African Queen, as my father called me when I was little, pure as the driven snow until I was twenty-two. Then I met Mr. Lawrence Bough Witherby." She turned and did see the expression on Lila's face this time, and laughed through her tears. "Yeah, he was everything his name says, and more. Old money, summer house on the Cape. And ultimately a total shit. But I thought I was in love and lost that virginal veil one night in the Chem Lab."

She hiccupped a few times and pulled over onto the shoulder, putting the truck in park. She reached past Lila and Frank, who continued to snore lightly, and took some tissues from the glove box. After blowing her nose, she looked at Lila, who changed her opinion from thinking Marina was pretty to knowing she was beautiful.

After a few deep breaths, Marina pulled back out onto the road. "Sorry, this isn't something I talk about," confirming Lila's suspicion. "The last person I told it to is sleeping next to you."

Marina seemed to be collecting her thoughts and Lila sat quietly, giving her whatever space she needed. After a few minutes, Marina went on.

"Five weeks later, my period is missing in action, and Lawrence is ignoring my calls and messages. A few weeks after that, I got a certified letter from his fucking lawyer." There was anger in her face as she said in a sing-song voice, "Further harassment will be cause for legal, blah, blah, blah." She shook her head.

"I had burned the bridge to my father, at least I thought I had. I was making enough to pay for tuition and one quarter of a shared apartment, but that was it. So, I made an appointment at a local clinic and...and that was it."

Lila didn't offer the standard *I'm sorry* most people would say was called for. Marina hadn't opened herself up looking for sympathy. She simply asked, "You came to the Market after that?"

A head shake. "Not right away. The school was in Lowell, just over the New Hampshire border in Mass. The last few months before graduation were hell, but I managed to make it through. I already had resumes out looking for a dietician job. I was lucky - got called for an interview at a clinic in Enfield a few weeks after graduation and was offered a job on the spot. Hell of a commute, but it was a job, and a lot of my classmates were looking at flipping burgers." A gentle chuckle. "Only problem was, they wanted me to start in two weeks. Being fresh out of school, I accepted, but my head was spinning on the way back to Lowell. I decided to make a pit stop to decompress. It was the Market and..." A pause. "And that was that," Marina finished.

'That' is never just 'that,' Lila thought, but Marina had shared more with her than anyone ever had, including Mama Elise. She felt a touch of embarrassment at how open Marina had been but was more touched that Marina had felt she could share it.

And it's a hell of a lot more than I've offered.

She swallowed. "I..." she started.

An extra loud snort from Frank, whose head popped up as he blinked the sleep from his eyes, cut her off.

"What time is it?" he squinted at the radio LED.

"You need glasses, old man," Marina quipped, giving Lila a wink.

"I'm not even fifty," was the retort.

"It's not the years..."

"Yeah, yeah, it's the mileage. I saw that movie before you were born."

Lila said, "I don't think you're helping yourself, Frank."

He didn't engage further, apparently sensing it was a losing proposition. "How far out are we?"

Marina replied, "Still another five hours to go, more or less."

"Ugh," he said, and tried to stretch in the confined space. "Let's pull off somewhere soon. I need to use the boy's room and get the kinks out." He was looking at Marina, but his eyes shifted to Lila as he added, "and I can relieve you for the last leg."

Lila knew he was thinking about her earlier reaction to not being allowed to help with the driving, and tried out a small smile at him to reassure him.

It wasn't as difficult as she thought it would be.

⸻

The GPS didn't show any rest stops for the next hundred miles, and it was late enough and the area sparsely populated enough that it was unlikely they would find an open gas station or convenient store. Marina grumbled about Frank's aversion to highways as she pulled off onto a wide shoulder bordered by trees.

"Your commode awaits," she said. Lila slid out behind Frank, and they all spent a few moments stretching.

Lila looked up at the star-lit sky. She knew diddly about constellations but assumed the pattern was a bit different here compared to South Dakota. Down the road, she saw a single steady light in the direction they were headed.

Probably a house.

Other than that, trees, dark, and more trees.

It even smells different than back home,

There was a wide openness out west that touched even the air. Here, things seemed...closer? She wasn't sure.

She checked her phone.

Cell signal, at least. Thank God I can call 911 if we're attacked by a bear, if nothing else.

Frank wandered down the slope to the trees and Marina waved a travel pack of wet wipes at Lila, inviting her to join her into a separate copse of shrubs; she was glad of that, not being a big fan of dark, scary woods.

Bladders empty, Frank slid behind the wheel with Lila in the middle and Marina taking the spot by to the passenger door.

Next stop, Olmsville, Ohio! Lila thought, feeling dozy as the truck moved smoothly down the black pavement. She wondered what the festival would be like. She was still wondering as she drifted off.

Cute, was Lila's thought as they approached the town in the early morning sun. There was a row of neat, connected brick and stone buildings running down both sides of the wide street of what appeared to be downtown. Most of the worn but clean structures appeared to be occupied by local shops and eateries.

The truck turned right just before they entered the downtown proper, swung around a roundabout and headed away from it on a bumpy, potholed side road.

"Just about half a mile down here on the left, if I remember correctly," said Frank, pointing. As they cleared a rise in the road, Lila saw open fields bordered by trees on both sides. Hanging across the road was a banner proclaiming "Annual Duck Tape Festival: April 30-May 5."

Cars filled the side of the field closest to them, as well as the opposite side of the road. Tent and canopy tops dotted the landscape further into the fields, past the cars.

Frank pulled down a dirt driveway on the left that snaked through the cars and led off through the trees.

"A lot of people," commented Lila.

"The festival is a big deal around here," replied Frank. "Olmsville has somewhere around eight thousand people. Last year, about twenty thousand came to celebrate all things duct tape."

"Wow," she said. "Who knew?"

She couldn't believe the number of duct tape-centric displays that crisscrossed both the fields. She craned her neck around as she spotted what appeared to be a ten-foot-tall statue of...

"Wait, is that...?"

Frank chuckled. "Yep, the Senator. He was born in Ohio."

Marina muttered, "I wonder if duct tape burns?"

That got both Frank and Lila laughing.

There was another clearing behind the trees. This one didn't have quite as many vehicles and Lila saw a line of wooden signs next to the pathway sticking up from the ground labeled "Vendors Only."

A bored looking older, heavy-set woman waved them into an open spot. Frank got out to speak to her. When he returned, he said, "Let's go check in. We can unload our stuff when we find out when the music starts and where we can set up the yurt."

They walked back the way they had come, heading toward the main road. Once again, Lila was in a bit of awe at the number of people that apparently came to pay their respects to the almighty duct tape. She had never used it much, but when she saw a booth showcasing its first uses, she decided to get a roll for her pack.

She almost bumped into the back of Marina, who had stopped with Frank at a table labeled, helpfully, "Vendor Check-in." The man sitting behind it was darker than Marina, with ham-sized hands that were scribbling some notes from the last group.

"Name?" He was looking at the clipboard as he spoke.

"Frank Pullman. And company," he added, wryly.

The man's head came up and an enormous grin split his face. "Frank! Glad you made it back!" His eyes shifted to Marina. "And the Sea Chick!"

Marina gave him a fake growl, "You damn well better remember me, Lark. Or do you need reminding who rolled you home last year?"

Both she and Lark laughed. He replied, "Good to see you, Marina." He turned to Lila. "But I really don't know this one."

Frank said, "This is Lila, um..."

Lila stepped up with her hand out. "Fortin. Lila Fortin." She flushed with embarrassment, realizing she hadn't told anyone at the Park her last name.

Lark returned the proffered handshake. "Good to meet you, Lila. You're a musician?"

"Damn straight she is," Marina replied firmly. Her hand came out and rested on Lila's shoulder.

"Great!" Lark said. He looked down at the clipboard on his table again. "Frank, I've got you scheduled to join the Bombastic Boomers at eleven-thirty, first act." He glanced up, "You remember Tuck Williams?" Frank nodded. "That's his new band. He requested you sit in, and I figured it went so well with him last year, you'd be okay with it." Another nod, along with a smile from Frank. "They're playing again tomorrow and through the week at three. I'll leave it to you and Tuck to work out if you want to sit in on every set or if you would prefer to do a bit more wandering between groups and keep things loose."

"And the parade?" Frank asked.

"Friday at ten am, same as last year."

"Good."

"Now," Lark pushed back from the table and stood. "Your call, of course, Frank, but...well, I left a slot open at seven tonight, tomorrow and Thursday too." Frank chewed his mustached as Lark hurriedly continued holding up his hand. "Hear me out. We had a last-minute cancelation last night. I can shuffle things around with the other groups if needed. Hell, I can leave it open entirely if I have to, but since I knew you were coming, I wanted to offer...no, ask... if you'd take it. I figured you could take your pick of musicians since I'm pretty sure they'd all love to back you." Eyes back to Lila and Marina. "But you brought your own band, so that's not even an issue."

He looked back somewhat anxiously at Frank. "What do you say?"

As Lark finished his pitch, Lila felt butterflies in her stomach, guessing Frank would have her take lead for part of a set. She looked at Frank, trying to gauge what his reaction might be, but she couldn't tell, still having a tough time reading him. He was a great musician, and a decent guy from everything she could tell and had been told, but...that pain Marina had mentioned, and that Lila had seen for herself at the Oddbow...performing seemed to hurt him almost as much as he enjoyed it. Sure, he had come all this way to play, but taking the starring slot wasn't what he had planned.

She saw him make a face, like he was biting down on aluminum foil, but he said, "Sure, Lark. Sounds good." He gestured to Lila and Marina. "I'll just have to beat Frank's Follies into shape before tomorrow night."

Lila exclaimed, "Follies?" She reached out and slapped Frank's arms. "Watch it, Mister. I'll duct tape you to the soundboard."

They all laughed, and Frank held up his hands in surrender and said he would work on the name. Lark handed him a map of the festival grounds with a red circle around where they could set up the yurt and store their equipment.

As they headed to their designated spot, rumbling along at almost a walking pace in the truck, Frank and Marina continued their joking, and Lila smiled along but kept thinking about the name Frank had tagged the group with. Had it been a mistake to run when she found Mama Elise's body? And who had killed her? She caught a memory-whiff of the close, cloying smell in the trailer and shivered, then reiterated the promise to herself to find out what had happened.

"Lila? You all right?" Frank was looking at her.

She looked over at him and realized she was frowning. She forced a smile. "Yeah, all good, Frank. Just thinking about our opening number tomorrow. Do you think..."

As she spoke, she tried to shake the image of Mama Elise in her chair. It was difficult, but by the time they were unloading the truck and pulling the support poles up for the yurt, she had been able to mostly put those thoughts aside. One thing hung with her, however.

Who did it, and why?

She knew she would run those questions to ground, no matter how long it took.

Chapter Nine

Lila plugged her guitar in to the amp in front of the mic stand and scanned the gathering crowd who were waiting for the Bombastic Boomers to start their performance, accompanied by Frank's Follies.

Why the hell would people travel hours, some of them days, to go to a duct tape party?

Frank gave her a wink as he walked past her, his own guitar in hand.

Him too? Why does he drive all over creation for these things? She shook her head.

And what the hell am I doing here? Well, there are special circumstances...

Mama Elise's voice echoed in the back of her mind.

There always are, little one.

At that, she gave one of those little frustrated *hmphs* Mama had always said reminded her of a camel and looked around at the other band members setting up.

Tucker Williams was a small, well-dressed man wearing a large cowboy hat that made his head appear smaller than it probably was. Lila guessed he was in his thirties. Anywhere else, she would have pegged him for an accountant or maybe a supermarket produce manager. There was something slightly off-putting about him as well, although Lila couldn't identify exactly what it was. But according to Frank, he was one of the best heavy metal bluegrass players he had ever met. Considering Lila didn't even know such a person or genre existed, she asked Frank exactly how many he knew.

He grumbled, which Lila had learned was his way of admitting he didn't have a good response, and Marina laughed. She had left her keyboard back at the campsite and planned on just doing harmonies with the Boomers, since Tuck had a keyboard player as well as a bass player, mandolin player, and drummer.

Lila remembered her lack of concern earlier when Lark offered the open slot to Frank. She had thought the Oddbow was a good breaking in for a bit of an impromptu jam session. But she had absolutely no idea what *metal-grass* might require of her and was more than a tad nervous.

Tuck came over, grinning. "Little lady, Frank tells me you are a solid rhythm guitarist and phenomenal singer, but a bit inexperienced." He took her hand in his and patted it with the other. She was nonplussed, but when he started stroking it with one finger, she yanked her hand back. It didn't appear to faze him. "You just do the best you can to follow along and maybe jump in on some of the choruses and you'll be fine. Easy as pie." His smile was as oversized as his hat and showed too many years of smoking and missed dental cleanings.

"Sure, sounds good," being polite since she was sitting in with his band and set, then turned away, hoping he would go back to the front of the stage. After a moment he did, clearly disappointed. She saw Marina, who shook her head, shrugged, and then put a finger to her open mouth and made a gagging motion.

Lila nodded and gave an exaggerated sigh at the shared understanding that Tucker was one of *those* men. Not dangerous, but annoyingly certain he was the savior of the fairer sex.

"Ok, ladies and gentlemen. Welcome to the first act of the world-famous Olmsville Duck Tape Festival!" Tuck started loud and ended in almost a scream into his mic, which complained by emitting a high-pitched scream as he finished. Then, in a volume at least slightly lower, "And introducing my new backup band, the Bombastic Boomers, guest starring Frank Pullman, Marina Agbo, and Lila Fortune."

"Fortin, numb nuts," Lila muttered, a tad too close to the mic. There was laughter from the audience, and Tuck's face turned red. Apparently, she wasn't the only one with that opinion of him.

"Lila Fortin," he corrected quickly and backed away from the mic. Picking up a jacked banjo, he turned to the others on the stage.

"One, two, one, two, three..."

Lila didn't join in right away. Not that she couldn't handle the key and chords. It was simply that, regardless of what a shithead Tuck Williams was as a person, he truly was a virtuoso on the banjo. She watched in growing admiration as he picked his way through the opening number at the speed of sound. Lila might never have heard of metal-grass before, but she was a fan halfway into the first number.

Mountain ain't big enough,
For Billy, Bob, and me,

Gonna get up early in the morn,
Kill 'em all, then some whiskey
Blood on the banjo, still in the moonlight
This here's my mountain,
For it, I'll always fight

The heavy beat laid down by the drummer was almost tribal, reminiscent of some gatherings back at Pine Ridge. Tuck might have been a small man, but he had a set of lungs on him, and Lila thought he could scream with the best of anyone who had ever hit the metal charts. She joined in after the second chorus of "Blood on the Banjo," singing and working hard to have her strumming keep up, although she knew no matter how loud she cranked the instrument it would barely be heard through the roaring of Frank's electric lead. Frank wasn't sweating, but she was sure he would be soon, as hard as fierce as he was going at it, trading licks back and forth with Tuck's picking. He couldn't, quite, keep up with the speed of the banjo player, but apparently, he was going to try damn hard to not get left too far behind.

It was mesmerizing; Lila knew she was watching two men who were as skilled in their art as any she had ever seen. And that beat...

She kept strumming staccato chords in the background as memories rolled through her mind. Arriving at Mama Elise's as an underfed, wispy five-year-old, belligerently pushing Mama's hand away when she reached to stroke Lila's tangled hair. Mama Elise patiently bringing meals to her on sagging paper plates in the small room she had been given, sitting next to her, gently encouraging her to eat, day after day and week after week.

Then, as time passed, accompanying her foster-mother out on errands, clinging to her hand and hiding behind her dress when someone stopped to chat, but inwardly feeling safe for the first time she could remember, although her past in Maine was only a fog in her memory.

Finally, the evening Mama Elise came back so angry from meeting with the Shaman who refused to perform the Hunka adoption ceremony for Mama. Later that night, as Lila pretended to be asleep, Mama stood over Lila's slim, thin cot and Lila listened as Mama Elise whispered words Lila didn't understand, lay her hands on Lila's forehead, and slipped something under her pillow. Lila pulled it out as soon as Mama left her room and saw it was a feather.

She had put the feather back under her pillow, taking it out now and again during hard, or harder than usual, times.

The same feather that was now in Lila's pack.

Blood on the Banjo built to an even higher volume as Lila struggled to keep up her backup rhythm and sweat was now flying from not only Frank's fevered brow, but Tuck's as well. They seemed to be in a death duel, bursts of notes fired and aimed flawlessly at each other, back and forth, over and over. Lila was amazed they had been able to keep up the pace this long.

One last chorus and it was over. Lila had been too taken with watching the guitar-banjo duel and trying to keep her own playing in time with theirs to have paid attention to Marina but as the final note echoed through the amps, she glanced over and saw a proud, and protective, gleam in Marina's eyes, which were locked on Frank's sweat-stained face.

Tuck was in no better shape, but the two men grinned at each other, nodding in mutual respect, then turned to the cheering audience. They took individual bows before coming together for a final joint one.

"All right, folks, not a bad start," Tuck almost panted into his mic, grinning. "Give us a minute to towel off and we will really get going."

He might be a slime, Lila thought, shaking her strumming hand to bring feeling back into it, *but, Jesus, he can play.*

Luckily for all the players, the rest of the set didn't exceed the kinetics of Blood. Otherwise, Lila was certain both men would require the ministrations of an Ohio version of Mike DeTony.

Not that the rest wasn't intense, Lila thought, following the final refrain of the closing number, *Country Demon Spawn.* She took Marina's proffered hand towel, but even a bath towel wouldn't have been enough to dry her completely.

Shit, who knew it got so hot in Ohio this time of year?

Marina had been speaking to her. "...freaking hot."

"What?"

"I said, why the hell is it so hot?"

Lila said, "Funny, I was just thinking the same thing. Early heat wave, I guess. Lucky us."

The festival schedule called for each band to do a single set with an hour break before the next group took the stage. A married couple, Quentin and Rose, were scheduled to go on next. Frank didn't know the duo, and the Follies hadn't been asked to sit in, so they would have at least a few hours before potentially playing again. As they headed toward the yurt, they had to stop constantly for Frank, who seemed to know everyone, to exchange greetings with other musicians.

The greetings were almost always accompanied by requests for Frank's Follies to sit in with the other act. Frank generally kept things non-committal, which suited Lila as she was hoping to do some exploring after giving her leg a bit of a rest. She had been able to cut down to one crutch upon arrival, but didn't want to push it too much.

After crossing the road that intersected the two festival fields, she saw the police tape that surrounded the section where various vendors and musicians had set up camp. RVs, SUVs with trailers attached, and a smattering of tents spread out and filled the space. Over to the left, Lila spotted the top of the yurt poking into the air and the group turned toward it.

When they reached their camp, she sat down on one of the lawn chairs.

"Oomph."

Marina joined her, smiling as she sat down across from her. "Quite." She offered Lila the now very damp shared towel. Lila made a face and declined with a shake of her head. "Interesting, isn't it?" Marina continued, laying the soggy cloth on the rocks circling the firepit, gesturing around the festival grounds.

Lila nodded. Frank poked his head into the yurt to check on their packs and the extra instruments they had brought with them, then joined them at the firepit. He was just settling into a camp chair when his cell phone buzzed.

"Welp, everything okay?"

Lila started to ask Marina a question about the rest of the week's schedule, but the other woman waved at her to wait. From Marina's concerned look, it appeared Welp calling Frank on the road was not a normal thing.

"Hmm, yeah, I understand why you're concerned. Hang on."

He looked at Lila, eyes steady. "I take it you don't have traveling companions following behind you that you didn't mention?"

Lila started. "What? No, of course not. Why?"

"Because two people, an older man and woman, were in Mike DeTony's liquor store and a couple of other places in town, apparently, asking about a young woman traveling on a scooter."

Shit!

It must have to do with Mama Elise. She didn't know for certain why Mama had been killed, but more than suspected it had to do with her foster-mother's involvement in the feather trade, a mostly legitimate business.

Mostly.

There certainly wasn't anything at the falling-apart four room shack that would have attracted a burglar. The obvious conclusion was that it was related to Mama's business.

Frank was still looking at her, and she knew he was trying to determine if she was telling the truth. After the shared road trip, she felt a stab of hurt at his questioning gaze, but admitted to herself that it was understandable under the circumstances.

She looked back just as steadily.

"Frank, it's possible someone might be looking for me related to the reason I left South Dakota. But I haven't done anything wrong or illegal."

He looked at her a moment longer, then nodded as he spoke to Welp on the phone again.

"Welp? Yeah, sorry about that. No, Lila has no idea. What does Mike think?"

Lila hadn't noticed Marina get up, but she offered a can of beer from the cooler, her own can in her other hand.

Lila popped it open as Frank continued his conversation with Welp.

"Ok, good. Well, then I'll leave it to Lila to decide. Thanks, Welp, good...what? Well, sure, of course, but... Welp, I said yes. But sit tight there until we get back, okay? Promise? All right, we'll talk then."

He ended the call and looked back at Lila.

"Mike says the two seemed to be okay. He didn't smell bullshit on them, and they aren't cops. He thinks they're harmless. They said they simply need to talk to you about something back at Pine Ridge."

Marina asked him about the other part of the conversation, at the end, but he waved it away.

"Later," he said.

Even with the reassurance, Lila's stomach was still in knots. "How good is he at smelling bullshit?"

Marina said, "Honey, if bullshit was a drug and he was a K9 dog, not a speck of dope would make it through an airport. And he deals with cops all the time as an EMT, so can tell a cop at a thousand yards."

The comment struck a chord and Lila winced inside but kept her face blank, wondering for the hundredth time since finding Mama Elise what the old woman had gotten herself involved in.

Oh, Mama! Was it your business? Or maybe drugs? No, it couldn't be. You were always cold death when it came to those. Too many friends lost over the years.

Frank grunted agreement with Marina's assessment of Mike's bullshit detector, continuing to watch Lila.

"All right, while I don't generally poke my nose into other people's business --" a noise from Marina interrupted him, but he kept going, "I think it's time for some sort of explanation." He settled himself back into his chair, put his legs out, folding his hands across his waist...and waited.

Lila took another drink from her beer. She had tried to leave South Dakota behind, emotionally as well as physically, but should have known that was impossible. Even without Mama's murder, the reservation was as much a part of her as her nose. She took a deep breath and gulped the rest of it down, slamming the empty can onto the little table next to her. Marina got up and pulled another one from the cooler and tossed it to Lila, who burped as she sat back down.

Lila cracked open the can as she remembered Frank's comment a couple of mornings ago.

In for a penny, in for a beer.

"I was mostly raised on the Pine Ridge Reservation, outside Rapid City," she started. Marina nodded at this, knowing at least that much. "But I was born in Maine."

This surprised both of her listeners. Frank said, "What..."

Lila waved her hand, needing to keep going now that she had started.

"A town called Adrianna, north of Bangor."

Another sip as Frank and Marina watched her. "I don't remember anything about it. Maine, I mean."

Marina said kindly, "I had the impression, though, you were really y—"

"I was five, almost six." Lila waved this off as well. She had been looking down at the can in her lap, but now looked up. "Pretty young, sure, but I should remember *something*. People, family, the place I lived. Something. All I have is the name of the place, and that's because my foster-mother, Mama Elise, told me when I graduated high school."

"Nothing at all?" Frank asked, squinting slightly at her.

"Diddly squat. Nada. Dagnee shnee."

"What was that last one?" Marina asked.

Lila said, "Lakota. And no, before you ask, I'm not technically Lakota. Not by blood."

She added, raising her drink, "But I am, by heart."

The others raised their beers, and they all took drinks.

"I don't even know why or how I ended up with Mama Elise. She is...was...Lakota." She felt her eyes filling.

No tears!

She took another swig to gather herself.

"When I asked, she would simply say God brought me to her."

The folding chair suddenly felt claustrophobic, and she stood up, putting most of her weight on her good leg. "If that's the case, then he was watching when she was murdered." She pulled her drink from the chair cup holder, raised it to her lips and finished the beer off in three large swallows. She looked at the can for a moment before crushing it and throwing it hard toward the fire pit.

"Fuck God."

Neither of her companions said anything. Lila limped over to the cooler, took out another beer, and cracked it open.

"She was my family. My entire family. And she's dead."

She could see Frank and Marina trying to take things in. After a minute, Frank said, "What happened? Does it involve Maine? Is that why you're headed there?"

A lot of questions at once and she didn't have all the answers, for them or herself. Her leg had started to throb again, too. Before responding, she hobbled back to her chair. "I don't know why she was killed. She ran a business selling Lakota souvenirs to shops and distributors around the region but," she shook her head, "and it could be connected, but I'm not sure." Lila looked toward the cold ashes in the fire ring, not really seeing them, the gray, dusty remains in contrast to the silver of the crumpled can. She looked back at Frank again. "Maine may or may not be connected. I just don't know. It's where I started, though, and Mama started her business not long after I went to live with her, so it might."

Marina said in a quiet voice, "You said you found her. Is it possible it was an accident or that..." she hesitated, "well, that she killed herself?"

Lila shook her head.

"I don't see how she could have been shot in the head accidentally alone in her own house. She didn't own a gun. And even if she did, she would never kill herself." She added firmly, "I'm sure of it."

Frank said, "You didn't report it, did you, Lila?" It was a statement, not a question.

Lila looked back with frustration, but reminded herself it wasn't their fault this had been dumped on their yurt-step. And Mike's. And Welp's and…

As calmly as she could, she said, "I've never been on the best terms with the Council that runs Pine Ridge, Frank. The head Council woman especially doesn't care for me, and it's mutual. Any time anything went wrong, and at Pine Ridge that was daily, I would get the blame. It was the main reason I moved to Rapid City as soon as I could after high school. Flipping burgers and doing occasional bar gigs didn't pay a lot, but it was enough to get by. I visited her every week to make sure she was doing okay."

It was Frank's turn to stand, and he paced, looking thoughtful.

Almost to himself, he said, "So they could be looking for you about her death."

She nodded and blew out a breath. "Yeah, they could be. I had just found Mama, and I heard someone outside. I…I snuck out a window." She gestured at her leg. "I got this in the process."

The enormity of everything that had happened, including that someone may have traveled across the country to pin Mama Elise's death on her, finally hit full force.

Her stomach heaved, and she limped as quickly as she could to behind the yurt, emptying her stomach. She stood for a couple of minutes, bent over, hands on her knees, until her head and stomach cleared. When she came back around to where Frank and Marina stood, the other woman came to her and without a word hugged her. Lila felt herself tense, but Marina stood unmoving and silent, her arms around Lila, and she felt herself relax. After a time, Marina pulled back, gave her a small smile, and stepped back next to Frank, who looked at her with concern.

His lips tightened, and he nodded. "All right. After we—"

"Hey, Frank!"

The three turned to see Lark approaching, clipboard in hand. He looked a little harried.

"The Quatrains asked me if you would be willing to join them onstage." He looked at the group. "All of you. Seems you made quite an impression with the Metal Grass set."

"I don't..." Lila started.

"Will they settle for me and Marina? I think Lila needs a bit of a break."

Lila looked at Frank gratefully.

Lark looked between them, then at Lila, and nodded. "Sure. Set starts in ten minutes. Grab your gear and I'll help lug it over. I'm on after them - you all - so need to check my equipment, anyway."

As Frank and Marina ducked into the yurt, Lark looked at her again. "All good?"

She thought she would throw up again if she tried to talk anymore, so tried to smile and nodded. She must have managed a decent job, as his face smoothed and he smiled back. Frank and Marina were back out shortly, carrying a trombone case and a small electric keyboard between them. They declined Lark's offer of help and set out, following him back toward the stage area. Before departing, Marina leaned over to her and whispered, "We'll figure this out. It will be okay," then kissed her quickly on the cheek and rejoined Lark and Frank.

She doubted it, but she appreciated Marina's concern and caring.

Alone now with her thoughts, she grappled with the idea that someone, two someones, had followed her from South Dakota. Mike didn't think they were police, which was good, assuming he was right.

Her head ached in addition to the throbbing from her overused leg. She stretched out the healing limb and wondered if another beer would help or hurt. She had just decided to skip it when she heard a call.

"Hey, little lady!"

You have to be kidding me.

Tucker Williams was waving at her, making his way across the field, heading in her direction. His smile was, if possible, even wider than it had been earlier, making him look like a big-eared, shrunken-headed jack-o'-lantern. She debated ignoring him, but knew that wouldn't work. He was cutting through and around campsites, leaving no doubt as to his destination.

She waited until he was close enough that she wouldn't have to shout.

"What do you want, Tuck?"

Tuck either didn't catch the tone in her voice or didn't care. Noticing the partially empty whiskey bottle dangling from his hand, she thought the former.

He stopped a few feet from her, and looked down, first at her, then at the two empty chairs nearby, apparently waiting for an invitation.

That's not going to happen.

"I saw Frank and Marina getting ready to sit in with the Quatrains and noticed you weren't with them. Thought I would come check on you."

"I'm fine, thanks. Just needed a bit of a break." Her voice was cool but polite.

Not dissuaded, the musician pulled over a chair. He sat down in it just in front of her and leaned forward.

"Know the feeling," he nodded. "A good session always takes it out of me." He winked and his hand reached out to pat her injured leg. "Like sex."

Her last frayed nerve snapped. "Not a fucking chance, you pig-eared slime." She stood so fast, a line of pain shot up her leg. "And I said I'm fine. You can leave now."

If she thought her response would make an impact, she was wrong. Apparently, Mr. Tucker Williams was accustomed to such reactions.

"Now, now, little lady," he said smoothly, standing as well. "Don't get your panties in a bunch. Ol' Tuck is here to make sure you have everything you need." He gave another wink, and she wondered if a head could split open from a grin that big.

Without looking, her hand found the crutch leaning against the chair behind her, brought it around, and continued an arch that ended between his legs. It was fortunate for him and any potential future little Tucks that she didn't have the room to get her full force behind it.

The liquor bottle dropped to the ground as both of his hands came around to grip his crotch.

"Time to leave, Tuck."

His face contorted, breath exploding, along with spittle, from his mouth. He looked like he wanted to say something else but either thought better of it or wasn't able to get enough oxygen in to manage it. His head bobbed up and down as he turned and slowly duck-walked away.

Tucking the crutch under her arm, Lila hobbled to the cooler.

She would have that beer, after all.

Chapter Ten

Frank enjoyed playing with the Quatrains. He and Marina had added their harmonies to the quartet's barbershop stylings and joined in instrumentally on a few numbers. It had been a change of pace from the Bombastic Boomers, and now he had their own headline act that evening to plan for.

But he couldn't get his mind off Lila. Even with Mike's assessment that the two people poking around asking questions were harmless and not cops, and Frank would bet his trailer on Mike's judgment, it still didn't explain why they had traipsed across the country looking for Lila.

And what she had seen...

Christ on a stick.

On top of that, not even knowing where she came from, except a name on a map, or how she ended up on a reservation...

There had been a time that Frank wished he didn't remember certain things, but this was at a whole different level.

Poor kid. But not really a kid. Twenty-something, Sloe's age, near enough. Both of them have been through a lot. Be good to help her if we can.

He shook his head at himself. He was doing it again. For every time he said he wouldn't get involved, he stepped right into things. But he couldn't *not*. He had realized some years before that he was constitutionally incapable of not helping, if he could.

Well, there's a step forward.

Damn it. Could you be quiet for a change?

Now and again, often when he was attempting to have a serious talk with himself, he would hear her. Jessie. He wasn't crazy, at least he didn't think so. Hers was the only voice except his own that bounced around his head. He tended to think it was his friend's way of looking down, or over or up, wherever she now was, to help him figure things out, in her own inimitable way.

He had given up any semblance of the Congregational faith he had been raised in long ago, but retained a belief, admittedly illogical, that when we die, we don't simply end.

Apparently, even in the afterlife, giving him shit was still Jessie's specialty.

He heard a brief trace of her cackling laugh, but it quickly faded as he considered Lila's situation.

Well, she can decide if she wants to meet with those people when we get back, assuming they're still hanging around. Either way, if she still wants to go to Maine after that, maybe she will hold off just a bit and I can tag along, or vice versa, on my trip to Hillford next month for their Bagel Bonanza.

He wasn't sure if Lila would be willing to delay her departure, but it was worth asking. She did a good job overall of hiding her pain, but he was an expert. And if he could do anything to help her avoid the path he had started down years before, trying to hide or avoid it, he would.

What was that town she mentioned? Andrea? Something like that.

Whatever its name, he could adjust his schedule to make sure she arrived safely and swing back to check in on her after the festival was over. If she wanted to head back to New Hampshire, or anyplace else, they could travel together on at least the first leg, depending on her plans.

Best I can do for the moment.

He saw her at that restaurant again, so angry at his offered help, now understanding the anger was partly to shield herself from the almost overwhelming grief. He knew that kind of pain.

An unwanted image now replaced the one of her. A teenage boy, smiling and laughing, teasing him...

He forced the image down, back into the dark corner of his mind from where it had come.

So young.

Not that much younger than you were when I found you puking next to your truck outside the Park.

Hush.

He turned his thoughts to his other current traveling companion. It shouldn't have surprised him when she crashed the trip. Since last summer she had been more open, and forceful, with him, and how she felt. And it wasn't as though he didn't have similar feelings, but it had been easier, and safer, to keep things at arm's length for a long time.

Wasn't arm's length at last year's Testicle Festival, though, was it? Or are you now comparing your size to an arm?

More cackling laughter.

Oh, will you shut up?

Frank sighed. He could have said no to Marina's self-invitation. But he hadn't really wanted to, had he? He wondered what that meant, immediately answered himself, and sighed again, picking up his trombone case.

"Ready, Frank?"

Marina stood looking at him, returned from chatting with the Quatrains, keyboard case strap strung crisscross on her back, her corkscrew curls sticking out, having escaped from the clips she put in her hair before the set. There was a sweaty gleam on her face. Her blue eyes, always a contrast to her dark complexion, seemed to be alight as he looked at her and he felt his heart pause for a moment, then do a double thump.

"Ah…"

He saw the questioning look on Marina's face as he unraveled competing and contrasting emotions and thoughts. Apparently of its own volition, his hand began to rise toward her, but whether from too many years spent in a self-imposed emotional prison or simply fear, he froze, and it came back down to his side.

He took a deep breath.

"Ready."

Marina gave him another smile, but he detected a touch of sadness in it.

Damn it, you idiot! She's right here and has been waiting for how long? How much longer will she?

He had no answer, not a good one, to Jessie's voice.

He nodded, dropping his eyes, and turned toward their campsite, Marina at his side.

Lila was next to the fire pit drinking a beer when they arrived. Lily said she was going to wander a bit since they had a couple of hours before their performance and Marina offered to join her. Frank nodded and watched their retreating backs for a minute before going into the yurt. He lay on the air mattress, staring up at the canvas.

The earlier image of a teenage boy crept into mental view. This time, though, he didn't clamp down on the memory. He followed it down a dark path he had avoided for a very long time, allowing it to take him back.

Back eighteen years.

Chapter Eleven

Frank knew he had carried a chip on his shoulder the size of a log in his earlier years, although if he had been confronted with it at the time, he would have simply said he was confident. Confident in his views, in his musical abilities, and in himself. And while his mother, Patty Pullman, never said it directly, he was now certain she had thought he was arrogant, but she had limited her comments to simply saying his saving grace was his idealism. She did warn him, though, that he tended to take things to extremes. If his pride was affronted, he could be an absolute roaring ass, even as a child. Not intentionally cruel, more condescending, which he could and, did, use like a knife. But he also felt others' pain as much as his own, never brooking a bully in his presence even toward people he didn't like and volunteering at food pantries and organizing charity events throughout high school.

And the times the arrogance came out, he regretted it afterwards, doing everything he could to make amends with whomever he had lashed out at. But even this he could take to an extreme, reminding his mother of a medieval monk whipping himself.

"Balance, grasshopper," his mother would tell him at these times, pushing his cowlicks back from his face. "I'm glad you recognize you were wrong, but throwing yourself in front of a metaphorical train isn't necessarily the best way to make up for it." And each time, his younger self would nod and say he would try to remember. And he would try. Until the next time it happened.

He had been a decent but not outstanding student throughout high school and during his four years at college, majoring in music. His high school band teacher had called him a phenom, with Frank's ability to pick up an instrument, any instrument, and shortly be playing it like he had studied for years. His friends used to tease him that they hoped he would consider hiring them for his backup band when he made it big.

So as his senior year at college approached, he debated going on the road and skipping his final few semesters. He had no illusions about the odds of becoming famous, even for someone with his ability, but becoming a working musician seemed the next logical step; he was certain he could at least make a decent living playing. And there was, of course, his ego, which reveled in the applause of an audience, even if he had occasional thoughts about the shallowness of bathing in the adulation of strangers. So he dithered, unable to decide what to do.

When his mother died a few weeks into his senior year, it crystalized things. Standing alone in the calling line at the funeral parlor, he heard from dozens of people about the impact she had had on them. "She was a great teacher," one of her former students from decades prior told him, tearing up. "Hell, I didn't even like history, but she always made it about the people, not just the big stuff and dates and kings and queens. Made it so you understood it was really about the regular folks, folks like us, just trying to get by. Everyone and everything connected. She made us care...because she cared. Not just about history. About us."

Person after person, sharing memories about her and the difference she had made to them and in their lives, sometimes minor, sometimes major.

That night, alone with his grief, he thought about the stories he had heard and remembered getting annoyed back in high school that kids who wouldn't give him the time of day otherwise, would come by the house to visit her, even over summer vacation. Sometimes they came for advice, sometimes just to be mothered by her in her own special way. She had had an aura of trust, respect, and non-judgment that surrounded her, regardless of circumstance. And then he thought about the roar of a crowd at the end of one of his performances. The tremendous rush he felt. But also, how quickly it passed.

And he realized he wanted to make an impact, too. Not to a crowd of cheering fans. A personal one, as she had.

So following graduation, he started work on obtaining a Master's of Education at another Boston college, taking gigs on weekends and school breaks to keep his chops up. Then had come the student teaching opportunity at Willowdale House, a private high school in the suburbs.

He did well with the students. He had much of his mother's natural ability to connect with people. His musical talent, however, caused friction with the class's actual teacher, who was responsible for grading his performance and, ultimately, determining whether he would get his teaching certification.

Mrs. Rhonda Clotis was not untalented. She had a fine soprano voice and offered private lessons for beginning violin. Before beginning her teaching career, Rhonda had dreams of being a Broadway star but had discovered her talent, praised by family and friends, was run of the mill compared to the vast majority she competed against at auditions.

So, she became a teacher, and a decent, if not outstanding, one. Then along came Frank with his mad skills and cocky attitude. It grated on her, as did the fact students flocked to him at the beginning and end of every class, asking for feedback, joking, even inviting him to one of their parents' anniversary parties.

She needled Frank, exaggerating mistakes he made and finding flaws where there weren't any. Not with anything music specific, of course. But if he graded someone an A, she would say he was being too easy on them. A B grade or lower would result in her saying he was being too hard on the student. She constantly pointed out there should be a proper distance between teacher and student, which, in her opinion, he constantly flaunted.

Frank knew what was happening and suspected why. He initially shrugged it off and tried harder. But a time came when she took him to task in front of the band for supposedly not keeping a steady beat in conducting and that pushed him over the edge.

He told her she was a half-baked, musical wannabe and challenged her in front of a class to a 'play-off,' instrument and song of her choice. Rhonda knew she had gone too far and, also knowing he would wipe the musical scale with her in head-to-head competition, declined and walked out, red-faced, as the entire class laughed.

Frank knew he had won the battle but didn't let it drop. He went out of his way to chat with the students, even hanging out with them after school. He became known as the *cool teacher* and it wasn't unusual for a group of high schoolers to be found at his apartment on any given Saturday afternoon, drinking soda, sometimes jamming, sometimes just bullshitting or talking about the future. Frank had moments of objectivity about the run-in with Rhonda, and realized he should apologize and make amends, but every time he saw her, she started ragging on him and then his dented pride and arrogance welled up again. So, the cycle continued.

Kenny Short was one of the students that had become a regular at Frank's apartment. He was a competent but not outstanding musician for his age, sitting first seat in the trumpet section. He was also well liked by his peers and teachers, confident, but lacking in arrogance.

Kenny was an only child and viewed Frank as more of a big brother than a teacher. Frank, the only baby Patty and Lou Pullman had managed to have before cancer took Lou, was fond of the high schooler as well and enjoyed the hero-like worship from the young man, although would have denied it if asked.

As the school year neared its end in early June, Kenny had come to Frank's apartment one Saturday, solo, and the two sat on Frank's balcony. Kenny started talking about his post-graduation plans. He had been accepted at the local community college, but was debating if it was the right choice.

"It's a tough business, Kenny," Frank said in response to Kenny telling him he what he really wanted to be was a professional musician.

"I know, Frank." His use, as well as the use by other students, of Frank's first name in lieu of Mr. Pullman was another thing that grated on Rhonda Clotis. "I'm not a world-class musician." He gave a shy smile. "I'm not you. But I'm not talking about being a rock super-star. Or even a studio musician, at least not right away, until I get more experience under my belt. I just want to see things. Play some good music, meet people, learn about, well, the world, I guess." He grinned. "You know, there's a festival somewhere out west I heard about. A Testicle Festival. Who the hell would think of something like that? I'd like to meet the folks who came up with that idea." He sat back for a moment, looking off over the edge of the balcony at the cars zooming past on the nearby highway. "There's just so much to see, do...experience, you know? I swear, there must be a parade in every little town in the country. So many people..." He shook his head and stood up. He checked his watch. "I better get home." He paused at the balcony door. "It's Senior Skip Day tomorrow."

Frank nodded. After years of ignoring Skip Day, the school administration had enacted a new policy following a student DUI the previous year. Any students without a valid doctor or parent excuse that day would be dropped a full grade rating on their year-end report card, which for some would put their graduation in jeopardy, depending on previous school infractions. Also, any faculty member made aware of a planned, bogus absence was obligated to report it. If not, they would be subject to disciplinary action.

"A bunch of us are going to the old quarry for a party. Tunes, some swimming." He grinned. "Refreshments." He looked at Frank. "If you want to join us, I know it would be cool with the others."

It was Kenny's way of letting Frank know he was 'one of them,' not part of the establishment.

Frank felt a flush of pride and had no intention of turning the kids in, but it would be pushing things too far to join them in their truancy.

The quarry thing, though, that concerned him a bit. He had heard a few people, and not just teenagers, had drowned there. He opened his mouth to give a stern warning, perhaps try to talk the teen out of going, but saw Kenny raise an eyebrow, as though waiting to see, and judge, how Frank would react. Frank bit off what he was going to say.

"Thanks, I'll have to pass. But...be careful, okay?"

The teenager laughed and told him not to be an old man and let himself out of the apartment.

Frank's phone rang about seven o'clock the following evening. When he heard Rhonda Coti's voice, he was stunned, then waited to hear whatever it was she thought he had done wrong this time.

"Frank, I know you've gotten close to many of the kids. Whether or not I agree with that, I didn't want you to be blindsided by a newspaper report or when you come into school Monday." There was a hitch in her voice as she spoke, and he realized she was trying not to cry.

"What is it, Rhonda? What happened?"

"The kids, Frank...oh my god, those poor kids."

Her anxiety transferring to him in a wave of dread, and he barked, "What, Rhonda? What the hell happened?"

"The kids, Frank. Damned Skip Day. I warned them yesterday, you heard me, the rules are clear, no excuses...""Rhonda!" He wanted to jump through the phone and shake her.

He heard her swallow then, "A bunch of them drove out to the Swarton quarry. A big party. I don't know for sure, but it sounds like they were drinking. A few of them decided to have a contest to see how far they could jump from the lip out toward the middle of the water." She was babbling by this point, and began explaining how the pit had been filled. "Between rain and ground seepage, over time the hole–."

"I know how they fill up with fucking water, Rhonda. What happened?"

Another gulp. "One of the kids managed to jump quite far out, apparently. Took a running leap that carried him almost to the center of the pit."

"And?" An icy chill ran from his scrotum up his back.

"Kenny, Frank. Kenny Short. There was an old earth mover shovel just under the surface. He...he came down on the fork, the tines of it."

The walls of his room wavered as she talked. He saw Kenny's teasing smile, telling Frank not to be an old man.

"He came down right on the spikes." Rhonda's voice hitched, and her next words came out in an explosive burst.

"Skewered. Like a piece of fucking meat."

He dropped the phone at that point. When he picked it up, she was still talking, describing panicked kids, firefighters, the two officers and a body bag lowered from a State Police helicopter to get Kenny's disfigured corpse wrapped up before transporting it to the county morgue.

He had fallen back onto the sofa, staring at nothing, and hung up as Rhonda began talking about the planned wake.

The following days were hazy. There had been the services with a closed casket, and a painful and awkward encounter with Kenny's parents. He had tried to avoid them, but they approached him, wanting to tell him how much Kenny had admired him and appreciated the guidance he had given him.

He had nodded numbly, and immediately staggered out of the funeral home. Two blocks away, he found a bar and spent the next ten hours drinking himself into oblivion.

Don't be an old man.

He wasn't old yet, although forty-six was a lot closer to it than the twenty-eight-year-old he had been when Kenny died. And Kenny would never even see that relatively young age.

He shook his head.

Enough.

What Marina called his walkabouts had started as a way to honor Kenny's memory and the dead student's desire to experience life, meet people, and get a glimpse into their worlds. Now, though, he acknowledged that whatever they had started out as, the trips had turned into a permanent penance for Kenny's death. He hadn't thought himself deserving forgiveness, even if no one else saw it that way.

Not even Rhonda Clotis.

He had spoken to her once more, a few days after bolting from Kenny's wake. He had returned to the school to pick up the few personal items from the office he shared with Rhonda behind the practice hall stage. Frank wasn't, quite, drunk, but he had spent the better part of a week in the suit he had attended the service in. He had already submitted his withdrawal from the teaching program and planned on going away. Somewhere, he wasn't sure where. When he entered the hall, he saw Rhonda sitting on the edge of the stage, legs dangling. It wouldn't have surprised him if the front office had notified her of his arrival. She didn't comment on his appearance, or smell, just looking over at him with pity in her eyes.

Don't, I don't deserve it!

But he said nothing, just started moving across the room toward the office door.

"Frank, I–."

"I'm just here to pick up my stuff, and I'll be gone," he replied, not making eye contact as he passed her.

"Frank."

He kept going.

"Goddamn it, Frank!" It was the tone that stopped him. It was a stuttered pleading mixed with the sobs she was trying to hold in. He turned slowly,

"It wasn't your fault."

Anger bubbled up. "You don't know what the fuck you're talking about."

She slid off the stage and stepped a few feet toward him, then stopped. "I knew about the party, too."

He stared at her.

She walked a few feet closer, approaching him slowly.

"And so did most of the other teachers. Marie Sneed, Larry Walton, a few others."

Rhonda shook her head at his apparent confusion. "What, Mr. Cool, you think we establishment-types are idiots? I grew up in this town. Skip Day at Swarton Quarry has been a tradition since before I was born. You think Kenny and the rest of the kids were the first?"

"But I—"

"Jesus, Frank." She snorted and shook her head, looking at him, then walked to the piano in front of the stage.

"I really don't like you." She looked down at the keyboard. Her index finger extended and came down on a black key.

Plink.

"Rhonda, what—"

Plink. "You can be an obnoxious ass." *Plink*.

She looked up at him.

"But I realize part of it is jealousy. I can admit that. You're good, Frank. Not just the music, the teaching. You...connect. In a way, I can't. I don't think many can.""I—"

He jumped as she slammed her hand down on the keys and the discord echoed across the empty hall.

"You're damn good, Frank," she repeated, then acidly, "When you're not too busy congratulating yourself on how wonderful you are."

He winced.

Rhonda's eyes softened. "But you didn't kill him, any more than I did. Or Marie. Or Larry."

She sniffed as she sat on the bench, head hanging down.

"Or maybe we all did," she almost whispered, but it seemed to echo even louder across the hall than had the piano.

He stared at her bent form for a moment and walked out.

His apartment was already empty, everything sold or donated apart from some clothing, a few instruments, and a yurt his friends at college had given him as a birthday present in his junior year, back when he talked about going on the road as a musician. *At least you'll always have a home*, they had laughed.

Indeed. The yurt, instruments, and his other few possessions were loaded into the truck he had purchased with some of the insurance money from his mother.

There was nothing for him back home in Kansas with his mother gone, except more painful memories, so he simply started driving, making his way across New England, its varied mountain ranges and craggy ocean cliffs so different from the plains he had grown up on.

But the memories followed.

The initial weeklong drunk that had followed Kenny's death quickly descended from an ongoing more or less functional buzz to blackouts and days when he woke in the truck's cab, head splitting, with no idea what towns he had driven through or which one he was in. Then one morning he woke up in his truck, dried puke in his lap and on the seat.

He blinked and shaded his eyes against the early morning sun as he peered through the windshield. He was parked on the side of a country road with no memory of anything after taking a swing at another bar patron the night before and the bouncer taking his role literally; Frank could feel what he was sure was a large bruise on his hip. A tall stockade fence ran in both directions next to the road. Turning, he saw a large metal sign hanging next to what appeared to be a large opening, possibly a driveway, through the fence.

He craned his neck to read the words on the sign, but that made his head swim. He groped under the front seat and came up with an empty bottle of Jim Beam.

Damn.

The wobbliness he felt as he stepped out of the truck was almost comforting, an old companion following months on the road.

He walked carefully toward the sign, squinting. It took a few seconds for the letters to stop moving around.

Sun Trailer Park

New Hampshire Easy Living

Home of the Sun Market – *Best Flea Market in New England!*

"Jesus, you stink!"

He turned slowly and saw a small woman staring up at him. Her sun-streaked hair pulled back in a ponytail, and freckles splayed across her nose. She could have been anywhere from his age to ten years older.

He didn't think she could be over five feet tall. But looking at her, there was bridled fierceness in her green eyes.

He looked down at his crusted clothes.

"Um...yeah. I guess I do."

She stared at him a few seconds longer, her eyes searching his eyes. For what, he didn't know, but she nodded, apparently having decided something, and waved her hand at him.

"Well, come on. I doubt you have a shower hidden in that truck over there. The Market opens in a couple of hours. If you wander around smelling like that, you'll scare all the tips away. You can clean up at my place."

She didn't wait for an answer but walked toward the opening into the Park, pulling a small cart behind her, overflowing with toys and games. She paused before entering, turning to see if he was following.

He stared back, bemused in his haziness.

What the hell.

It wasn't as though he had any place to be. And even in his half sober state, he could smell himself.

He locked the truck and joined her at the open gate.

"Thank you. I appreciate the hospitality." He held out his hand. "I'm Frank Pullman."

Her eyes crinkled at his formality, at such odds with his alley-dweller appearance, and held her own out to shake with him.

"You're very welcome, Frank. Nice to meet you. Although it will be much nicer, for both of us, once you've hosed off." She dropped his hand and turned toward the Park again, grabbing her cart.

"I'm Jessie Blunt," she said, and started walking.

Chapter Twelve

Sometime during his walk down the dark corridors of time, he had gotten up, he wasn't sure quite when, and gone out into the late afternoon. He stood staring into the firepit, poking the half-burned logs with a stick.

"Did the old man have a nice nap?" He looked up and saw Marina and Lila, arms around each other. Lila was grinning at him.

He chewed his mustache and grumbled *Damn women*, which only made them laugh more, and he joined them after another attempt at a frown. He thought if Lila stayed around the Market, he better get used to more teasing.

Shit, the Market.

There were still the repercussions of Jessie's letter to deal with back home. He hadn't forgotten about it, of course, but his trip down the dusky tunnels of his memory had pushed it aside temporarily. And then there was Welp and Sloe's situation.

One thing at a time.

He said, "Looks like it's about time to get our stuff together for the evening show. Now, here's what I'm thinking..."

What Frank was thinking was, simply put, "winging it." He figured they had just enough time to tie themselves into knots if they attempted to rehearse.

"What's the worst that can happen?" He asked them rhetorically, giving a smile meant to be reassuring. But Lila's wide-eyed stare told him it hadn't worked. As she put the acoustic guitar in its case, frowning, he popped into the yurt and grabbed another, wider and shorter case, this one hard-shelled, and came back and handed it to her.

"Here," he said. "Thought we would mix it up a bit tonight."

She looked questioningly at him, popped it open, and shut it again.

"But I haven't..." Lila trailed off, as she looked at him, one side of his mustache raised in his own version of a smile.

"Fine." She took the case from him and stomped back over to Marina, who was shoving a few harmonicas into her pants pockets. Around her neck was what Frank called a 'hamburger eater,' a neck brace contraption that held harmonicas in place while a musician's hands were otherwise occupied.

They made their way to the stage and Frank and Marina helped boost Lila up. She settled herself into the chair set up for her. As Tucker bantered with the crowd to warm them up, she wet the reed of the unfamiliar sax and stretched her fingers, blowing a short up and down scale to check the valve action.

She looked up as Tucker cleared his throat into a mic and introduced them.

"Without further ado, ladies and gentlemen, please welcome...The Stallers!"

Frank wouldn't make eye contact, but Lila was sure there was a twinkle in his eye as he made a couple of final adjustments on the panel for his electric guitar. She felt an unexpected flush of warmth at the group's new name.

Frank turned up the reverb on his guitar and started playing. Lila knew the words of the old song but had never played it. He seemed to sense it and repeated the opening instrumental stanza a few times as her body swayed with the rhythm. Her fingers moved on the sax valves, getting a feel for things, and she nodded to let him know she was ready. She glanced over at Marina, who seemed to be studying Frank as he started singing.

To everything turn, turn, turn

She and Marina came in on the final repeated words. Over at her keyboard, Marina continued to watch Frank, her fingers moving smoothly across her instrument as she played along with Frank's ringing lead.

There is a season turn, turn, turn

Lila looked out at the middle-aged and older crowd. Most were either singing along, nodding their heads along with the lyrics, or both. She smiled to herself as she lifted the sax to her mouth, thinking Frank had pegged the vibe for tonight just right.

She let loose with a short, punctuated solo before the next verse and felt a flush at the applause that followed.

They finished in a three-way harmony that was as in sync as a group that had practiced together for years.

She swung around to watch Frank and Marina for the cut-off on the last note, and as they sang the last line about there being a time for peace, she thought there was a shininess in Marina's eyes.

The next handful of songs were from a couple of decades, at least, before Lila was born. Some she knew, some she picked up as they played. Then, following a bluesy tune where Marina surprised Lila with the depth of her harmonica chops, Marina called out, *I've got this one.* She started a melancholy, slow melody on her keyboard and Frank stood back from his mic; Lila realized Marina would be doing this one solo.

Lila had heard it before, but only as an upbeat tune. Focusing on the lyrics, she realized they really lent themselves to Marina's rendition, which came across more emotional. And when she saw Frank's eyes glued to Marina, she realized that she, and the crowd, were in the middle of a private conversation, the details to which only Frank and Marina were privy.

I think I'm falling, in love too fast,
It's got me hoping for the future, and worrying about the past

As Marina finished the song, Lila wondered if she would have to throw something at Frank, who continued staring at Marina. For her part, Marina busied herself playing with dials on her keyboard, not looking up.

Finally, he turned back toward the audience, cleared his throat, and said the Stallers were going to take a break.

The three of them got drinks at a small wooden kiosk. Their talk was light-hearted and mostly centered on the upcoming second set, but Lila thought if she reached out and touched either of her bandmates, blue sparks would fly off their bodies.

The second set was solid, Lila thought. More than solid. They grooved together as though they had been performing together for years and she felt the sizzle in the air that happened when everything and everyone came together during a performance.

And leaving the stage, she thought the electricity hovering between and around Marina and Frank was, if anything, higher than it had been, like lightning captured in a bottle, desperately trying to get out. She studied them as they made small talk. It was obvious they both wanted to discuss something more substantial than the tempo of the last song they did, but neither seemed willing to take the step toward that. Frank, more than Marina, seemed almost jittery compared to his usual laconic self, responding just a tad too quickly when Marina said something, and louder than usual.

When they got back to the yurt, Lila offered to take her sleeping bag outside by the firepit, thinking a bit of privacy might help them sort through whatever appeared to be coming to a head.

Marina simply shook her head. "Don't worry about it, Lila. It's chilly tonight."

Lila thought she saw relief in Frank's eyes. After storing away the instruments in the back of the truck, they all settled onto their respective air mattresses.

Lila would think back to the days that followed as some of the happiest she had ever had. Additional performances, both as the Stallers and as invitees with other groups, were interspersed with her wandering the grounds of the festival and meeting people, sometimes alone, sometimes with one or both of her yurt-mates. And while the three had brought food with them to cook, there were unlimited munchies, mostly fried, available for free, 'payment' for performing.

Contrary to Frank's comments, as he handed her yet another napkin to wipe powdered sugar from her face, Lila didn't know that anyone had ever died from too much bread dough, but was willing to risk it.

The day before the festival close-out, one of the other bands approached Lila and asked if she would sit in with them. Not the Stallers, her personally. The thrill she felt as she nodded enthusiastically in reply was the perfect topper to the trip for her.

So what if it was a polka band? Lila loved it and managed a somewhat awkward but fun waltz with the elderly glockenspiel player when the set was over.

The final day, they were all up early. Frank doing muted scales on the trumpet he would play during the festival-ending parade. According to Marina, it was the only time he played it, at the closing parade or ceremony of every festival he attended. Then the keyboardist pulled out a triangle, telling them she had missed out playing in the parade last year, only having her keyboard at the time, so she had come prepared this time.

Lila decided to watch from the sidelines. Realistically, she wouldn't be able to use her crutch and didn't want to tax her leg, especially since the ongoing antibiotics seemed to be working and the leg was well on its way to healing.

Frank and Marina left to meet up with the musicians marching in the parade. Shortly, the waltzing glockenspiel player pulled up beside the yurt, having offered her a ride downtown. He dropped her off a block from the Main Street parade route and she hobbled the rest of the way, finding a likely spot at the curb. She looked around and spotted a number of new acquaintances scattered up and down the street and exchanged waves.

As the sound of horns and sirens reached her, she saw firetrucks slowly turning onto the main drag from a side street four or five blocks away. She waved and cheered along with everyone else as the trucks made their way past her. The fire department was followed by a Girl Scout troop, then a unicycle club, along with some costumed characters, throwing candy at the onlookers. A squalling toddler next to her with his mother quieted when she held up a Tootsie Roll to show his mother and, at her nod, handed it to him.

The first musical group, the Olmsville High School Marching Band, approached, followed by a small cadre of elderly veterans with drums, a bugle, and cymbals, following behind the flag carrier. Cheers followed them as they passed Lila, and she turned to see what was next. It was Frank out in front of three columns of musicians. Looming behind them was a float being pulled by a pickup. It was an enormous donut, made of, naturally, duct tape. The sign on the side proclaimed, "Dipping Donuts – Proud Sponsor of the Olmsville Duck Tape Festival!"

Frank had the trumpet in one hand, a baton in the other as he marched backwards, facing the band which included musicians from the various festival bands.

Although he looked somber, she could see a sparkle in his eyes. He raised the baton, and the eclectic group brought their instruments up. The baton came down, and they began to play. After the first stanza during which Frank conducted walking backwards, he turned forward again and joined in on his horn. Lila recognized the song from a kids' movie a few years before.

Rolling slowly behind the group was a single police car, signifying the end of the parade.

Around her, people gathered up their children, chairs, and other parade supplies, and began dispersing.

An unexpected wave of sadness hit her as she realized the festival was over.

Back to reality, she thought, and started her lopsided crutch-walk to the agreed upon rendezvous with the glockenspiel player.

The ride back from Ohio felt different from the outward journey. When Frank offered to buy lunch for the group, Lila found she had no more than a twinge of angst and defensive anger, which she was able to quickly put aside. She simply smiled at him as she said thanks. And while the charge between Marina and Frank was still there, it seemed to have subsided, or at least they were handling it better.

Leaning against the passenger door as they made their way through Vermont, she tried to enjoy the ride and view of forest and intermittent old farmhouses, but the thought of the visitors back in Bridgett began gnawing at her the closer they got to New Hampshire. She still didn't know what they wanted but told herself to have faith in Mike DeTony's belief they weren't some type of police sent to bring her back to Pine Ridge, planning on somehow tying her to Mama Elise's murder.

She glanced over at Frank and Marina, who were sharing some inside joke regarding fried bull testicles, Marina slapping the steering wheel as she laughed. Lila shook her head, smiling.

And realized that she did have faith, something never in abundant supply for her at the best of times. Welp had scooped her up, more or less, and the next thing she knew, although she was a stranger, they had patched her up and taken her in as part of their odd group.

Their family.

She looked over at Frank, certain that if he had made any sort of case against getting involved with the suspicious wandering woman with a leg wound from an unknown source, the others would have gone along with him, even if they disagreed.

She wondered if it occurred to Frank that he was the patriarch of the Staller clan.

Frank glanced over with a raised questioning eyebrow when she gave a small chuckle, and Lila shook her head. He gave a grunt and returned to his conversation with Marina.

Reluctant patriarch, if he even knows, although I doubt he does. He doesn't think in those terms. He just does what he thinks is right. And takes care of people that need it.

Like her.

As they passed the sign indicating they had just entered New Hampshire, a frisson of nervousness hit her, and she mentally reviewed yet again through what Frank had recounted from the phone conversation with Welp. When she got to the latter part of the call in her mind, when Frank had told Welp to not do anything until they returned to the Park, she turned and asked Frank about it. She wondered if it had something to do with the visitors.

"Frank, what did you tell Welp to sit tight about?"

He looked over from his current ongoing conversation with Marina and frowned.

"He asked me if he could stay at my place a couple of days. Apparently, he moved out from his and Sloe's trailer and said he needed a bit of time to find alternate arrangements. I told him he could use my trailer, but asked him to stay put there until we got back."

He had apparently already filled Marina in, as she kept her eyes on the road and didn't react.

Lila said in surprise, "Oh no. Is it because of Welp's drug problem?"

At that, both Marina and Frank stared blankly at her.

Marina said, "What are you talking about? What drug problem?""The first day at their trailer. Welp said you were there for an intervention. I figured it must be drugs."

Marina's laughter echoed in the truck cabin. Frank had to reply as Marina tried to get control of herself.

"No drug problems, Lila. It's that Welp wants to leave the Market and Sloe doesn't. Sloe asked me to talk to Welp to see if things could be smoothed over."

Luckily it was dark and the two couldn't see Lila's cheeks burning bright red. She was only glad she had never said anything to Sloe about it.

"Oh. Well. I'm glad he isn't an addict." Then, "Do you think they will stay together?" She was hoping the answer was yes. Sloe and Welp obviously loved each other and seemed to be good for each other.

Frank told her he didn't know; Sloe had come by her stubbornness honestly, and Welp was just as obstinate in his own way.

Marina added to his comment. "I hope they do. Some people just belong with each other," echoing Lilia's thoughts, but Lila didn't think she was only talking about the couple back at the Market. She noticed Frank kept his eyes firmly on the road.

They turned off County Line Road onto Phelps and she could see dots of light flickering in the darkness behind the Park stockade fence a hundred yards down the road. It was good to be back.

Home?

No, it wasn't home. At least, not right now. But there was a hominess about it that made her glad to be pulling in. The sound of the tires on the gravel thru-road seemed too loud to Lila; it was going on midnight and most residents were tucked in. They pulled up to Frank's place and Marina, who was currently driving, put the truck in reverse and backed into her own driveway behind her small SUV. They all got out and

Lila headed to the back of the truck to pull out the canvas bag containing the yurt.

"Lila, we can give you a hand setting that up if that's your preference," the keyboardist said, stepping up behind her with Frank. "Otherwise, I have a spare bedroom that *isn't* filled with instruments if you'd like a real bed for a change."

She was on the verge of saying she didn't want to intrude any more than she already had or was necessary, but looking at Frank and Marina, she realized it didn't matter. As far as they were concerned, it was expected. Lila was a Staller.

She felt a warmth she hadn't felt since before that day in the trailer, finding Mama Elise's body.

"How could I pass up the chance to sleep on something other than an inner tube?"

"Watch it," Frank growled. "Or I'll make sure the air mattress has a slow leak the next time you need it."

"Yeah, yeah," she grinned in the dark at him. Then she paused and asked if she could talk to him for a minute. He raised his eyebrow, but nodded. Marina told her to come over when she was ready and walked across the roadway.

Frank motioned toward his picnic table and sat on its edge, his legs propped on the bench seat. She walked slowly over, already regretting asking to talk.

He pulled a half-smoked cheroot from his shirt pocket, examined it, apparently decided it was still worth smoking, and stuck it in his mouth, lighting it with a stick match that sent little sparks into the night sky as he scraped it across the wooden table. Thankfully, he didn't seem in a hurry since she wasn't sure what she wanted to say, or at least how to say it.

She rocked back and forth for a minute as he took a long drag and blew smoke rings which shimmered in and out of sight in the spotlight shining from his trailer.

Finally, she said, "Thank you."

To her relief, he didn't ask for what. He looked over at her and said, "You're welcome."

But she wanted, needed, to say more, and she tried to get her thoughts straight.

"Frank, you didn't have to–" he waved it away, and her voice got firmer. "No, please, listen."

He put his hand down and looked back at her intently, nodding.

"You didn't have to take me in. I mean, I know Welp dragged me to the Park and Mike patched me up, but, well, you could have left it at that." She paused. "But you didn't."

He tried to wave this away as well, saying, "The others had their own minds, anyway, Lila. I just–"

"No." She cut him off, more curtly than she intended and took a deep breath as he looked at her in surprise. She said it again, more gently this time. "No. You could have sloughed me off, maybe gotten me a ride into town, whatever. And all the others may not have liked it, but they would have done it. Because you asked them to. They follow your lead. "

His eyes seemed to grow brighter, but he said nothing, watching her.

"All the Stallers, they look to you to, I don't know, set the tone. The path." She gave a wry smile. "The key. You set the key, and they come in doing their own thing, but you're playing lead. Like in the festival parades."

He looked down at the smoldering stub in his hand for a moment, then threw it to the ground violently and stood, looking back toward his trailer.

Lila realized she had triggered something in him. She was debating reaching out to him when his voice, gruff and filled with pain, came to her through the semi-darkness.

"I'm no good lead, or example, for anyone."

She did reach out now, putting her hand gently on his arm.

"Frank...I don't know what made you come here to the Park, but whatever it was, I've spent enough time with your family," He stiffened at the word but kept looking toward the trailer, "and heard stories about you..." his turned to her in surprise as she said this "...yes, everyone seems to have a Frank story. Not just the family. Almost all the Stallers. And every single story comes down to *Frank did this for me or us*." She squeezed his arm. "Do you know how rare that is? I mean, don't get a big head. They also think you're a masochist and can't get out of your own way to enjoy life, but...damn it, Frank, you've made a difference to everyone here."

She saw his eyes were as misty as her own.

"So, thank you. For everything. And everyone."

He stood, just looking at her. She stepped up to him, put her head against his chest, and hugged him.

After a moment, his arms came up and wrapped around her as he stood looking across at Marina's trailer.

Chapter Thirteen

Lila paused in the hall outside Marina's spare bedroom, taking in the smell of fresh brewed coffee.

Mmmm.

She made her way to the kitchen, poured a cup, and joined her hostess, already sitting at the dinette table.

"See Frank yet?" she asked her yawning host.

Marina gave a slightly wistful shake of her head and, not for the first time, Lila wished Frank would do what every Staller she had encountered knew he should.

Lila smiled and Marina gave her a chagrined look, realizing Lila knew what she was thinking, stood, and looked out the window over the kitchen sink.

"Speak of the mustached devil. He, Welp, and Sloe are talking outside Frank's place." Marina's lips tightened. "Let's hope it helps." She stretched, turning back to Lila. "Nice to be back in a real bed."

"Yeah," Lila said. "Thanks for the use of the room last night."

Marina gave a bright smile in return. "No problem. You can stay as long as you like, you know."

She nodded. "I know, but I really don't want to be any more of a nuisance than I have been." She stuck her mostly healed leg out; the crutch in the bedroom. "Besides, my leg is a lot better, and I should be making my way to Maine." Her face fell. "Assuming I'm not in jail."

"About that, Lila. Frank and I were talking–"

The opening of the trailer door interrupted Marina. Frank walked in, closely followed by Welp, with Sloe on her husband's heels.

"Welp, the two of you have to decide what's best. I just don't want either of you to make a rash decision. I think you should both keep talking." He walked into the kitchen, giving Marina and Lila a nod as he passed. He grabbed a mug from the cupboard and poured himself a cup.

"Does it really matter?" Welp had an almost petulant tone as he sat down in the chair next to Lila. Sloe pulled the one out on her other side. "I keep trying to tell her what I want—"

"I know what you want, you big idiot!" interjected his wife, leaning forward to look around Lila, who felt she was center court of a verbal tennis match.

"You see?" Welp slapped his hand on the table. "She won't let me explain and thinks–"

"You've told me already, Welp!" Sloe's frustration was evident in both her volume and tone, cutting him off again. "You want to leave, and I told you I'm not going anywhere! I just...can't."

Welp made a strangling noise and stood again, gripping the back of his chair tightly.

After a moment Lila said quietly, "Welp, it really isn't my business but, well, can I ask *why* you want to leave?"

Dead silence.

Frank leaned against the counter, blowing on his cup, a raised eyebrow showing his curiosity as well. She was sure he had more background than she did, but apparently there were gaps in his understanding, too.

She saw Marina leaning back, expectantly as well. Sloe stared down at the table.

Welp let out a breath and sat back down, facing across the table, looking out the kitchen window.

"It's a trap," he started, and Lila saw Sloe open her mouth.

Frank cut her off with a stern, "Sloe, let the man speak." For a moment she thought Sloe was going to ignore him, but then the Staller seemed to think better of it and closed her mouth again.

Prompting Welp to continue, Lila said gently, "A trap?"

He waved his hand in a partial circle. "This, the Park. The Market. All of it. It's like flypaper. You're born here, or you come to the Park, or are dumped here because you don't have anywhere else to go, you don't have any other choice. But once you're here for a while, you're stuck."

More animated than Lila had seen him before, she watched as he paced a small circle like a newly caught wild animal in a cage. "Sure, some leave. But most don't. You spend your days just trying to get by, paddling in place. Yeah, I know it's the same for a lot of people, but, well, let's be honest. Living and working at Sun Market and Trailer Park doesn't present a lot of choices, does it? Even if you do lift your feet to try to do something else, something different, you're stuck in place."

Lila thought Sloe would explode at that, but when she turned her head, she saw Sloe had looked up from the table, her eyes brimming with tears.

"Is that what you think?" Sloe said slowly. "Of *me?* Paddling in place? You didn't have a choice?"

Her husband shook his head, hard, "Not about you...us...Sloe. Never. It's...Look, I run a used bicycle business, for Christ's sake. We get by, between us and the repair business I do outside the Market but...you're so smart, Sloe. And I'm good. Damn good. Not just bikes, you know that. My father was a magician when it came to anything mechanical, with or without a motor. I've got a lot of him in me. I'm sure I could–"

Shouting outside interrupted him. It sounded like it was coming from across the graveled roadway, over at Frank's.

"Frank! Frank, goddamn it, I know you're back. I want to talk to you." Loud banging followed.

Frank stepped to the window and peeked out.

"Christ on a stick. Egan has come visiting," he said, giving a weary sigh.

Lila heard a growl emanating from Sloe.

The banging and yelling continued. Frank turned back to them, focused on Sloe.

"I don't think we'll get any peace unless I talk to him," he said.

Sloe issued another growl, along with some mutterings about Egan. Lila was pretty sure what Sloe was proposing was anatomically impossible.

Gruffly, Sloe finally huffed, "Fine."

Frank walked to the door and swung it open.

"Top of the mornin' to you, Egan," he called out, overly cheerful and with such a bad Irish accent that Sloe gave a laughing snort despite herself. "Care to join us for a cup of coffee?"

There was a pause in Egan's yelling, then footsteps. Frank stepped back from the door, his arm extended to keep it open, and Lila saw Egan glare at him from the small deck before stepping inside.

Upon entering, the Park owner looked around the group at the kitchen table, realizing Frank wasn't alone nor just with Marina. He came to himself and said to Frank, "We need to talk. Privately."

Frank sauntered casually over to the coffeemaker. Filling a mug, he held it out to the new arrival and said, "I believe you take it black?"

Egan hesitated, then walked over and took the proffered cup.

"Thank you."

Sloe, who had apparently been tightly holding her temper to that point, burst up from her chair.

"Well, look who has learned some manners, Mr. Fucking Park Manager Lothe. And 'private' chat, my freckled ass. This involves me as well as Frank. She was my mother."

Egan winced.

"Sloe...Ginny. You're part of this, of course. When I said private, I meant including you, too."

"Oh, were you, you..."

Welp had stepped to Sloe's side when Egan entered and now set his hand set gently on her shoulder. She looked up, at first thinking he was going to interrupt her just-getting-started tirade, but saw only support for her and anger at the interloper in his eyes. She smiled gratefully at him.

They better stay together, Lila thought.

Welp may not have planned on interrupting his wife, but she had paused when he put his hand on her. This gave Frank a chance to step in before things escalated.

"Sloe, work on your sailor-talk later."

She started to respond, but seeing Frank's expression, closed her mouth and nodded.

"Thank you," Egan repeated to Frank. "Perhaps you, Ginny, and I can go somewhere to talk?"

"No." Sloe's voice was quiet, measured, but final.

Egan looked at her.

"Everyone here is family, Egan. If we're going to discuss anything, we can do it right here, right now."

Egan stared back then his eyes moved to each of the rest of the group, one at a time. His eyes stopped briefly on Marina, noting the arm she around Frank and then they moved on to Lila.

"She's not. She isn't even a Staller."

That jolted her, like she had touched a bug zapper, but Lila silently agreed, Frank's joking band name aside. She also suddenly wished she was one of them. These people, these *friends*, were as much family as she had and she realized how much she wanted to be here, with them, to help, if she could.

But she wasn't one of them, and didn't want to be a distraction or cause problems.

Frank, however, had a different view.

"Yes. She is," he said. His eyes held Egan's as he spoke.

Egan looked back at him just as steadily but then nodded slowly.

"Fine, one big happy fucking family, all around," he said as he pulled out a piece of crumpled paper that Lila assumed must be the letter from Sloe's mother, Jessie.

"We need to settle this, Frank. Now. I've been waiting five years and this," he shook the paper angrily, "this is just bullshit." He glared at Frank. "What's your price?"

Lila's head swiveled back and forth between the men. Before she could stop herself, she said, "Wait, what? His price for what?"

Egan looked at her consideringly for a moment, then answered.

"Well, *cousin*, Frank is now half owner of the Park and Market, courtesy of my sister."

Lila was totally lost, but wasn't sure she should ask any more questions. Sloe saved her the trouble, though, turning to her to explain.

"My mother inherited joint ownership of the Market and Park from my grandfather along with free tenancy to her immediate family and descendants, in perpetuity. Apparently as disgusted as he was by Mama walking away from managing things and, well, me being born, he still had something that passed for a heart."

Welp shook his head and murmured, "Two sizes too small."

Sloe continued. "I think he hoped she would be tempted back into the 'family business', but that didn't happen. She made a deal with him," she gestured disparagingly at Egan with her chin, "that he could run things with a few conditions."

Egan's scowl was bigger now, but Sloe ignored it as she laid out the conditions. "No evictions without her express approval, no major modifications, except for upgrades and upkeep, to the place without her giving express, written permission...and that the property couldn't be sold."

Egan seemed ready to explode, shaking his head in disbelief, and turned to all of them. "Do you know how much this land is worth? Enough to set me up for life, and Jessie and you, too! What the hell was she thinking?"

Sloe calmly replied, "She was thinking this was, and is, home."

"Idiot!" was Egan's response.

Welp's hand on Sloe's shoulder tightened, and he managed to keep her grounded as his wife tried to launch herself across the table.

"Don't ever talk about my mother like that again," she spat at Egan.

Egan started to reply in kind but then stopped, taking a deep breath. The anger in his eyes cleared, replaced with something closer to regret.

He looked at Frank. "I assumed, and based on reactions to the letter, I think we all assumed, that the trust Jessie set up for five years was to give Ginny time to acclimate and decide if she wanted to stay or leave. During the five years, I would continue to run the Park under the previous agreement Jessie and I had. At the end of the five years, if Ginny decided to leave, everything would come to me, with a payout to her." His lip curled. "Again, I assumed." He shook his head. "That will teach me."

"Wait." Lila didn't understand. "Why wouldn't her portion just go to Sloe, period?" She looked at the tanned woman questioningly.

"Because Mama knew I didn't want to run the Park but left open the option if I changed my mind in the first five years."

Sloe glanced at Welp. "Welp and I can live here free for the rest of our lives but her will stated I would have to make a final decision five years after her death. Otherwise, her ownership portion would transfer to someone else."

"Yes, me, goddamn it!" Egan became animated again. "Not him!" His finger came up, pointing at Frank like an ancient prophet calling down the wrath of God on a heretic.

Frank ignored him and said to Sloe quietly, "It's still yours, if you want it."

Sloe shook her head. "You know better, Frank. The Market and Park are and always will be home, but I don't want to be in charge." She tipped her chin up, staring at Egan. "I'm a Staller."

Frank nodded. He looked back at the Park manager. "So that's that, then." He added, "And I'm not interested in selling. Partner."

Egan made a sputtering sound, then exclaimed, "Idiots!"

This time Sloe was too quick for Welp and made it across the table, hand stretched out in a claw toward Egan, but Frank stepped in front of her until Welp could haul her back.

Egan hadn't moved but had the good grace to look chastised as she took her seat again.

He held up a hand. "Ginny, I apologize. Look, I loved Jessie. For all of her stup...her way of doing things her own way, she was my sister." His eyes softened. "I idolized her when we were kids. And when she and Daddy fell out and she left, it was like she had cut me off too."

Sloe opened her mouth to say something, but he added, "And trapped me."

She closed her mouth and looked up at Welp, who looked at Egan with surprise, then nodded slowly.

Sloe looked back at Egan and asked in a soft voice, "What do you mean, trapped you?"

Egan pursed his lips and blew out. He motioned to a chair, and at her nod, sat down.

"My mother, Jessie's and my mother, your grandmother, died when we were both very young. I was still in diapers. Daddy had a very specific view of the world. I'm sure Jessie told you. You were either on Team Lothe or the enemy, someone to grind into dust or to make money from. Preferably both. And there was only one person in charge on Team Lothe."

Sloe nodded.

"After boarding school, he sent me to college to hone my business skills. He expected me to take over running things one distant day when he got tired of playing the game himself. In the meantime, I was expected to help out when I was home, collecting rent, throwing out dead...people who weren't able to pay. Strictly according to his way, his rules. No discussion, no arguments. And when you worked for him, there was no disappointing him. No one dared. Except Jessie."

His brown eyes softened for just a moment. In that moment, Lila knew he really had loved his sister. And that may be the prevailing view of him around the Market and Park was more seeing him through the ghost of his father than Egan himself.

"She had moved into the Park a few years before I graduated from the University of New Hampshire." He paused and smiled. "When I came back and started working for Dad full-time, you were about three and the cutest goddamn critter I had ever seen, running all over the Park in those ridiculous Hello Kitty outfits."

Sloe's eyes widened. "You were watching me?"

Egan nodded. "And Jessie kept me filled in when I saw her every month."

Sloe stared at him for a moment, then scowled. "Liar. You turned your back on her when your father did!"

To Lila's surprise, Frank shook his head and replied, "No, Sloe. He didn't."

Sloe's head whipsawed back and forth between the two men. "I don't understand."

Egan said, "Ginny, you're right, at least initially. I was angry. No, I was *pissed*. But I told you, she was my big sister, and I missed her. So, after I took over collecting rent, about once a month we would meet after hours. At Frank's."

"Frank!" Sloe's shock and hurt were obvious on her face.

"Sloe, it was Jessie's decision to not tell you, and she asked me to keep it to myself as well. Your grandfather was still alive, and she worried it would get back to him. That would have been very bad for Egan."

Egan muttered, "Maybe that would have been better."

Sloe looked at him for a moment, then nodded, anger gone. "All right." Not anger this time, more hurt non-understanding. "And fine. So you kept up on the goings on with your banished sister and her bastard. Whoop de doo.

What about when she got sick? Where were you then? You could have helped."

Egan glanced at Frank. "The stubbornness is strong in this one."

Lila wasn't the only one surprised at Egan making anything resembling a joke. Welp let out one of his guffaws and Sloe and Marina looked shocked. Frank simply gave one of his patented *hmmph* sounds and said, "She comes by it honestly," looking out of the corner of his eye at Sloe.

Egan sighed and turned back to Sloe.

"I would have, if she would have allowed it, Ginny. But," a resentful glance toward Frank, "she had Frank, and he kept me posted. I worked around the edges, based on what he told me, to make sure things were taken care of if he or she couldn't handle something."

Frank was chewing on his mustache. "Egan, I loved your sister too, you know that. She was a combination sister and, well, let's say, a foul-mouthed, brash spiritual guide that continues to help me, even in her physical absence. But I never tried to take your place. You'll remember I was the one that came to you and suggested if you wanted to, you could use my place to meet."

Egan said nothing but after a few moments, nodded.

"She loved you, Egan. And worried about you. For myself, I couldn't have given a rat's ass, but... she *missed* you, for Christ's sake. And, well, I hated seeing her in pain."

As Egan sat silent, Lila saw the resemblance between him and Sloe for the first time. It was in their eyes. A depth that both their sometimes-loud outbursts of emotion masked. But the outbursts themselves showed they cared. It might be about different things, but the caring was genuine.

There's more to him than it seems at first.

She continued to watch him as he spoke again.

"I know you hate me, Ginny. But I did what I could."

Sloe looked back at him, her gaze softening, and she sighed. "All right, so you tried to help. But it doesn't change anything."

"I didn't expect it to." There was sadness behind the words.

Egan directed his next comment to Frank.

"Let me buy you out, Frank."

Frank shook his head. "I already told you, no."

"Then buy me out."

Frank's laugh was dry. "Where the hell do you think I'd come up with the money to do that?" He shook his head again and said simply, "No."

"Fuck."

"Look," Frank said, his lip quirking up, "it could be worse."

Egan looked almost affronted by the comment and said, "Really, Frank? Really? You like it here. I've been trying to get out of this fucking place since I was sixteen."

"Why?" It was Welp. His head was cocked slightly to the side as he studied Egan.

Egan appeared to have a hard time registering that the up-to-now silent large, furry man had actually spoken.

"What?"

"Why have you been trying to leave? I mean, you *own* the place. Or might as well, since you run things. Big house, don't have to even show your face around the Park or Market unless you want to. How bad could it be?"

Lila waited for a condescending and probably sneering response, but the overall conversation had apparently caused Egan to put aside the persona of big and scary Park Manager; he seemed to consider the question.

"It doesn't matter," Egan finally said.

"Actually, it does." Sloe spoke.

Egan looked at her. "Why would you care?"

"I...just do." Sloe looked up at Welp, then back to Egan.

Lila saw Welp give Sloe's shoulder a small squeeze.

Egan looked at the two of them over his cup of coffee as he took a sip, then nodded, perhaps sensing, whatever the reason, how important it was to Sloe.

"Look, this place has been my life, aside from school and even then, I was tied to it. Before Dad informed me that I'd be going to the State University, so I could come home on weekends to work, I had looked into schools in Florida, California, even England and France. Almost anywhere away from *here* that offered what I wanted to study."

"And what was that? That you wanted to study?" Lila asked, curiously.

He looked over at her for the first time since shortly after entering the trailer. "Architecture." More hesitation, and his cheeks turned pink. She stifled a smile, thinking it was cute, but not wanting to embarrass him more than he already obviously was. "My dream was to work for one of the big theme parks, designing new attractions."

"You wanted to be a Mouseketeer?" Sloe guffawed as she said it.

Egan glared at Sloe. "That's an *Imagineer.*" The fire in his eyes reminded her of Sloe when she was ready to go on a tear.

He is definitely her uncle.

"Oh. Right." Sloe tried to blank her face, without much success.

Egan turned back to Lila. "Dad had other plans, though. I ended up majoring in business management. He did let me take a couple of engineering classes as electives. Throwing the dog a bone, essentially. But in return, he told me he expected me to come up with a way to squeeze more tenants into the Park. He never quite forgave me for not doing that."

"Quite the sweetheart," Marina spoke up, making a puckering face. "Sorry I missed meeting him."

Egan snorted and looked around at the group.

"Look, it's not that I hate the Park, or Market." He saw Sloe's eyes narrow and headed off her likely rebuttal. "No, really. It's just..." his voice dropped. "I hate that I didn't have a choice." Lila saw Welp nodding. Sloe looked thoughtful as Frank and Marina stood silent. "Maybe I would have gone off to California and after a while and decided Bridgett, New Hampshire was the place for me. I doubt it, but who the hell knows?

I never will." The comment came out with both pain and long simmering anger.

Sloe had one hand on Welp's, resting on her shoulder. The other hand now joined it, and she craned her neck to look up at him. Lila saw the tears that she had suspected Sloe was holding back, and they finally cut loose.

"Oh God, Welp. Oh, love, I hadn't..."

Egan looked confused then over at Frank, Marina standing at his side.

"What..."

A knock interrupted him. It was followed by a voice, slightly muffled by the door.

"Ms. Agbo? I understand you were traveling with Lila Fortin. Is she with you, by any chance?"

Chapter Fourteen

Lila shivered, recognizing the voice, and stared at the door. "Fuck." Welp stifled a chuckle, thinking it was an almost perfect imitation of Egan from a few minutes prior.

He saw Frank lean over and whisper something to Marina, then motioned Lila toward the hallway. Lila headed down the hall to the spare bedroom, leaving its door open a crack behind her.

Welp was nervous. He didn't know how this would shake out and tried to remind himself Mike D thought the visitors were harmless. He hoped so, for Lila's sake. For everyone's sakes, actually.

All things considered, he'd rather be tinkering with a bike.

Egan looked around, confused. He said to no one in particular, "I don't–"

"Uncle Egan, *please!*"

Egan started and looked wide-eyed at Sloe, then slowly nodded and was silent.

Welp looked down at Sloe in the chair in front of him and felt the same tingling in his stomach as he had the first day he met her. He promised himself that they would finish their aborted conversation when everything died down.

I'm not going to lose you, regardless of what happens.

Marina looked at the group around the table and nodded. As she stepped to the door, Welp sent out a prayer to whatever gods that might be listening and willing to help flea market dwellers and scooter riding women that Mike was right about the visitors.

Marina tried out a couple of different versions of a smile, settled on one, and opened the door. A man and a woman, both upper middle-aged or older, stood on her stoop. They had the look of people used to working outside and Welp noticed each had braided plaits hanging down to their shoulders, although the man's was partially hidden under a cowboy hat. Behind them in front of the trailer was an older truck camper with South Dakota plates.

"Hi," Marina said brightly.

"Ms. Abgo?" the woman asked, eyes slitting slightly as she asked. Welp guessed they weren't aware Marina was not black. Not the type of person anyone would expect to run into in the bowels of New Hampshire.

"I'm Marina Agbo, yes. Can I help you?"

The man glanced at Marina, then looked past her, scanning the group in the kitchen, obviously trying to spot Lila.

Marina repeated, ignoring the man peering around her into the trailer, "Is there something I can help you folks with?" She was standing very straight, and her body language made it clear she wasn't about to invite the two in.

The man finished his scan and shook his head slightly at his companion. The woman said, "We're looking for Lila Fortin." Although a good foot shorter than Marina, she didn't seem intimidated in the least by Marina's tall stature. "Is she here?"

Marina's return stare was just as steady.

"Nope."

The woman held her gaze for a moment. "I see," her reply as succinct as Marina's. She let it hang there for a moment, perhaps hoping Marina would expand upon the single syllable. When it became apparent no more information would be forthcoming, she spoke again.

"We had heard she was traveling with you. And you're back." She waited, looking steadily at Marina.

Marina responded, not denying Lila had been with her. Welp thought that was probably best. Too many lies tended to trip you up. "Yep, I'm back. But Lila decided it was time to move on. Somewhere south, I believe. Virginia, West Virginia, somewhere around there. I don't quite remember."

There was a pause, then the woman said again, "I see."

"I don't know that I'll hear from her, but if I do, I could pass along a message if you'd like." Marina said it casually, but Welp knew she was trying to get a sense of the visitors' intent.

The man spoke up for the first time, having completed his scan of the trailer.

"We're here–"

The woman made a motion with her hand. It was only a twitch, but it was enough for him to stop talking.

"I'd rather speak to her in person," she said. "It's rather complicated. Just tell her it has to do with Woweechala."

Welp had no idea what that last word meant and doubted anyone else in the group knew either, but Marina said, "Well, if I hear from her, I'll let her know."

The woman nodded. "We'll be around for a couple more days. We've been parking in the open field next door. Mr.

DeTony at the liquor store told us it shouldn't be a problem. Hopefully, no one minds." She looked pointedly toward Egan, who opened his mouth to say something, but immediately closed it again at a glance from Sloe.

The woman put her hand on the man's arm and turned to leave. She paused and looked back at Marina.

"I do hope she is all right. It will take her some time to get to Maine on foot."

Marina's face remained blank. "Maine? On foot?"

The woman gave a dry smile. "Yes, I believe that was her destination when she left South Dakota." She pointed over toward Frank's place. "And unless she has sprouted wings, she must be walking seeing that her, ah, borrowed, scooter is sitting across the way, leaning against that trailer."

With that, the visitors departed and Marina closed the door, turning to the group and leaning against it.

She blew out a breath. "Damn."

Egan stood, waving his arms. "Now, can someone tell me what the hell is going on? Who are those people? And, maybe only important to me, what the fuck are they doing camping out in my field?"

Welp saw Frank had pulled out his cell phone and Sloe was hugging Lila, who had come out from the back room, tears on her face. He caught Marina's eye, but she simply shrugged, so he decided it was his turn in the barrel.

He gave Egan a brief breakdown of how Lila came to be at the Market and a rather vague description of her departure from South Dakota, leaving out the part about her foster-mother's possible illegal activities and her death.

Lila stepped back from Marina, snuffling. "Tell it all, Welp, it's part of it. Maybe an important part. She's dead. It doesn't matter at this point."

So, he filled Egan in about Lila finding Mama Elise's body, the old woman's possible illicit activities, and about Lila's escape, finishing with the possibility someone might try to blame her foster-mother's death on the young woman.

Lila was back at the table. Marina handed around bottles of beer from the fridge. Egan looked at the label and made a face but took a swig.

"So, your foster-mother had some sort of business, and you think that might be tied, legally or not, to why she was killed?" He asked. "What was the business?"

"Eagle feathers," Lila responded.

"Feathers?" Egan was in disbelief. "She might have been killed over feathers? Why the hell would anyone want eagle feathers, let alone kill someone for them?"

Lila explained, "They're used by tribal members for ceremonial purposes. Eagles are sacred to my people...the Lakota, messengers between people and the gods. They've been used in traditional dress for centuries. Not just the feathers, but body parts and sometimes the whole bird. Totally legal but also very hard to get. They come from ones that have been poached and confiscated or from ones that die of natural causes. For an entire eagle, it could be two years to get them from Fish and Wildlife." She took a sip of her beer. "Powwows have contests for traditional dances which include wearing traditional costumes. The prize money is big, sometimes in the thousands. A reservation doesn't have much in the way of job prospects and not much of anything else either. That kind of money would tempt almost anyone." The sadness on her face as she said this changed to anger, and Lila's mouth curled up in disgust. "Mama Elise didn't sell to other Lakota, though. Only white dealers who wanted them for 'authentic' Native American souvenirs. Maybe someone wanted her stock. I just don't know."

She lifted her beer again, bile in her throat. "God bless America." She slammed the bottle back down on the table, drops flying out the top.

"Jesus," Egan said. "That's...insane."

Lila's eyes grew dark, and she spat out, "What part? The part where a family tries to support themselves performing dances that were outlawed at one point by the same group of people who now pay big money to buy 'traditional' trinkets and watch the people whose land they stole perform like circus animals?"

Although not directed at Welp, he took a step back at the vitriol in Lila's voice.

Egan shook his head, holding up a hand. "Lila, no. I mean... yes, but only in the sense of people having to do that to try to get by. And that your foster-mother was possibly killed over it."

He leaned toward her. "I'm sorry." There was a gentleness in his voice that surprised Welp. Admittedly, he had very few past direct dealings with Egan aside from handing him a check at the end of the month. No one at the Park really did, with the now known exception of Frank. He was simply a looming presence, like an endemic disease whose presence was constant but that you hoped wouldn't pop up anytime soon.

Not quite that black and white, though, is it?

Egan's earlier comments had resonated with him, and Welp was surprised to have anything in common with the man, let alone sharing a sense of being trapped.

Frank hung up from his call and turned back to them. "That was Mike. He was the one that suggested they park their camper in the field. Thought it was better to know where they were, than not."

Egan bit his lip. "All right, that makes sense, under the circumstances." He smirked. "I won't even charge them rent."

Frank gave a *hmmph* and Marina asked, "Lila, do you know them?"

She nodded and said, "The woman, at least. Winchapi, Margaret Elmhurst. She is the district medicine woman, the phejúta winyela, and president of the Tribal Council."

Frank said, "Ok, but I won't even try to pronounce...Fehoota? Medicine woman. And the man? He seemed to be taking orders from her."

This time Lila shook her head. "I couldn't see anything from back there and he didn't say enough for me to be sure." She cocked her head. "Although, at a guess, it's probably James Tokalu Taylor. He usually follows her around. Sort of a lapdog."

Frank repeated, "Okay. Last question, for now. What was that word she used? She said their visit has to do with... Woweech...?"

Lila closed her eyes for a moment, and when she opened them, they were glistening again. "Woweechala. It's Lakota for Faithful." Tears began scrolling down her cheeks again. "It's...it was Mama Elise's Lakota name."

She took a couple of deep breaths to steady herself, and Frank cleared his throat. "Welp?"

"Yeah, Frank?"

"What shape is Lila's scooter in? Were you able to fix it?"

"Yes, but it might only be temporary." He looked at Lila. "That beastie must be twenty years old and it has been hammered. The carburetor is shot. I cleaned it the best I could, but it really needs to be replaced and I haven't been able to find a match yet."

Frank nodded. "Ok, so maybe we can find her some alternate transportation. We can all work on keeping the two visitors distracted, tell them we heard from Lila and she is coming back. That will keep them here while Lila heads out." He turned to Lila. "Not Maine, though. At least, not right now. We'll want to make sure–"

"Frank," Lila said, but Frank kept speaking.

"—they've lost interest or are headed–"

"Frank." There was growing frustration in Lila's voice.

"—in the wrong–"

"Frank!"

The musician stopped and looked in surprise at Lila.

"I'm not going anywhere."

"Well, of course–"

Welp interrupted him this time. "Frank, don't even try." He grinned. "I know that look. Hell, you should know it even better than me, having been around Sloe for as long as you have. You're staring down the barrel of a Lila-shotgun loaded with prime-A stubbornness."

Frank looked at Welp, then Marina, who looked like she was trying not to laugh, then back to Lila, who simply stared back. Sloe was shaking her head slowly at him.

Frank sighed.

"Damn women."

"Ain't that the truth," Welp said, and Sloe elbowed him.

"Fine, Lila isn't going anywhere," Frank said, agreeing with an annoyed tone. He looked around at all of them. "What do we do about the visitors, then?"

Lila had known this would be coming. The only question had been who would bring it up first.

"Nothing," she said firmly. "At least you all aren't. I'm going to talk to them."

The rest of the group erupted.

Not a chance!

Are you crazy?

It's too dangerous!

No fucking way. Are you a complete idiot?

The last comment was from Egan, who immediately blushed and muttered, "Sorry."

Lila raised an eyebrow and tried not to smile. "Thank you. All of you, really. But it's the only way to figure out what they want. And while I've never gotten along all that well with Wichapi, she isn't a murderer. Neither is Tokalu. I'm sure whatever they want is related to Mama Elise's death, but I don't see them coming all this way to hurt me."

Frank spoke up. "They could be here to lead the police to you."

She nodded. "They could be, but I still don't see it. First, it would be the Department of Public Safety at Pine Ridge doing any investigation. The reservation has its own rules as a sovereign territory. Depending on the crime, they may or may not decide to get the FBI involved."

Frank asked, "Wouldn't they in this case?"

Another nod. "I'm sure they would. But," she put up a finger, "number one, they may not right away. There isn't a lot of love between the DPS and the Feds, and," putting up her middle finger, "number two, the FBI has a reputation for not being overly enthusiastic about jumping on reports from the reservation."

"Even murder?" Egan questioned doubtfully.

"Pretty much anything, including murder," she responded.

The half owner of the Park shook his head. "Jesus, what a place."

"Yeah, it is," she readily agreed. "Poor as dirt, only Haiti has us beat in this part of the world," she continued, frowning. Then more softly, "But there are good people there, Egan. Some of the best. Mama Elise was..." her breath caught, and she sniffed.

Egan reached over and touched her gently on the arm. "I'm sure there are, Lila. And I'm sure Mama Elise was, too."

She nodded and said, "Thank you."

Frank said, not happily. "Lila, you're a grown woman, so it's obviously your choice how you want to handle things." He glared a bit. "I don't agree, but it is your call. But–" he pointed at her, "you are not going alone, period."

Frank had leaned toward Lila as he spoke, seeming to expect an argument and ready to respond, but Lila said simply, "Okay, Frank."

Frank went on, obviously ready to rebut her expected refusal. He stood and said loudly, "I don't care...wait...what?" He looked at Lila, confused.

"I said okay. I don't think Wichapi or Tokalu would do anything to me, but even so, having someone with me isn't a bad idea." She paused. "I'm getting to like the idea of having friends."

Frank's tanned cheeks darkened, and he turned away, giving a 'Hrmpph' as he did.

Welp spoke up.

"Someones."

She turned to him.

"What?"

"Someones. Plural," he said.

Lila furrowed her brows at him.

Sloe poked him in the ribs and said, "He's cute, but not necessarily the best with grammar. He means we're going too." She stepped closer to Lila. "And we're family, not just friends."

As Lila gave Sloe a hug, Egan said, "I'm in, too."

Lila jerked back from the hug.

"What? Why? This doesn't have anything to do with you, Egan."

The man looked annoyed at the question.

"Egan?" Frank asked, prompted.

"Well, those two are squatting on my property."

Frank snorted. "That's one damn lousy reason. They'll be gone soon enough anyway, or you could simply eject them."

Egan shook his head. "You and Mike made the point that we don't know what mischief they would get into then."

"Right. Mischief. Having to do with Lila. Not you. So why?"

The entire group looked intently at him, waiting for an answer.

With a huff, Egan finally said, "Because...well, because it's family." He looked at Sloe, then back to Lila. "Right?"

For the second time that night, Sloe launched herself at Egan. This time, it wasn't to do bodily harm. She threw her arms around him and said, "Thank you, Uncle Egan."

At first Egan resembled a statue, not moving. After a few seconds, his arms came up awkwardly, and he returned the embrace, patting his niece on the back. He stared up at the ceiling as he said. "You're welcome, Sloe."

Frank cleared his throat. "Marina, I assume you wouldn't be left out of this, short of hog-tying you?" He turned, but she wasn't in the kitchen. He looked around. "Marina?"

Welp cut through the living room toward the bedrooms and bathroom, calling her name. There was no response.

"Anyone see her leave?" Frank asked, concern on his face.

On cue, the trailer door opened, and Marina came in.

"Where --?" Frank started, but she was replying already.

"Decided to do some reconnoitering," she said. "Popped out and over behind their camper to see what I could find out."

Frank growled, "Damn it, that was foolish. We still don't know for sure what they want. Don't do that again without checking!"

Marina's temper was far from Sloe's mercurial one. But her expression was flat. She stepped toward Frank, nostrils flaring.

"Oh, really, Mr. Pullman?" Her face was inches from his. "Well, let's get something crystal clear for now and forevermore. I will not be *checking* with you or anyone else before I do something that needs doing. You may be the best damn musician I've ever known, and I may love you, but you are not now and never will be in charge of what I do or don't do. Are we clear on that?"

Lila's eyes widened.

Whoa.

Frank didn't move and Lila felt a shiver run up her spine at Marina's quiet, deadly tone. But her bald statement of her feelings for Frank also hung in the air between the two, and Lila wondered how Frank would respond.

Don't blow this, Frank.

He continued looking at Marina, who stared back, motionless. Finally, he came out with what Lila thought was the only answer he could. At least, she thought, knowing he felt the same way toward Marina and if he wanted to avoid being buried at the edge of the field by moonrise.

"I love you, too," he said, his pale blue eyes holding steady into her bright ones.

Marina's head tilted back, like a strong wind had rocked her. Her eyes lost the flatness, the usual bright sparkle back. She whooped and her lips crushed his as their arms went around each other.

"I will be dipped in the deepest pool of shit in all of New Hampshire," Egan muttered. "Never thought I'd see the day."

Sloe, still standing at Egan's side and having released him from her bear hug, bumped her hip into his and smiled.

"Me either," she said, wiping away a tear.

Frank and Marina finally separated but held each other's hands as Egan asked, "So what did you find out?"

Marina shook her head. "Not a damn thing. They were inside the camper when I got there. I squatted under a window, hoping I'd hear them talking, but after a few minutes of moving around, the lights turned off and that was it.

"So, we still have no idea."

"Except it's something to do with Mama Elise," Lila said.

"Right," Egan agreed. "Lila..." he trailed off.

"What?" she asked.

"Well...from what you've shared, it sounds like her murder was related to her souvenir business. Could you be tied to whatever was going on in any way?" Obviously fearing an explosion, he quickly followed with, "I don't mean that you had anything to do with it. I mean, could anyone try to connect you to it since she was your foster-mother?"

Lila felt her cheeks redden at his first question, but she quickly calmed down as he clarified what he actually meant. She thought for a minute.

"I'm sure they could try. I lived there up until last year and she made most of the various pieces at the house. I was never involved with the eagle trade, though. She was adamant that I never 'touch' her business. I always wondered why, but she said I was meant for bigger and better things. She...fuck!"

Sloe said, "What is it, Lila?"

Instead of replying, she got up and went back to the spare room. She returned with her backpack, put it on the table, and pulled out some bills from a side pocket. There were a few twenties, a ten, and a bunch of ones.

"A couple of times a month Mama Elise would disappear for the day, taking care of what she called a 'special' customer. And she would come home with cash."

"Not a ton, but a lot more than she ever got from the other customers that either sent checks or came to the house to pick stuff up." Lila spread the bills on the table. "This is what's left of the stash she kept at the house." She reached into her pocket and counted out a few bills and coins. "Plus, what I got from my last bar gig in Rapid City."

She looked up. "There was another hundred or so when I started, but I spent that getting here."

Frank, scanning the table, said, "You drove...scootered, across the country with less than two hundred dollars?" His voice was incredulous.

Egan had a different reaction. "So, you could be charged with money laundering if her money was from an illegal business, and possibly aiding and abetting. All righty, then." He shook his head.

Lila first turned to Frank. "Not as though I had many other options, Frank." Then, to Egan, "I guess so, if that's what taking the money means. I guess you could add robbery to the list, then."

Egan shook his head. "Not sure about robbery. If it was from illicit activities, I don't think you taking it would be considered stealing." A sour grin. "Besides, who would accuse you?"

He took out his cell phone.

"You aren't calling the police, I assume?" Lila asked, half joking, wondering if she had totally misread Egan.

"No," he replied. "I'm in over my head. We all are. I'm calling a twat."

Frank's eyes widened. "Holy–"

"Knock it off, Frank," Egan said, then spoke into his phone. "Jerry, it's Egan Lothe. Yeah, yeah, I don't know, check the weather channel, maybe they cover snowfall in hell. No, I'm not calling about the Park." He glanced at Frank as he said this. "No, Frank, Sloe, and I will work that out together. I'm calling because I need to hire you, on retainer."

Welp could hear an incredulous, deep voiced exclamation on the other end of the phone.

Egan held the phone away from his ear for a moment until the voice quieted. "Like I said, it's been a day filled with never-happens. Now let me fill you in on the background of the situation and what I might need from you, then you can tell me how much blood you're going to suck from me."

He stood and walked toward the trailer door as he continued talking.

Lila had listened with confusion when Egan began the call with the 'twat.' Then, the pieces fell into place. 'Jerry' was the name of the lawyer Egan had said delivered that letter from Jessie. He was calling him to hire him, presumably to handle any legal angles that might come up related to Wichapi's tracking Lila down. Lila's guts clenched, and old anger and resentment bubbled.

She must have shown it on her face as Marina looked at her in concern and said. "Lila, what is it? You look like you're going to be sick, honey."

"I don't have money to pay a lawyer." She gestured at the bills scattered in front of her. "When I said Mama Elise never made a lot, I wasn't kidding. This is all the money I have left." She shook her head, trying to not let her emotions get ahead of her. "I–"

Egan re-entered the trailer.

"We are all set with Jerry. And the retainer wasn't as bad as I thought it would be. I suppose I'll have to stop calling him a twat now that he's our twat."

"Egan."

Egan's smile disappeared as caught sight of Lila's face. "What's wrong? Jerry may not be a big city lawyer, but he is good and, insults aside, he's trustworthy. At least when you're his client."

Lila took a deep breath. "If you hired him as your lawyer, in case you get dragged into anything having to do with me, I understand, but—"

He interrupted her. "Of course not. I said he's *our* lawyer. Just in case, and depending on what happens when we meet with Winnie and Toke."

"Wichapi and Tokalu," Lila corrected. "But, like I started to say, if you hired him for me, I can't afford it. Him. A lawyer I mean, and I—"

Egan looked taken aback and said "Lila, of course you can't, you're broke. I mean," he waved at her cache of money, "I'm amazed you got all the way here from South Dakota with what you started with, let alone having anything left. I–"

That stung, although she knew Egan hadn't meant it as an insult. She cut him off.

"Egan, please!"

He stared at her, mouth still open.

"I will *not...*" She realized she was about to come down hard on him, her wounded pride screaming to tell him to take the lawyer and shove it. But she knew that wasn't fair. He was simply trying to help. He was, in fact, the total opposite of how she had initially viewed him. A bit tone deaf, but weren't all men?

"Egan," she started again, calmly, "thank you. Really. But I don't accept charity. I don't have much, but I do have my pride."

Before Egan could respond, and Lila saw he was going to respond, and probably make things worse, Frank jumped in.

"Lila, you have a hell of a voice. Very professional. You were working in a bar band, you said, back in Rapid City?"

She blinked at this.

"Um...thanks? I mean, thanks. And yeah, not many gigs yet, though. But what–"

Frank was nodding. "Okay. So assuming the going rate out there isn't much different than here, and we did...what? A two-hour set at the Oddbow? That would be–" He was reaching for his wallet.

"Oh no you don't!" She wasn't angry now, but almost panicked. She saw what he was doing and while it was sweet, she absolutely would not allow it. Mama Elise had always managed on her own, always, and she did too. "I did that because I wanted to. And if anything, I owed you, all of you and Mike DeTony, for helping me with my leg. And Oddbow wasn't a paying gig for anyone. I know that."

As she spoke, a little voice in her head said,

What about the trip to Ohio and those meals on the road? And Welp working on the scooter and replacing parts?

She told herself to shut up, rationalizing those were different situations. Totally different.

Wasn't it?

"Lila?"

It was Egan.

"Yeah?" she said dubiously. She broke off from arguing with herself.

There was almost a pleading in his eyes as he explained quietly. "First, the lawyer isn't *your* lawyer. He's *our* lawyer. I said it before, I'm out of my element. We all are. But we are in this together, so don't you think it makes sense to have someone who understands the law on our side?"

"Well, sure. Yes, but–"

He held his hand up, palm toward her, his voice continuing in the same gentle tone.

"Second, we aren't friends. As Sloe pointed out earlier, you're family." He looked around at everyone's faces, pausing when his eyes met Frank's. "We all are." The resigned sigh that followed this elicited a group chuckle. "And frankly, the family isn't so big that I want to lose a member. Or have to visit one in jail on alternate Sundays."

"Jail? I'm not going–"

His hand was still up, and he waggled his pointer finger to cut her off yet again.

Annoyance warred with a sudden absurd thought that he looked cute when he was trying to be calm and serious. Then, an even more absurd thought.

I wonder how he'd feel if I leaned over and bit that finger?

She stifled a giggle. Her mind did tend to go in weird directions when she was uncomfortable or nervous, but as she took a deep breath to steady herself, she realized she owed him, all of them, the chance to lay things out from their perspective.

"Fine, go ahead and finish," she said, looking anywhere but at his finger.

"I don't think you are going to jail. But that's it. I don't *think*. What the hell do I know, though?"

A chortle from Frank caused Egan to scowl at him before continuing.

"About the *law*. But I do think someone with a hard-on about your foster-mother's business and death could try to pin something on you and possibly make a decent case of it. So we..*we...* need a lawyer. For the family. Which includes you."

He seemed to have exhausted his reserve of patience as he blew out his breath and said in a stern tone, "So will you just shut up, stop arguing, and tell us if you have a plan for the meeting?"

Her mouth opened. Then closed as she saw the slight twinkle in his eyes.

She laughed, her mental argument about accepting help settled. She made a private promise, though, that his finger was toast, or maybe finger food, at some point in the future. At the moment, though, Lila wasn't sure if she wanted to hug or slap him, so nodded and stuck out her hand. He looked at it for a moment, then extended his own and they shook.

"Okay, Egan," she said, and looked around the group. "As for a plan, it's simple..."

As Lila ran through her 'plan,' a line from one of Frank's favorite movies came to his mind.

I don't think that word means what you think it means.

It *was* simple, though, he gave her that.

Lila was going to meet, or confront, the two visitors and see what developed from there. Frank could almost hear a flushing sound as she told the group this.

But he had said and really believed that it was her choice to make. However foolish he thought she was being.

He had done his own share of foolishness over the years.

Everyone nodded when she told them what she was going to do, although none of them looked happy about it, so he knew at least he wasn't alone in his concerns.

Before they broke up, she at least agreed that he could do some contingency planning, just in case. Then, there were so many hugs passed around for a moment he flashed back to a revival meeting his mother had brought him to in his youth.

As he took a last look around, he felt a warmth. Marina, who had waited so patiently, mostly, for him to pull his head out of his rear, Welp and Sloe, who were holding hands and once again stood as a single entity ready to battle the world together and who, per Welp, would be both sleeping at their trailer tonight, Egan, a man with a good heart but still and always as far as Frank was concerned, an ass, but now *their* ass, And Lila...

She will get through this, whatever it is. She's tough. Tougher than I was.

The contingency planning didn't take long. He asked Welp to go chat with Mike DeTony, who was taking the night shift at his and his husband's liquor store. He also asked him to stop by

Amanda Fleming's trailer to let her know about Lila's planned meeting with the visitors and asked Marina to do the same with Forrie. Frank was certain that by the time Amanda and Forrie went to bed, every Staller would have the basics of the situation and would come up with their own way to help Lila out. There had been no point in trying to mandate any specific plan to the Stallers. You might as well try to herd a bunch of feral, drunk cats.

Once that was done, he headed over to his place and sat on the edge of the weathered picnic table. He was fairly confident things would work out, one way or another, and, more than a little surprising to him, he felt more at peace than he had in many years.

A lot of water under a lot of bridges. More whiskey than water for a while, though. Jessie...

He waited, expecting to hear her voice, chastising him about anything and everything, but for a change, he was alone with his own thoughts.

You got me through it, though, didn't you, old friend? In your foul-mouthed, special way. I was more than done when I first showed up at the Market...

Chapter Fifteen

As Frank followed Jessie into the Park that first time, still suffering the effects from his previous night's alcoholic masochism, he had looked around wondering about the odd combination of a trailer park and flea market advertised out front. What he saw was nothing special. The opposite, in fact. Trailers in various states of decoration and repair or disrepair with a few people about their own business. Jessie stopped in front of a mint-green trailer surrounded by a white picket fence. She made her way up to the door, opened it and entered, the screen door slamming behind her before Frank had gotten onto the little attached porch. He stood, wondering if he should follow, when Jessie's face suddenly appeared up against the screen.

"Well, haul it inside."

He did.

After taking the promised, or perhaps threatened, shower, he found sweatpants and a T-shirt laid on the bathroom sink. There was a small plastic dinosaur sitting on top of them. He studied it for a moment and slid it into the pocket of the sweatpants. They were baggy but by cinching the draw string as tight as it would go, Frank was pretty sure they wouldn't fall off. When he exited the bathroom and turned to go down the hall to the living room, he thought he saw a flash of movement under a closed door and stopped, but heard and saw nothing else. Jessie wasn't in the living room, so he assumed it must have been her.

He should have felt awkward, standing in borrowed clothes in a stranger's trailer, but somehow didn't. Jessie's straight-forward but breezy attitude seemed to permeate her small home. He sat down in an ugly green recliner to wait for her. If she was out burning his puke-covered clothes, he would understand, but he didn't want to leave wearing the loaners without at least thanking her for the hospitality. Frank just hoped she wouldn't be too long. He was at least three quarters sober now and wanted to find a liquor store to rectify that and get back on the road.

The trailer door opened, and Jessie walked in carrying an armful of board games. He got up to help her and was hit from behind by something knee-height.

"Mama!"

A flash similar to the one he had seen under the door whipped past him. A tiny creature threw its arms around Jessie's legs and started jumping up and down.

"Mama, Mama! Pick me up!"

While he couldn't see the small girl's face, he could see the little pink Hello Kitty sundress bouncing as she jumped, long brown hair swishing back and forth.

"Sloe, knock it off," Jessie said, not unkindly. She tried to stagger toward the dining table, her daughter still wrapped around her legs.

Frank reached out and took the boxes from her. Arms free, Jessie reached down and hoisted the girl up.

"Frank, this is Ginny Jean, otherwise known as Sloe."

Sloe buried her head in her mother's shoulder for a moment in feigned shyness, then turned back around, grinning at Frank.

"Hi Frank," she said.

He couldn't help but smile in return. "Hi Sloe." He reached into the sweatpants pocket and pulled out the dinosaur. "Is this yours?"

Sloe nodded her head.

He held it out to her.

She started to reach out, but stopped and shook her head. She said in a serious voice, "It's a present. Besides, Mama says when you give someone something, it's not fair to take it back." She looked at her mother for confirmation, who nodded her head in agreement.

"Hmm..." Frank said, holding the small toy up, pretending to inspect it. "That is a good rule." He thought for a moment. "How about this? It's my present, but you keep it safe for me for now, okay?" He motioned at his outfit. "At least until I get my regular clothes back on."

Sloe looked back at her mother again, who nodded, and reached out to pluck the pink T-Rex from Frank's hand.

"Ok," Sloe replied, agreeably.

Jessie put her down, saying, "Market opens in a bit, little one. Can you bring our chairs down to the table?"

"Sure, Mama," Sloe replied. She tucked the dino into the breast pocket of her dress and skipped out the door, humming.

Frank realized he was still smiling as he watched her leave.

Jessie let out a sigh. "She is something."

Frank said, "Yes, she's quite the cute little button."

Jessie said, "She's actually seven. Can't imagine where she gets her vertical challenge from."

They both chuckled at this.

Frank asked about his clothes, thanking the woman for the loaners. He planned on following that with goodbyes, getting changed into some of his own duds, and heading out. He was also hoping she could point him toward a local liquor store. But he didn't get further than the thanks. Jessie told him his clothes were just finishing up in a dryer at the Park laundry as she gestured at the games on the table, indicating he should pick them up. He did, still trying to move on to the goodbye when she turned toward the door. "You can change when they're done." She shook her head. "Took three rinse cycles to get the puke off them." She went to the door and held it open. "Now come along."

He stood for a moment, then followed her out. He assumed they were going to the laundry, but as they weaved between other trailers dotting the landscape, he saw they were approaching another fence and driveway with a sign tacked up that read Sun Market.

"Jessie," he started, "If you can point me toward the laundry, I'll swap the clothes for your sweats and get going, I need to get going."

She didn't stop as they entered the Market but replied easily, "Of course. I could use a bit more help before you do, though. There are a couple more loads of games and such in my shed that I need to get down to my stall."

He was going to tell her no, and remembered the three washer runs and the hot shower, as well as the disposable razor she had supplied. He decided it was the least he could do.

I'll leave a bit later.

His stomach tightened, the desire for a drink flaring up again. Maybe she has a bottle back in the trailer. Better ask before I make a trip back to her shed.

But he didn't get a chance to ask. Jessie was some sort of empathic ninja in her own way. She and Frank's mother had that in common, although the quietness of Patty Pullman was at the other end of the spectrum from Jessie's personality.

As he set that first load on a side table at Jessie's selling station, which was two picnic tables set at right angles to each other, Jessie pointed him back toward her trailer, telling him the shed was out back. Before he could ask about that possible drink, she took off again, muttering, "Now, where is that girl?"

So, Frank made the round trip. He briefly considered letting himself into her place to search for a bottle, or even a beer, but felt guilty at the thought. Neither Jessie nor her daughter was at their table when he came back, nor were they following his next three trips. On his fourth, both were resident, but apparently the Market had opened, and Jessie was in negotiations with a rotund, goateed man about a dusty wooden doll house.

There was a tug on Frank's pants. He lowered his gaze and saw Sloe looking up at him.

"Frank, a man wants to buy a firetruck and Mama says I'm not good enough with change yet. Can you help?"

Her brown eyes looked impossibly huge for such a little girl, and she batted her eyelashes at him as she spoke.

He gently ruffled her hair and said, "Sure, Sloe."

During breaks in the crowd, Jessie quizzed him gently on his background as she organized and reorganized her wares. Balancing between being polite and not wanting to talk about how he killed a kid at his last job, he simply told her he was a musician.

Even that was too much, though, and he saw Kenny's smiling face hovering in front of him, pushing his need for a drink even higher. He was on the verge of insisting he needed to leave when Jessie handed him a cup of homemade iced tea and asked him to help a woman holding a life-sized doll, waiting to pay for her find as she was pitching to another potential customer interested in an old wooden rocking horse.

His hand trembled as he completed the transaction with the woman and when she walked away with the doll, he leaned against the nearby tree, wiping the slick coating of sweat from his face.

The pattern repeated throughout the afternoon. His longing for the burning taste of Jim Beam, or anything else of similar proof would spike, and he would approach Jessie to let her know he needed to leave, but each time, before he could say the words, she would tell him she could really use his help again, digging for a specific item buried in a box, bringing a cup of iced tea to a blind vendor a few tables away, escorting Sloe back to the trailer to use the bathroom so she wouldn't wander off into the crowd of customers...the list of tasks was as varied as it was never ending.

Later in the afternoon, one of those customers was looking at a child-sized guitar, a handwritten price tag hanging from the neck declaring "$5." It was wooden, giving it the appearance of an actual instrument, but Frank could tell at a glance it was a toy, not something to be really played. The man said his young son wanted to take lessons. Without thinking about how Jessie would feel losing a sale, Frank told the man not to buy it and explained to him how to tell the difference between an actual instrument, even a half-size one, and a toy.

"Well," the man said glumly, "it's his birthday in two days. I'm on the road a lot for work and in the last week I've been through three states and hit half a dozen music stores, but everyone I found would break the bank for me." His face sagged even more. "I didn't quite promise him I'd get him one. Maybe a video game…" His voice tapered off.

Jessie had just finished with another customer and stepped over, but said nothing as she listened to Frank and the man talking.

Frank felt bad. He had not only burst the guy's bubble, but now his kid was in for a letdown. He looked over at Jessie, her face inscrutable. There didn't seem to be disapproval in her eyes, though, so Frank turned back to the man.

"I might have something you can use. Can you hang out for five minutes? I want to get something out of my truck."

The man was more than willing to.

Jessie finally spoke. "Take your time, Frank." She smiled at the man as she offered him a cup of iced tea and said, "Perhaps your son would also enjoy getting a gently used chess set?"

Frank took off at a brisk pace toward the Park and his truck.

He hadn't played since Kenny had died. Playing had always been a way of expressing his feelings, but they were currently bottled up, and he had no intention of pouring anything unless it was at least eighty proof.

He still had his instruments, though. Among them was a half-size travel guitar he had picked up at a flea market, not unlike this one. It was pretty beat up, but it was also a full-fledged instrument, meant to be played.

He brought it back to the Jessie's stall and found her engaged in a negotiation with a snippy woman who he was sure would not be getting the deal of the century, based on the flash he saw in Jessie's eyes. The would-be guitar purchaser was sitting behind the table in a lawn chair, looking relaxed, cup in hand.

He stood up when he saw Frank and smiled at the guitar-shaped cloth bag in his hands.

Frank took it out, pointed to the shallow chips in the lacquer, explaining that they wouldn't interfere with the sound, but the man interrupted him.

"Buddy, don't bother." He pointed over his shoulder at Jessie, who was contentedly counting out bills, the snippy woman walking away carrying a small record player. "Jessie here tells me you aren't a vendor and anything you came back with is your own personal property. I assume you wouldn't own anything you didn't think was decent, you being a musician and all. My only question is, how much?"

Frank gave a little start at the question. It hadn't occurred to him that the man would pay him for it. He had planned on simply giving it to him for his son. Before he could reply, he saw Jessie staring at him from behind the man, waving the bills she held at him, then pointing at Frank, then the man.

Frank assumed she was trying to tell him not to screw things up for the vendors. If customers thought they could start wheedling freebies from people, there would probably be a riot.

"Um, well..." He had paid twenty-five dollars for it. "Twenty dollars?"

The man pulled out his wallet and slid two twenties from it.

"No, I said twenty," Frank protested as the bills being waved at him.

"Forty it is," the man replied. "And a hell of a lot cheaper than anything I've seen for a real one anywhere else."

He added, "Throw in the bag, though, would you? I don't want it getting any more nicked in the trunk."

Frank agreed, and the man was soon on his way. He tried to offer Jessie one of the bills, but she gave a cackling laugh.

"Frank, honey," she said, shaking her head. "That's not how it works. And don't feel bad about him not buying the toy guitar. I only paid fifty cents for the thing."

He pocketed the money, still feeling guilty, but telling himself that the insurance money wouldn't last forever. The forty dollars would at least fill his gas tank when he got back on the road.

He looked around. The crowds were thinning out and, according to Jessie, the Market would close in less than an hour. Sloe was dozing in one of the lawn chairs behind the table, curled into a tiny ball, the dinosaur she was keeping safe for him hanging limply from her hand.

"Jessie, I–" He was going to offer to help her clean up, then get back to his truck.

"I'm sure glad you came along, Frank," she interrupted him. "Thank you."

He looked at her, startled. "I'm the one that owes you the thanks. You not only took care of my clothes, which I would like to get back, by the way, but let me clean up. Hell, I even made a few bucks today."

She was piling things into boxes and stacking the games up.

"You earned the money. And fine, we can do mutual thank-yous while we get my stuff back to the shed." She glanced up through the canopy of the tree shading the stall. "Market again tomorrow, but it might rain tonight. I don't want everything getting wet." She picked up a box and held it out to him. "Here," she said, and gestured at the sleeping girl. "I'll wake this one up and have her get your clothes on her way back to the house. You can change after everything is put away."

She headed back toward the Park carrying a small pile of games. Frank stared after her for a moment, then followed along.

He didn't leave that day, of course. First, Jessie told him he couldn't possibly leave without her giving him a good meal for his help. Then, as he was sipping a cup of coffee following the bowl of chili she served him, Sloe found her way onto his lap, holding out the dinosaur in what would become a multi-year swapping game. An hour plus was spent playing Destructo-Dinos. Then, per Jessie, it was too late to drive anywhere, what with the "idiot drunks" that careened around the unlit country roads in the area. He looked sharply at her when she said that, but there was no reproval in her words.

Sloe moved into her mother's room after dinner and Frank fell asleep surrounded by an odd but endearing assortment of dinosaurs and Hello Kitty dolls.

The next day he found himself following her around the Market and Park grounds, making trips between the shed and vendor setup and helping handle customers.

In the quiet moments, few and far between, a wave would hit him, and his throat would tighten as the image of an amber filled bottle popped into his head. And each time, Jessie would need help with boxes, errands, or Sloe. By the time the sun was getting low on the horizon, and they had moved everything back to the shed, he was bone tired. The few months he had spent driving between bar stools worn down his resilience. He lay his head down on a T-Rex adorned pillow and was quickly out.

Jessie took him around just before the Market opening the next day, introducing him to other vendors, some of whom Jessie referred to as Stallers. Everyone was friendly and seemed to know he was staying with Jessie. Many thanked him for helping her out.

The rest of the day was spent once again playing assistant, gopher, and Sloe-minder, his hands and mind kept occupied by Jessie's regular requests. At dinner that night, Jessie asked him if he could drive around with her and Sloe the next day while she looked for goods to sell.

"I use non-Market days to replenish my stock, and that pickup would be a godsend, Frank. It can fit so much more than my little hatchback."

Thus, after a few hurried sips from the mug of coffee Sloe pushed into his hands the next morning, Frank found himself chauffeuring Jessie and Sloe around the area, stopping at a few houses Jessie had pre-arranged visits to and then making the hour drive into Lebanon. As they hit the town line, Jessie directed him to their next stop.

As they turned down the wide gravel pull-in, he saw a warehouse ahead, its large sliding doors open. Inside were stacks of boxes forming a lane back as far back as Frank could see. Jessie hopped out of the truck, and he followed as Sloe continued doodling on a pad in the rear jump seat.

"Hey, Chuck!"

"Heya, Jessie."

Chuck was an older, pasty looking man, a large brown growth jutting out from one cheek. He was lugging large cardboard boxes back and forth between a panel van and the warehouse.

"Anything good this time around?" Jessie asked the question as she poked her head into the back of the van.

"I've got a bunch of stuff set aside for you, just inside the door. Poke around and make me an offer."

Frank and Jessie walked over to the warehouse and inside he saw ten-foot-high piles of miscellaneous household goods, each with its own theme: lamps, furniture, small appliances, mattresses, every type of item he could imagine.

Just inside the doors was a smaller pile, about his height. It contained toys, games, and other assorted kid-centric items.

Jessie gave it a practiced eye, then yelled out, "Twenty!"

Chuck was just coming in and put down the box he was carrying.

"Now, Jessie, how the hell am I supposed to make a living if I start giving everything away?" He shook his head, but had a smile on his face.

"Twenty-five," was her response.

Chuck whistled. "When I get home, I'll tell Rebbie we'll be moving into the warehouse since I won't be able to pay the mortgage." He cocked his head. "Seventy-five."

She *tsked*. "How far do we go back, Chuck? And you, a classmate of Daddy's. Thirty-five."

This back and forth continued for a few more minutes. Frank enjoyed the gentle, mutual teasing as the numbers grew closer together until they both agreed to fifty. Money changed hands and Frank began carrying things from the pile back to his truck. Jessie told Chuck she would see him the following week and grabbed an armful of her new merchandise. The loading didn't take long, and they headed back toward Bridgett and the Park. As he got into the truck, Frank saw Sloe had fallen asleep. He smiled at her curled up form, her thumb firmly in her mouth.

"Interesting guy," Frank said, a few minutes later. "You said he's a friend of your father?" Jessie hadn't mentioned any family other than Sloe.

Jessie's horsey laugh filled the cab, and Sloe stirred but didn't wake up.

"Not a friend, no. My father doesn't have any friends. Simply employees and acquaintances."

"Well, he has family. He has you and Sloe," Frank replied. "Right?"

"I would put me more in the former employee, Frank." There was a trace, but not much, of bitterness in her answer. Like a wound that had healed but that had left an empty hole.

She reached over and petted Sloe's head. "And he's never met Sloe."

Frank pursed his lips. Multiple questions popped into his head, but Jessie continued talking, still stroking her daughter's hair.

"My father, Egan Lothe Senior, my brother is Egan Junior, owns the Sun Market and Trailer Park," she said. Frank's eyebrows threatened to touch his hairline with this comment. "Have you noticed the big brick house across the road from the back gate?" Frank nodded. "I grew up there. My father, and brother, when he's home from boarding school, still do. The Market used to be a car sales lot, Sunshine Cars. He converted it when I was a kid, for a tax shelter. He made quite a tidy sum with the car dealership. When he first mentioned getting rid of it, I didn't believe it. Egan Lothe give up being the piranha? Never happen. The Lothe's have been in Bridgett since before there was a Bridgett and have generally been the big fish in a small pond, feeding on anyone and anything not fast or smart enough to stay out of their way."

Frank noticed any time Jessie talked about her father or the Lothe family in general, it was always one step removed. Like you would talk about neighbors or someone you had read about.

"It wasn't until after he sold off the last of the car inventory, had the first few trailers delivered, and opened the Park and Market that I figured it out." She grimaced. "He views the whole thing as partial retirement and total entertainment." She shook her head. "I used to manage things for him, starting when I was in high school. I refused to go to boarding school, so he thought it best to put me to work to offset what he called the 'corrupting' influence of the local public school.

That was one of our many disagreements. I collected rent, handled evictions." Her expression darkened. "Other things."

"What happened?"

"Nothing specific. It was more...everything. I never had any illusions of who or what my father is. But by the time I was in college, still working for him on weekends and breaks, I had a much clearer picture of how petty and soulless he was. Lording over everyone who lives and works at the Park and Market. Squeezing people, not for the money so much as to make himself feel important and them feel small. Inconsequential. Me included. He would gloat over it." Jessie sighed. "I just couldn't take it anymore. After I graduated, I quit and told him I was moving into the Park, which sent him into a fit. He argued with me but," she gave a predatory smile, "he shut up when I said it was that or I would call the state attorney general's office and share all the info I had gathered about his business practices."

"Wow," Frank replied. He thought for a moment. A lot of questions occurred to him. Did she stay to keep an eye on her father? To atone for what she had done while working for him?

"So, you have a brother?"

Jessie apparently hadn't expected the question and laughed. "Right. Egan Lothe Junior. And I'm sure if he reproduces there will be an Egan Lothe the third. He's a chip off the old Egan block." She stopped and shook her head.

"No, I shouldn't say that. He isn't dark, like my father. Not yet. Just off-white, I guess. Always wanted to be a daddy's boy and figured out the closest he could come to getting attention, never real affection, is to mimic the old man." Another sigh. "Hopefully, he figures things out."

"Jessie," Frank had to ask the next question, not knowing if it was going too far. "Sloe." He left it at the single word.

Jessie's hand moved from the top of the little girl's head to her nose, but continued to pet her. "Her father?" Frank nodded. "She never knew him. Neither did I, for that matter. Thomas Blunt, county fair barker and sperm donor. It happened right after I moved out. July fourth celebration over in Ashland. Had one of those traveling carnivals set up. Short version, I got drunk, married, sober, annulled, and pregnant all in the space of about four days."

Frank couldn't help himself. "Jesus, Jessie!"

She gave him a prim look. "Do you disapprove, Mr. Pullman?"

"Ah, well, I mean, I, um...no. It's just–"

Her horsey laugh filled the cabin on the truck. "Just about drove my father over the edge. And when I refused to get an abortion, that was the final straw for him. Bad enough, I had already tarnished the family name by moving into the Park. But having, and this is a quote, a carnival freak's spawn, plus me keeping the name Blunt, admittedly out of spite, well, it was too much for him. We haven't spoken since before she was born."

She grew quieter. "I thought about an abortion. It would have been simpler, maybe. But ultimately, I decided it wasn't something I could do."

Her hand left her daughter, and she clasped both in her lap, uncharacteristically, in Frank's brief experience, looking worried. "I just hope I can stick around to see her through."

Frank was quiet. He wasn't sure what she meant by her last comment, except sharing every parent's fear, he supposed.

It wasn't until a few years later that she received the ALS diagnosis, but she told him later that even back when they first met, she sensed something wasn't quite right with her, with her body.

At the time, though, the story still touched a nerve, and Frank got a lump in his throat. When faced with a choice, Jessie had picked the harder path. You could argue whether it was the right choice, but Jessie thought it was and took it, even knowing what she was giving up. What could he say to that?

"I killed a boy. One of my students."

It just came out.

Jessie reached her hand out again, this time putting it on his arm, as gently as she had rested it on the little girl's head.

"Talk to me."

Chapter Sixteen

Welp was not feeling overly optimistic as he left Marina's trailer after hearing Lila's 'plan.' She had agreed, at least, to Frank's suggestion about having a backup in place, which was something. But Frank's idea to leave the actual details of the backup plan to the Staller collective didn't give him much more of a warm and fuzzy feeling than he had had upon Lila telling them all she was simply going to go talk to the visitors.

His trip to fill Mike DeTony in didn't take long. As he left the liquor store, Mike was already on the phone to his husband, Larry, passing along the information.

Mission accomplished, Welp pointed his truck back out of town toward the Park and headed home.

Home. Yes, it is. As long as Sloe is there, at least.

It wasn't a case of trying to come up with the right words anymore. There was only one word, and person, that mattered. Sloe.

He bumped along the rutted road for a few more minutes, letting his mind wander.

Egan was certainly right. It's been a day of never-would'a-thunk its. And if I didn't know better, there was some sort of vibe between Egan and Lila.

He made the turn back into the Park and then down and around to Marina's place.

The lights were on, but there was no answer to his knock. He looked over and saw Frank's light flick off.

Good for you guys.

He noticed a glow of light emanating around the corner of Frank's trailer and figured it must be from the yurt. He wondered if Lila had changed her mind about sleeping arrangements and walked toward the yurt. As he got close, he could make out Egan's and Lila's voices coming from the structure.

"Damn Egan, really? It can't be as big as you claim." Lila said.

"Oh yes, it is," came the reply. "I've measured it enough times. Why don't you come over to the house and I'll show you?"

Welp stood stock-still.

"It takes a few minutes to warm up but once it gets going, it's full throttle all the way," Egan continued.

Lila laughed. "I'm sure it is."

Welp felt trapped between feelings of embarrassment and protectiveness. Part of him wanted to leave them to the intimate conversation and whatever the hell else was happening, or about to happen. But damn it, Lila was family, and he felt obligated to save her from herself, no matter how angry he knew she would be at any intrusion or attempt to tell her what to do. Egan had turned out to be human, after all, but...well, he was still Egan.

Finally, embarrassment won out, just, mostly because he was certain Lila would kick his ass for interfering with her personal affairs. He turned to skulk away to his trailer and wash his mouth out with either Scope or half a bottle of bourbon when another voice inside caused him to whirl back toward the yurt.

Sloe's voice.

"Uncle Egan, you've got my curiosity aroused. Can I join you and Lila?"

What? No! After I've decided I'll stay, come hell or high water...

"Sure, Sloe. I'd love that."

Whipping the door covering back, Welp stormed inside, a bear's roar shaking the fabric of the yurt.

"Like hell!"

His large hands were balled into fists as he stood in the doorway, glaring at the three of them.

Sloe jumped up from her seat between Lila and Egan. "Welp? What..."

"Egan, you slimy son of a–"

"Welp! What's going on? What's wrong? Did you talk to Mike? Did --"

"Stay out of this, Sloe."

His wife's mouth snapped shut in shock. "Egan, you had me going for a while," Welp growled. "Egan Lothe, decent human being, trapped by life. I had actually started to like you, you sick..."

Welp stepped toward the park manager, who looked calmly up at him, seemingly oblivious to Welp's intent, as Welp's arm came back, ready to lay Egan out.

"Welp, knock it off!" Lila had stepped up between them, hands on hips, and stood looking up at him.

"Lila, not now, I'm–"

"Welp, back the hell off and tell me what is going on."

His eyes never leaving Egan, he said, "Look, it's none of my business if you decide to go off and play Johnson measuring games with him, but I will be damned if my wife–"

"What the *fuck* are you babbling about?" This came from Sloe, who was now next to Lila, her eyes blazing. "Johnson measuring games? Are you out of your mind?"

She poked Welp in the chest.

"Do you think," poke, "that I," poke, poke, poke, managing to hit the same spot each time, "am planning on *screwing* Uncle Egan?" For all her fury and poking, she was still two feet shorter than him, and he had not moved an inch, but he now stepped back at her unbridled fury.

He stuttered, "Sloe, I, ah, I heard..."

She stepped forward again, finger at the ready, "I don't know what you *think* you heard, but whatever it was, you," poke, "are out," poke, poke, "of your mind!" The last few words were punctuated by a shove instead of a poke.

It had no more physical effect than if she had tried to shove a bus, but the act itself, along with her words, cut through his red fog.

His fists dropped to his sides.

"You're not?"

Egan, who still hadn't moved to that point, reached out and pulled the two women apart to stand directly in front of Welp.

"She's not. They're not. And I'm not, you idiot."

"You're not?" He repeated it numbly, looking between the three.

"No," replied Egan, with emphatic head shakes from Sloe and Lila.

"But I heard you --"

"I assume what you heard had to do with how large my model is."

Welp's face tightened again.

"I've never heard one called a model before, but if that floats–"

"Welp!" Sloe again, poking his chest yet again. He wondered how she managed to keep hitting the same spot; he thought he would have a bruise by tomorrow morning. "Egan was talking about an actual model, not his dick. Christ, how could you even think that?" She turned away from him.

Welp, totally befuddled now, reached down and rubbed his chest.

"His model? Of what?"

Egan responded. "A dream."

He agreed, with more than a touch of chagrin, to accompany Egan, Sloe, and Lila across the road to Lothe's house to see whatever the hell the 'dream' was. On the way, he tried to take Sloe's hand, but she huffed and moved to walk next to Lila on the other side of Egan.

As they walked down the long, winding driveway toward the three-story brick house, Welp felt a surrealness. In all his years at the Park, he never would have imagined he would be going over to the Lothe house, unless it was to TP it on Halloween.

Come to think of it, a bunch of us did that one year when I was a teenager. Egan Senior's reaction the next morning…

He smiled ruefully at the memory and then looked up. They were standing on a cobblestone semi-circle that surrounded the steps leading up to the front door. Tasteful plantings ran off from either side down the length of the house. Lights were on inside, but drawn shades blocked the view.

Egan turned to them and smiled as he opened the front door. "Welcome."

Welp saw the slightly dazed look on Sloe's face and knew she was feeling as odd about the visit as he was. More so, he realized. After all, this was the house her mother had grown up in, and left, cutting off her own branch from the family tree. As far as he knew, she had never been here either.

They stood in a large foyer, a massive, carpeted staircase half a dozen paces in front of them. The staircase's ornate polished dark wooden bannisters matched the lower portion of the walls in the foyer, which segued to the ivory colored upper wall. White, yellow, and steel blue patterned tile covered the floor and ran off down a hall past the stairs and under a closed door on their right, as well as into another room on the left whose sliding door was just cracked open.

Lila whistled beside him.

"Wow, Egan. Nice digs."

Sloe nodded her head in agreement, looking around with wide eyes.

"Thanks. It's a lot bigger than I need, so I mostly use just a few rooms. But Daddy's will dictated either Jessie or I had to continue to live here. And Jessie…" he trailed off.

Welp thought back to his outburst a little while before.

"Egan, I'm sorry."

The other man raised his eyebrows.

"I mean, for earlier. Hell, for the last ten years. I..." he glanced at his wife. "We were wrong. About you."

Egan shook his head. "No, you weren't, Welp. Not totally. I've been an asshole. I know it. Acting like a spoiled, entitled shithead."

"But," Welp argued, surprised, "you said it yourself. You didn't have a choice. At least, not about being here. At the Park. I can understand why you acted like a pissed off wet cat."

Egan studied him a moment. "Thank you." Then he sighed. "But here's the thing. I did have choices. The same ones we all have. The same ones my sister had."

He turned and headed toward the sliding door, opening it to reveal a large room. "I just wouldn't admit it to myself."

Welp looked over at Sloe, who was looking back at him, then she took his hand. She turned, and they followed Egan into the adjoining room, Lila behind him.

The fireplace across the room drew his eye immediately. It almost, but not quite, overwhelmed the room and looked big enough to roast a yak. To one side of it was a well-worn leather chair, a sofa behind it. He noticed the room itself wasn't as pristine as the hall had been. Turning to the other end of the room, he did a double take. He squinted, thinking his eyes were playing tricks but...

"An amusement park?" He was astonished.

The model sat on a large table, at least twenty feet wide on each side, with a narrow space between three of its sides and the walls.

Sloe squealed like a little girl, clapping her hands as she danced up to it. Lila gave a full-blown smile, which he now knew was her equivalent to Sloe's reaction. He walked up to it, Egan standing to one side motioning with his hands like a game show host.

"Tada," he said to his visitors.

The level of detail was amazing, Welp thought. Miniature carousel, Ferris wheel, a 'loop-de-loop' roller coaster. And the mountain in the middle had an opening with a track and small tube running down the middle of it, leading down to a blue-painted bowl-shaped depression.

He asked, "Is that...?"

Egan clicked a switch on the side of the table and water started trickling down the tube. The merry-go-round and Ferris wheel also started rotating, along with a dozen other tiny rides spread across the display.

"A perfectly scaled and functional flume ride." It was obvious how proud Egan was of the model. They all watched as a tiny log-shaped capsule came out of the mountain, swooshed down the track into the bowl, and bobbed around.

Welp felt like an even bigger ass for thinking what he had been thinking. Put aside Egan for a minute. How could he have thought Sloe would do something like that? With anyone?

The excitement on Sloe's face as she and Lila took turns pointing out different aspects of the miniature amusement park made him smile. He reached over and brushed Sloe's hair back gently. She looked up at him, still smiling, and winked.

Choices, he thought and smiled back.

Chapter Seventeen

As much as Lila enjoyed seeing all the details of the mini-amusement park, she was enjoying watching Egan show it off even more. For the first time since she had met him, he seemed totally at ease, and she thought she was seeing the real person behind the Park manager facade. She smiled as he pointed out the working water guns in the tiny shooting gallery and inadvertently shot a burst of water into his face, wiping it off with a grin.

"Damn, I almost forgot." Egan reached under the table. A moment later, the tinny sound of calliope music emanated from under the model.

"Speakers are under the table," he said a bit sheepishly, blushing, and busied himself adjusting the speed of the merry-go-round, avoiding their looks.

She wanted to laugh but stifled it, not wanting him to think she was laughing at him and have him put back on the mask he wore much of the time.

Like the one I wear.

It was the first time she admitted it to herself.

She knew she often came across as stubborn, even harsh, even when she didn't mean to. It was self-defense, based on her history. But the Stallers weren't the Elders who wouldn't allow her to take part in tribal ceremonies, giving grudging permission a handful of times, for her to observe as though she were an outsider. Nor were they the men, white tourists, who seemed to think the women at Pine Ridge were for sale, along with the trinkets sold at the souvenir shop. No, these were good people, like most back at Pine Ridge.

Even Wichapi, the Council President, the medicine woman who had ruled Lila could not be formally adopted by Mama. It still stung the little girl buried inside Lila when she thought about it, but she now admitted to herself that the Elder made her decision based on what she thought was in the best interest of the Oglala overall. Even if Lila still didn't understand why or agree with the decision.

She realized she was still smiling when Egan glanced up and saw her watching him and this time she was the one who turned away, cheeks burning.

"Do you think Frank and Marina will be back soon?" she asked Sloe, not looking at Egan, who was still studying her.

"They should be. Their plan was to do a sort of game of telephone and have word pass along so they didn't have to speak with everyone."

Welp said, "Any time I played that game, the last person getting the message heard something entirely different from the original."

Sloe said, "My pessimist," and patted his cheek just as they heard chimes from the front of the house.

"Doorbell," Egan said, walking into the front hall. Lila heard the door open, then Frank's voice as the sound of footsteps approached. "Did you kidnap them, Egan?"

As Frank, Marina, and Egan entered the room, Marina said, "Nice place."

Just inside the room, they stopped and stared.

"Wow," Frank said. "That's quite the layout. Is it to scale?"

Welp shifted uncomfortably as Egan responded, deadpan but with a gleam in his eyes. "Oh yes, I've carefully measured every inch of it."

Sloe interjected, saving her husband from further embarrassment. "Everybody on board, Frank?"

He nodded. "Yep. Marina couldn't find Forrie, but I have faith in Amanda. She said she would make the rounds to everybody personally."

"She sells soda at the front gate, right? With the dog?" Lila said and Marina nodded. "Isn't she…ah…blind?" Another nod from Marina. Lila hesitated. "Ah, how is she…?"

Marina finished for her. "Going to make the rounds? She could call some people, but I doubt she will. Knowing Amanda, she will hit up every Staller at their trailers. As to how, she knows the Park as well as anyone. And then there's her furry guardian, Velcro. Not only will he get her wherever she wants to go, even if she has never been there before, but I swear he speaks English. One of these days, I'm going to catch him out."

The group chuckled at that, and Frank continued. "Also, I tried telling her that passing the word was more than enough help, but she was quite insistent that whatever happens, she is going to be part of it." He shook his head and mimicked the throaty, tobacco-worn voice of the blind refreshment seller. "*If that pompous ass Egan is helping, you can bet your fanny I won't be sitting on the sidelines.*"

Egan said, "How sweet," giving a chagrined smile. "But I can't argue with her character assessment."

There was an uncomfortable pause, finally broken by Frank, who pulled out his phone and checked the time. "Getting late. Things tee off at eight am. Think it's time to get some rest. Lila, we'll leave the door open for you. Marina?"

Marina nodded, and they walked out of the room. A moment later, Lila heard the front door open, then close.

Sloe turned to Welp. "Our turn, husband, mine. Let's get home." Welp took her outstretched hand.

"Sure thing," he replied. "Lila, do you want to walk–"

Sloe said, "She can find her own way back at this point, I'm sure," and tugged his hand.

Welp looked at her for a moment, then at Lila, then back to his wife. After a brief hesitation, he said, "Oh, right. I'm sure she can." As Sloe pulled him gently along with her, he said over his shoulder, 'Night, Lila, 'night Egan. Many thanks for the hospitality."

Egan called out, "Good night. And I'd like to talk to you about something when you have a few minutes. Maybe after things settle down."

Welp only had time to nod back at him before he and Sloe disappeared around the doorway, then out of the house.

The exchange between Sloe, Welp, and Egan had been quick enough that it took Lila a moment to process and realize she and Egan were now alone.

"Um...well, it is getting late. I should get going too."

Egan looked at her before saying, "Of course. Good night, Lila." He held out his hand.

She looked at it dumbly before it came to her that he was offering to shake hands, as she had offered earlier. She held her hand out rather stiffly next to his and said, "Good night, Egan."

He looked down and grasped her hand, holding it a few seconds longer than necessary and, she realized, less than she wanted.

She left, feeling a slight buzz, although she hadn't been drinking.

———

The hands grabbed her, forcing her toward the closet. She thrashed, trying to pull away, but he was too strong. Her name was being shouted as she tried to pry the hands loose, and dug her nails in, managing to get one off her shoulder, and bit down on a finger.

"Christ on a stick!"

Lila sat up.

"What the hell?"

"Why did you bite me?!"

Frank was standing next to the bed, cradling his left hand.

"Frank? What's wrong? What's wrong with your hand?"

"You bit me!" he repeated. Marina appeared in the bedroom doorway.

"Frank, everything all right?" She looked at his dangling hand. "What happened to your hand?"

Muttering from the wounded man. "Nothing. Everything is ducky."

Marina looked at him for a moment then, sighed and said to Lila. "It's almost seven, Lila. Thought you might want a cup of coffee before we go to see your visitors."

She looked back and forth between Frank and Marina. "Sure, thanks." To Frank, "Frank, I'm sorry. I must have been having a nightmare."

He shook his hand and grunted. "No kidding." Examining it, he said, "The skin isn't broken, so at least I don't have to worry about rabies."

She grinned. "I've had my shots, anyway." Then, more seriously, "I really am sorry, Frank."

Another grunt. "Come on, let's get some caffeine into you. And a Band Aid for me."

Sitting in the kitchen a few minutes later, she asked, "So this contingency plan you put together, in case the talk doesn't go well...exactly what are the Stallers going to do?"

He shrugged and said, "Depends. Whatever they think makes sense, I reckon."

She blinked. "That doesn't seem much of a plan."

Frank said, "Says the woman who thinks just walking up to people who might want to kill or arrest her and saying hi is a good idea."

Marina gave him a dirty look and patted Lila's hand, "It's okay, Lila. Really. You're family and a Staller. And Stallers take care of their own."

Silence.

"Thank you," she finally managed and left it at that.

The trailer door opened, and Sloe and Welp came in. "Almost time," Sloe said.

Lila stood and took one more sip from her mug, then a deep breath. "I'm ready."

Welp said, "We should wait for Egan."

The door opened again, and Welp looked over and said, "Speak of the devil."

Egan replied dryly, "I prefer misunderstood angel, but have it your way." He glanced at Lila and smiled, then turned to Frank. "Time to go."

"Way ahead of you, Egan," Frank said.

Egan nodded and held open the trailer door, ushering them out.

Chapter Eighteen

Something seemed off to Lila as they made their way toward the hedges leading to the field adjoining the Park and Market. Then it hit her. The Park was quiet, with no sound or sight of bustling Stallers getting their wares set up.

"Where is everyone? It's a Market day, right? Shouldn't they be getting ready to open?"

Next to her, Frank hesitated as Marina, walking on his other side, made a show of picking pollen off her shirt. She turned to her left and looked at Sloe and Welp, both of whom continued looking forward as they all followed Egan toward the hedge.

"Well?" she asked, turning back to Frank.

Egan stopped and turned to face her as they all halted. Lila saw he had on what she thought of as his business face.

"The Market is closed today, Lila."

She stared at him, then looked around at the others.

"What? It can't be closed. How are people going to make a living?"

Sloe said, "No, Lila. I mean, yes, we need to work, but this is more important. I got word a little while ago. It was a unanimous decision by the Stallers based on whatever it is they decided on as a backup plan. Although how Amanda got them all to agree to anything is beyond me. Besides–" A lump had formed in Lila's throat as Sloe talked and now all the pent-up anger, and pain, Lila had felt since finding Mama Elise's body exploded. She whirled to face Egan, cutting off Sloe.

"You can't let them do this! Their biggest bills are probably from you for their stall and lot rent. It just isn't right!"

Egan said nothing, which only made her angrier.

She lashed out. "No." She shook her head. "No, I won't allow it." Egan now tried to speak, but she didn't give him a chance. "These people don't really even know me and are sticking their necks out for me. They shouldn't lose out for that. And you? You're only worried about getting your monthly rent check. Poor Egan, acting all hurt and misunderstood, but you're like the rest of them. You don't give a damn. You're just...just..." Tears blurred her eyes she wiped them, her emotions tangling up her words.

The group had stopped, staring at her, and she unloaded on Egan. He looked back at her calmly. When she didn't continue, he said, "Can I talk now?"

She glared at him angrily, wiping her eyes again, but nodded her head.

"As Sloe was about to say, that although the Market is going to be closed today, I'm going to pay everyone. Or the equivalent. I'm deducting twenty-five percent of everyone's lot rent this month for one day's lost sales. And if someone can show me their average day's take is higher than that, doubtful but possible, I'll make up the difference out of my own pocket."

"A...a quarter for..."

He nodded, not breaking eye contact. "For a day's lost sales. Yes."

Before she could say anything else, he turned, never having raised his voice or shown any emotion, and started walking again toward the field.

She scanned the faces of the others who had watched the exchange silently. Then Sloe came to her. She hugged Lila and stood back, holding her arms. "I was wrong, Lila. And whatever he did, or didn't do, in the past, he *is* trying." She looked embarrassed for a moment and repeated, "I was wrong."

"I...I'm sorry. I–"

"Don't tell me. Tell him." Sloe pointed at Egan's receding back. Then, in a brighter tone, "But not right now. Let's get this done and hope it doesn't go sideways."

She took Welp's hand and she, her husband, Frank, and Marina began walking down the path behind Egan. Lila stood for a moment, then jogged to catch up to them.

Welp called ahead. "Egan, you mentioned you wanted to talk?" Egan stopped and turned, waiting for the rest of them. He made a point of not looking at Lila and she felt another stab of guilt, but knew now wasn't the time to try to make amends.

"I do, but there isn't enough time to get into it right now. Short version, I want to know if you would be interested in a business relationship." They had reached the hedge opening leading to the field, and he waved them through ahead of him.

Welp looked at his wife, who had to take two steps to each one of Welp's. Sloe shrugged, apparently also clueless.

"Business relationship?" Welp asked. "In what?"

Egan simply said, "We'll talk," and entered the opening in the shrubs. As they made their way through the five-foot-wide hedge, Lila thought she could hear a continuous staccato popping sound from the field side and wondered what it was.

***

When Frank and Marina had told Lila there was no specific plan of action for the Stallers, they had been telling the truth. They just knew there was no more point in trying to dictate to the Park residents than trying to herd a bunch of cats; the Stallers would take in the information given and then put their creativity and resourcefulness to work in making sure Lila, and her companions, stayed safe. And Stallers were, if nothing else, creative and resourceful.

But even Frank was surprised at what greeted them when they stepped out onto the field. The Market had essentially been duplicated, spreading across the field with a particularly dense cluster of tables ringing the visitor's truck camper just off center in the field, only leaving enough space near its doorway for someone to go in and out.

There was even a sign, in the form of a flag waving from a tall PVC pipe planted in the middle of the field. Instead of Sun Market the words Sun Gun Show were emblazoned in big, sloppy, red letters across it. Frank scanned the vendor tables, noticing that, in keeping with the doppelgänger banner, the usual Market day wares were nowhere to be seen. Harvey Kettle stood behind a table covered, not in pipes and plumbing supplies, but hunting rifles. And while Marty Florchet's doilies were not totally absent from her station, their presence was limited to a few fluttering decoratively around the edge of her table, the usual lace on display replaced with numerous handguns and ammunition clips.

There was more of the popping sound, and he looked to his left. Near the tree line on that side of the field were about a dozen poles about fifteen feet apart, each with a large person-shaped paper target. The silhouettes had concentric circles inside them, descending in size, each with a heart-shaped bullseye in the center. Some distance back from the targets were hay bales with a few Stallers standing behind them, just finishing a round of shooting at the targets. A woman was standing at one end of the bales, calling out to the shooters. A small, wire-haired dog stood on top of the hay next to her, as though keeping track of the shots fired.

"Ok everyone, reload! Forrie, you were way off that time. Check your sites! Willie, great shooting! You won that round! The rest of you, good work!"

"What the hell?" As accustomed as he was to the idiosyncrasies of his fellow Park denizens, even Frank felt awe. Welp, Sloe, Egan, and Lila were also looking at the woman running the shooting range with amazement.

"Amanda!" Marina shouted at her and began quickly walking toward her, the rest of the group following.

The woman turned upon hearing her name.

"Marina? How you doing?"

Marina said, "Amanda, what the hell is going on?"

Amanda held her arms out, and the dog leaped into them. She stroked his head as she replied.

"What does it look like?"

"It looks like you've all lost your minds," Frank said.

"You said you wanted to make sure things didn't go off the rails when Lila met with those strangers," came Amanda's response, turning to him then nodding toward Lila, somehow detecting both her presence and where she was standing.

"And *this* is what everyone came up with? A *gun show?*" came his retort.

Amanda bowed her head slightly and said with some modesty. "And firing range. That part was my idea. Harvey came up with the initial gun idea." She gave a wicked grin and chortled. "No one is going to cause any trouble with a bunch of armed Stallers around."

"Amanda," Lila said, looking around in shock, then back to her. "How are you, um…"

"Running the range?" came the laughing response. "Hell, honey, it's easy. Everyone is using six shots per round so I can keep count."

"But I heard you tell a couple of them how they were shooting!"

"Lila, I've known most of them for years. In Forrie's case, he's used the bathroom at my place more than once. If he can't manage to piss straight enough to hit the bowl, there's no way he can shoot a target at fifty yards. As for Willie, he's young and shy, and can use all the building up he can get."

"Ok," Lila continued, shaking her head. "But where did all the guns come from?"

Egan answered that one, wariness in his eyes, probably trying to gauge if she was still upset, and Frank saw her give a smile in return.

"Lila, this is New Hampshire. Probably as many guns in the state as black flies in the summer. I'm only surprised there isn't a bazooka somewhere around."

Amanda said off-handedly, "I think Jam Candis has a small one," and turned back to face down range. "Now, if you'll excuse me, I believe everyone is locked and loaded and ready for the next round." She held her arms out again, and the dog jumped down to take his position on the hay bale. "Why don't you all go take care of that visit? We'll keep an eye on things."

They made their way between tables toward the camper, the blind woman's call of "Clear the range!" following them. As they passed the various tables, they exchanged nods and words of greeting from the Stallers. Frank thought they seemed more enthusiastic about the day's events than he had ever seen them on a regular Market day.

And although he had lived in New Hampshire and at the Park for many years, he had to shake his head at the sheer number of weapons on display. He was even more surprised as they passed Jamaica "Jam" Candis's table and saw the man polishing what did indeed appear to be a small rocket launcher. He had no time to ponder it, though, as the camper was a few feet behind Jam's table.

They stood looking at the battered old Winnebago, and Lila wondered if anyone was home. She saw Marina nudge Frank and motion toward the camper and looked up to see a man's face peering out of one of the windows. It was Tokalu. He looked pale and unhappy but, in her experience, that wasn't at all unusual. She thought he existed to be unhappy about something. Although, in this case, he probably had a right to be.

"Hello inside!" Frank called out.

Tokalu's face disappeared from the window, and Lila heard muttering, then Wichapi speaking sternly.

"Open the door, Tokalu. We have visitors."

"But Wichapi...," came Tokalu's reply.

"Open the door," the voice continued, firmly. It swung open, Tokalu frowned down at them from inside. They stepped up into the dimness of the camper, Marina in front, Lila trailing at the rear.

Although it was an average New England spring day, cool but not cold, the camper was quite warm. Lila assumed the heat was cranked up for the benefit of the old woman seated in a recliner. Wichapi motioned toward the facing small sofa as she scanned the group, her gaze ending and staying on Lila. They continued to stand in front of the couch, none wanting to get too comfortable.

Marina started, "Wichapi, this is–"

"I believe I know everyone, Ms. Agbo." She looked at each in turn. "Frank Pullman, Ginny 'Sloe' Blunt, Welp Francis, Egan Lothe, and, of course, Lila Fortin." She nodded at her as she spoke her name. "Lila, I'm glad your trip to Maine was delayed. It's good to see you."

She gave an angry snort. "Right."

The older woman pursed her lips and nodded slightly. "Understandable." She leaned forward and continued, "There are things to discuss." She paused. "And amends to make."

Lila stood. "I have no intention of making amends for anything. I haven't done anything."

Wichapi looked up at the angry woman calmly. "No, you haven't. But I have." She motioned again to the sofa, but no one sat, and the medicine woman sighed.

Amanda's voice echoed faintly from outside. *Forrie, I swear you couldn't hit the floor with your feet without help!*

Wichapi turned to Egan, "Is the gun swap and firing range an annual event?"

Egan cleared his throat and said, "This, ah, is the first one. I'm not sure how often it will be held."

Wichapi's lips tightened. "Then how fortunate our visit coincided with its occurrence. Although it is rather cozily situated to where we are camped." Still facing Egan, she said, "It's very kind of you to allow us to stay here, Mr. Lothe."

"You seem to know all about us. How did you–?"

"Oh, come, Mr. Lothe. You run your enterprise, I oversee the functioning of the Tribal Council. In both our positions, it behooves us to understand who we are dealing with, doesn't it?"

Egan looked back at her for a moment then dipped his head a fraction, acknowledging her point.

Wichapi turned to Welp, "And Mr. Francis, it was also very kind of you to assist Lila when she broke down." She scanned the entire group. "It was generous of all of you, actually."

Sloe stepped forward from Welp's side. "Lila is family."

The Elder paused, then nodded. "I've heard the term 'Stallers.' I assume it has to do with those who sell their wares at the various Market stalls?"

Marina said, "And live here. Some of us, anyway."

Another pursing of the lips. "And you all consider yourselves, as well as Lila, Stallers?"

Frank picked up the conversation. He said flatly. "Yes, we do. And she is."

Wichapi nodded. "I understand. And I believe Stallers are both born one and also may become one?" Frank raised an eyebrow, obviously not knowing where the question was leading, but nodded in return.

Wichapi said. "Just right. With my people, you are either born Lakota or you are not." She looked at Lila as she made this comment.

Visibly tiring of the oblique nature of the visitor's comments, Frank said, "Is there a point to your comment?"

Wichapi ignored him, still focused on Lila. "Being Lakota means helping other tribe members. Protecting, when necessary. When there is a conflict, the tribe's needs must outweigh any individual members. It is how we have survived."

Lila replied in a clipped tone, "I'm aware of Lakota responsibilities, Wichapi. And yours. Even if I am not Lakota."

The old woman squinted at Lila and settled back in her chair, apparently changing the topic.

"Woweechala came to me the first year you were with us and asked me to perform the Hunka ceremony."

Dulled pain and anger. "I know. And you turned her down. She performed it herself that same night after she thought I was asleep."

For the first time, Wichapi showed emotion, raising her eyebrows. She nodded slowly.

The old woman said, staring down at her tanned and parchment-like hands, "I should have expected that." She looked back up at Lila. "Not that it would have changed anything."

"What–," she began.

"Protecting the tribe," Wichapi went on, "has been my priority since I became phejuta winyela." At the puzzled looks from the New Englanders, she added, "Medicine Woman."

"I already said I know what your responsibilities are," she grated, her annoyance moving toward anger.

"I said Woweechala's decision to perform the Hunka ritual changed nothing. That is because you are Lakota, Lila Lowanwee. Daughter of Allison Wachiwi, granddaughter of Maureen Wivyaka, who was my sister."

Numbness.

She stepped toward the couch, reaching out for the tattered sofa arm, and lowered herself. Egan joined her. The tick of a clock sounded loud in the silence.

Welp was the first to break the silence.

"Holy Flying Bat Shit."

Lila finally spoke, emotions roiling inside her. "No...I mean...I don't understand. I'm Lakota? And my mother was...your niece?"

A nod from Wichapi. "And you are my grandniece."

She reached out and took Egan's hand in hers. Shaking her head she said, "No. It doesn't make sense. How–"

Wichapi held up her hand and said, "Please."

Lila sat back, watching the old woman.

Wichapi looked away toward the small window next to the camper door as she spoke. "Life on Pine Ridge has always been challenging, as you know. Poverty, drugs, an early death in far too many cases. Even as a young girl, my sister knew that life all too well. She wanted to help, as did I. But as we grew, I determined the best way to help was by joining the Council. Wivyaka, however, always felt the Council was ineffective. Too hemmed in by regulations, many imposed by the same people who had forced us onto the reservation to begin with. She chose a different path."

She turned back to face the group. "But there are repercussions, always, to our choices. And sometimes those repercussions ripple out, as from a stone thrown into a river.

For the first time since arriving at Pine Ridge as a small girl, Lila heard the sadness and pain behind the words Wichapi spoke. And realized that, like her own life's journey to date, a long, twisted road had led to Wichapi being the person she was.

Much more gently than she had yet spoken to the old woman, she said, "Me? I'm a repercussion? Wichapi, I don't understand."

Wichapi said, "Your mother lived with her parents at Pine Ridge until she was fourteen. She was beautiful, as was Wivyaka, her mother and my sister. Your mother's Lakota name, Wachiwi, means Dancing Girl. And dance she did, even as a wisp of a girl. Every movement seemed to be to her own internal song, from the time she could walk." She looked toward Lila, but Lila thought she was looking at, seeing, something else.

Wichapi blinked and focused again on Lila. "You are angry. I understand."

Lila's emotions bubbled over again. "Do you? Do you, really, Wichapi?" Reflexively she squeezed Egan's hand so hard he winced and said fiercely, "I doubt it. I've spent most of my life feeling like I didn't belong because I'm not Lakota, but it turns out I am. And oh yeah, my mother was your niece? All of which you hid from me. What the fuck, old woman?"

Tokalu, standing by the wall and silent to this point, spoke for the first time since the Park residents had entered. He stood rigid as he said in a harshly chastising tone, "You should show respect. She is phejúta winyela, as well as your family elder."

Egan launched himself from the couch and lunged toward him. The Lakota jumped back so quickly his head bounced against the wall.

"Keep out of this, buddy. Or that firing range out there can start using a live target." Tokalu's pallor turned pale, but he said nothing.

Wichapi ignored the entire exchange and spoke to Lila again.

"I don't know what you remember from your life before you came to us, but—"

"Nothing. I remember nothing." She could taste the bitterness as she spoke.

"I'm not surprised," Wichapi said. "You were almost catatonic when you arrived at Pine Ridge the week following the murder."

Lila shot up. "Murder? My mother? By whom? Why? Does it have anything to do with Mama Elise's death?" She was overwhelmed with the apparently never-ending revelations but had to know everything.

Wichapi answered the last question. "And your grandparents, my sister and her husband. I'm uncertain if there was a direct connection, but...it seems likely."

Before she could respond to that, Egan interjected. "Wichapi, you said Lila's mother's name meant Dancing Girl. What did her grandmother's name mean?"

Lila looked up at Egan, not understanding the apparent non sequitur. She looked to Wichapi, who sat looking back at him, then it clicked.

She said, "Feather." All eyes turned to her. "Wiyaka means feather."

"Yes, feather," Wichapi agreed softly.

"My mother was involved in Mama Elise's business?"

"It would be more accurate to say Woweechala was involved in your grandparents' business. To my knowledge, your mother was not involved. She was simply home the day your grandparents were killed. As were you."

Wichapi answered her next question, shaking her head, before Lila could utter it. "I don't know who your father is or was."

She should have expected that, but it still gave her a pang of disappointment.

Wichapi continued. "My sister was married to an outsider, a part-time ranch hand from Spearfish. He was a good man and cared deeply about people, including our people. I considered him a friend. They moved to Spearfish and Wiyaka started the business shortly after they married. She supplied eagle feathers and parts both to our people for ceremonies and to dealers around the state. She practically gave them away to our people on Pine Ridge, refusing to make a profit from her own. The whites were a different matter. To them, those that have taken so much from us for so long, she charged as much as she could. But the bureaucratic hoops that must be jumped through to obtain even a single wanbli from the sacred bird meant she could only get one, sometimes two, carcasses a year. Even so, the money she made from selling to dealers was used to start a fund to assist those in the most desperate need at Pine Ridge."

Lila started. "The MAAS?" she asked. She explained to the others, "Mutual Aid and Support fund. It's used to help cover everything from school supplies for kids at Pine Ridge to heating bills to...well, just about anything when people run short. Which happens a lot." Back to Wichapi. "That's where that money comes from?"

Wichapi responded, "Initially, yes. The seed money for it came from your grandparents and has grown from there. But until they and your mother died, they continued to funnel most of their profits into it."

Lila's thoughts were a jumble, and she was still sorting through them when Marina asked a question.

"Wichapi, you said your sister was only able to get one or two birds a year. I know Lila told us there is a lot of money made on selling eagle parts, but with only a couple of eagles a year, it doesn't seem like there would have been enough to really build a big fund, not the size that you seem to be implying."

Tokalu spoke up again. "Wichapi." There was both a warning and a fear in his voice as he said the Elder's name.

The Elder responded to him. "Tokalu, this is why we are here."

"To speak with Lila yes, but these," he motioned at the group, "wasicun are not Oglala."

"No, but they are her family. More than we have been, in many ways." The small man tried to hold Wichapi's stare for a moment, then gave up and sank back into silence against the wall.

Welp, who seemed to have been contemplating something for the last few minutes, turned to Sloe. "Red-tailed?"

"Maybe," Sloe nodded. "Or possibly Osprey?"

They both looked at Wichapi, saying, "We enjoy bird watching when we can."

Wichapi leaned back, nodding. "Red-tailed hawks, osprey, buteos. Anything that could, with a little work, be passed off as an eagle."

Lila said, "Great, so they were liars and poachers."

The old woman shook her head. "Any lies were never to our people, only whites looking to profit from us as they always have. As for poaching, no, I'm certain they were not. They simply used easier to obtain carcasses."

"But you don't *know*, do you?" She grimaced, frustrated by Wichapi's calmness and certainty about things Lila had not even known about until now.

The Elder smiled for the first time in Lila's memory. "Oh, I know, Lowanwee. She was my sister and would no more have killed animals simply for profit than she would have sold false goods to Oglala."

The birds came from somewhere, though, didn't they?

Lila thought there was a lot of flexibility in Wichapi's, and apparently her own grandparents' view, of right and wrong, but this wasn't the time to get into that. She did want to pursue one aspect, though.

"But she did sell the bogus items to the white dealers."

Wichapi sighed. "Not at first, but yes. And as it was with my approval, I take responsibility for all that followed."

Lila waited, sensing there was more.

There was. "Shortly after Wiyaka and Thomas married, things were worse than usual at Pine Ridge. More children going hungry, more mothers and fathers turning to alcohol and other substances to blunt the pain of being unable to care for their families. The money that my sister and her husband were putting into the emergency fund helped, but not enough. As your friend pointed out, the small number of available wanbli limited the amount of money that could be made. It was during that time that Wiyaka came to me with an idea. It was tearing her apart to see family, friends, so many being destroyed. She spoke to me about expanding the business to sell to dealers across the country. I questioned how that could be done with the limited supply of sacred birds available. It was then that she proposed using other species to fulfill those orders."

Lila saw the familiar haughtiness Wichapi carried with her as the medicine woman went on. "I was not entirely comfortable with the idea, but I had, and still have, little concern for those making money from the Lakota, and many of our people were in genuine need. I did, however, see the potential risks." He paused, and her eyes seemed to have a touch of regret. "Or so I thought. I told Wiyaka that there needed to be a separation between the business and Pine Ridge. So–"

"You sent her away," Lila almost murmured. "Your own sister." Her anger about being lied to all these years faded to a dull, throbbing ache in her heart.

The Elder nodded. "Yes, I sent Wiyaka and Thomas away."

"And my mother."

"Yes, Wachiwi accompanied them to Maine, although I did offer to have her stay here with Woweechala, who had been as close to your grandmother as another sister. Your grandparents, and Wachiwi, refused to be separated. You were born three years later."

She remembered the old woman had said her mother had been at Pine Ridge until she was fourteen. "She was only seventeen when I was born? But that means she died when—"

Again, Wichapi nodded, saying, "She was only twenty-two when she was killed. Younger than you are now."

Lila's eyes welled with tears. Next to her, Egan asked, "What happened, Wichapi? Did someone find out about the fakes? Were they killed for revenge?"

"I do not know, although I suspect that was the reason. When it happened, I was contacted as next of kin since Thomas had no relatives. Arrangements were made to have you brought to Pine Ridge. However, based on my suspicions about your mother's and grandparents' deaths, I deemed it appropriate to avoid drawing any connection between you and them. The authorities and Council knew, of course, and Woweechala, but to all others at Pine Ridge and anyone else, you were a wasicun foundling, fostered to her."

There was a roaring in Lila's head as she screamed, "And you didn't tell me!"

Wichapi was unperturbed by her outburst. "No, I didn't. You were a young girl, badly traumatized. If your memories returned on their own, so be it. Otherwise, I saw no advantage in speaking of it."

She realized her palms were hurting and unclenched her fists, but there was still bile in her throat.

"Advantage. That's all it's ever been about, isn't it? Advantage to the tribe. But it was really an advantage for you to be able to take credit for the fund. Advantage to you to send my mother and grandparents away, to keep your hands clean." She was still standing, tears streaming down her cheeks now, and her voice rose to almost a scream. "It's your fault they were killed. And Mama Elise too. And that I...I..." Her voice trailed off, her mind unable to make sense anymore of the flood of thoughts, emotions. An arm slid around her waist, and she was pulled into an embrace that she initially pushed back against. Strong arms held her though and after a moment, she pressed her head against Egan's shirt.

No one said a word. Muted voices from the ad hoc gun show outside carried into the room as murmurs, punctuated now and again by the popping on the target range. Egan didn't move but simply kept his arms wrapped around her and her tears finally slowed.

And now she was embarrassed, not wanting to face the pitying looks from her friends. She tried to light the pilot of her anger, the armor, but found she couldn't. She was more tired than she remembered ever feeling. Pulling away from Egan, she steeled herself to deal with unwanted sympathy and looked around. To her surprise, what she saw in her friend's eyes was anger. But not at her. They were all focused on Wichapi.

Welp, of all people, looked like he was ready to launch himself at the old woman.

He growled, "Who the *hell* do you think you are? God?"

Wichapi stared back stonily, straightened in the chair, and tipped her head up. "I am head of the Pine Ridge Council and therefore have responsibility–"

"Yeah, yeah, responsibility to the tribe, blah, blah. You've done real well with that, haven't you?" He turned away in disgust. "Jesus."

"Why did you come here?" Marina's eyes were flat. "I mean, Lila's mother and your sister are long dead. Mama Elise is dead, and it doesn't sound like there is anyone trying to tie Lila to her murder. So why are you here?"

The Elder seemed to be preparing another officious statement, but Marina waved her hand dismissively and said, "Really."

Wichapi paused and leaned back.

Finally, "Because while I have done my best to fulfill my responsibilities to the tribe, I realize now I have failed in my responsibility to my family...to Lila." She looked back at Lila, uncomfortably. "I have failed you. And...I am sorry."

The apology washed over Lila like a wave. Wichapi never apologized. *Never.* As shocked as Lila was at finding out she was actually Lakota, she was equally rocked by the Elder's words.

But she couldn't accept the apology. Not with everything that had happened. Not right now, at least. She knew she had to respond, though, and managed, "I...I appreciate that, Wichapi." It was an acknowledgment of the apology, but not an acceptance.

From Wichapi's return gaze and slight nod, her great aunt appeared to understand.

But Lila still had so many unanswered questions.

Who was my father? Is he still alive? Who killed Mama Elise? And why?

But she was done for the moment. Drained. Too much in such a few minutes. As she stared at the woman who had been responsible for the path Lila's life had followed for so long, she realized there was only one more question she wanted answered right now.

"So with that out of the way, you'll be leaving now?"

There was no question Wichapi heard the anger in Lila's tone, but Wichapi simply said, "There is one more piece of business to complete first." She looked over at her erstwhile guardian, still standing rigidly against the wall, and held out her hand. From his back pocket he extracted a small, folded piece of paper which he handed to the Elder. She took it and held it out to Lila.

Lila looked at it for a moment and took it. Unfolding it, she saw it was a check made out to her for thirty thousand dollars. The bank stamp on it was from the Pine Ridge Credit Union.

Confused, she looked back at Wichapi.

"When your mother and grandparents died, and the decision was made for Woweechala to continue the business, she requested a small percentage of the profits be put into an account for you. It was her version of a life insurance policy." She finished simply, "The money is yours."

Lila stared back at the check for a moment. Tears ran down her cheeks and a familiar emotion filled her as she looked back, cheeks burning, at Wichapi. Before she could respond, Egan squeezed her arm and said, "Lila, think it through. It's what Mama Elise wanted. Because she loved you."

Lila's breath hitched. She couldn't speak as she tried to keep control. She nodded and put the check in her pocket.

"We are done here," Wichapi said, sitting back again. "We will leave this evening. That is," she looked at Egan, "assuming the gun show will be over by then?"

"Oh, I think it's about ready to wrap up," Egan said wryly.

"Good. You can show yourselves out, then."

Chapter Nineteen

Frank scanned the tables as they stepped down out of the camper. He spotted Willie and called to him.

"Hey, Willie! Go tell Amanda to wrap things up. We're all set."

The teenager, who had been making a show of cleaning a musket, looked from him to Lila then back. He lay the revolutionary weapon on the table, called back, "You got it," and took off at a trot toward the firing range. Those close enough to have heard Frank's comment began closing up shop immediately, putting their various and eclectic assortment of firearms in bins, loading vehicles, and headed back to toward the Park side.

Frank noticed Mike DeTony and his husband, Larry, moving boxes of ammunition off their table into plastic totes, then into the back of their car. He walked over to them as Lila and the others moved away from the camper to debrief.

"Hi Frank. All good?" Larry asked.

He nodded, looking at the variety and quantity of ammunition. "You looking to equip a marauding band of vigilantes?"

Larry smiled. "Probably could, at that. This is from our inventory at the shop." He was referring to the Bridgett Tobacco Haven, which adjoined the Bridgett Liquor Store, both of which the couple owned. Tobacco Haven carried ammunition in addition to its obvious wares.

As Mike put another tote in the car backseat, he said, "New Hampshire is a funny place."

"Hey, Masshole, I was born here," Larry chided him.

"My point is made," Mike responded. Frank had heard this repartee for years, but still smiled.

Mike asked Larry, "Can you finish getting everything loaded, hon? I want to check that my patient hasn't done anything stupid, too stupid, and messed up my work."

His husband picked up the last tote and loaded it into the front seat of their car. "Go for it. Lucy can cover at the shop. Just don't leave me stranded at the store for too long. It's Mr. Nichols' weekly bourbon run today, and I don't think I can handle hearing about how Jesus can turn us from our wicked ways one more time."

As Frank and Mike turned and headed toward Lila and the others that had visited the camper, Larry called out, "Glad everything is copasetic with your adoptee, Frank."

Frank stopped and stared back at Larry, then at Mike. "My *adoptee?*"

Mike gave a small laugh. "That's what everyone is calling her."

Frank grunted and started walking again.

As they approached the group, Marina was saying, "You don't have to decide right away, Lila."

He gave Marina a questioning look, and she explained. "I was telling Lila that Maine, South Dakota, wherever, aren't going anywhere. She should give herself time to think about what she wants to do before she leaves."

Mike pointed at Lila, then a nearby recently vacated table. "Upsydaisy, girl."

Lila knew better than to argue, and stepped over, planting herself on the edge of the table, legs dangling. Mike squatted down and rolled her yoga pants leg up as far as he could. A thin scabbed scar ran up her calf and disappeared further up under her pants. The EMT ran his fingers along it, examining and pressing with his fingers around its periphery.

"Well, it looks like you get to keep the leg," he said at last.

Lila shook her head and blinked. "Was there ever a question?"

"Just a bit, but I didn't want to worry you."

"How nice of you," came her reply, as he stepped away and she tugged her pants leg back down. She slid to the ground.

"Mike, thanks again, really. Can I–"

He was already shaking his

head. "Nope, not a chance. I don't charge Stallers, although," he shot Sloe a glance, "I've been tempted a few times. Just try not to need my services too often."

Sloe had stuck her tongue out at his comment but was prevented from saying anything as Amanda Fleming came around the corner, Velcro trotting next to her.

"Frank? Willie said things are all set. Need anything else?" He noticed a very large handgun haphazardly dangling from her free hand. He stepped to her side and gently took the weapon from her hand. He breathed a sigh of relief seeing the safety was on.

"Thanks, Amanda. No, I think our business with the visitors is all done. Pass the word to everyone if you would that they did a great job."

"And that there will be a barbeque tonight," added Egan.

Frank looked at him and Egan looked away, blushing.

"Least I can do under the circumstances," Egan muttered.

Amanda turned toward the sound of his voice and said, "Beer, too." It wasn't a question.

Egan turned to her and sighed. "Fine, beer too."

The blind woman cackled and said, "Egan, I will never again say that you don't do the least you can do." She clucked at Velcro to follow her and left to spread Frank's thanks along with the more important news about the free food and beer.

Egan shook his head and said, "She is something."

"That she is," Frank replied. To Lila he said, "Marina's right, you know. Don't rush anything. And when you do leave, consider the Park a safe harbor any time you need it."

To his surprise, Lila wrapped her arms around him.

He brought his arms up awkwardly and returned the hug.

Egan had enough barbeque and sides delivered to feed double the number of Park residents, but no one complained and what was left following the *chow down,* as Amanda called it, was carted away by various residents for later snacking and meals.

Now, about halfway through the evening, Welp was admiring the dueling bonfires on either end of the field which had hosted the Sun Gun Show earlier and where everyone now congregated. People were dancing around the stone pits in what reminded him of some ancient ceremony, although he doubted baseball caps had been particularly common a thousand years ago.

He saw Egan and Lila talking, off to one side, heads close together. Based on what had gone on in the camper and Lila's giggle at something the smiling Park manager said, he suspected not only had the fence been mended between them, but there were flowers growing up an arbor between the two. Then he saw Sloe headed back from the keg, two red plastic cups sloshing as she made her way toward him. She was staring at the drinks as though trying to will them to not spill any more than they already had. The barbeque had kicked off hours before, so Sloe, and most other adults, were well into the refreshments by this point.

Not the best night to discuss things. Good.

He had decided that while he had made up his mind, he and Sloe still needed to talk. And he wanted to make sure he said things the right way for a change. Half in the bag probably wasn't the best time to do that.

Sloe thrust a cup into his hand, beer splashing up to his wrist.

"So, what are you going to do?"

Well, guess we are going to talk about it

"Um...what?" He knew he had only bought himself about three seconds.

About two seconds later, he followed that up with, "Ouch!"

He rubbed the arm Sloe had punched.

"You know exactly what I'm asking, Welp. What are you going to do? About us?" The fire he so loved was in her eyes, but it was mixed with more than a hint of trepidation.

He took a deep breath.

Don't screw this up.

"Sloe, I love you. That's the beginning and end of everything for me." She was watching him quietly now, and he knew she was waiting for a follow-up.

He paused.

She finally came out with it.

"But?"

He shook his head.

"There is no but. My life is with you. *Is* you. I'm not sure what the hell I want to do, but any figuring out, we will do together. Like I said, it all starts and ends with you - us. I'm not going anywhere."

He reached out and stroked her cheek. "OK?"

She dropped her cup and threw herself at him. Her head may have only come up to his rib cage, but the fierceness of her hug could have come from a Kodiak bear.

Through her snuffles, he heard a muffled, "Ok,"

Thank God.

He wrapped his arms around her, being careful to not dump his own cup. Beer was beer and free beer, especially free beer supplied by Egan, was a gift from the powers that be.

As if reading his mind, Egan's voice rang out from just behind Sloe. "Wasting my beer?"

Welp looked over Sloe's head and saw the Park manager and Lila.

"Hi, Egan." He nodded at Lila.

"Sorry to interrupt, but I wanted to see if we could have that conversation about the business venture I mentioned."

Between the visit with Wichapi and trying to wrap his head around his and Sloe's situation, Welp had temporarily forgotten Egan's cryptic comments. His arms loosened on his wife, who pulled away with a final snuffle. Looking down at her dumped cup, she said, "Lila, do you want to go get a refill with me while the men-folk talk business?" There was heavy sarcasm in the question, but Lila knew Sloe simply wanted to give her husband space.

To Welp's surprise, Lila shook her head and said, "No, it involves both of you. And me too."

Welp's curiosity was more than piqued.

He tipped his cup back and gulped a sip. "Shoot."

"I'm going to build an amusement park, including having a bike motocross racetrack for nighttime and weekend events. And I want you to run it, taking care of the day-to-day operations of the whole thing, making sure all the equipment works, oversee the racing, whatever else needs doing."

Welp took a second gulp from the cup. Then a third.

Egan waited for him to process the offer.

Welp brought the cup up to his mouth again, but Sloe blocked it with her hand.

"Welp."

He looked at her, then back to Egan. Lila watched with an amused expression.

He took a deep breath. "What exactly do you have in mind?"

The talk continued over at Egan's house. Welp still felt out of place as he looked around the dining room at the mahogany paneling and paintings that Welp was certain had not been done at a sip and paint date night. Sloe, on the other hand, seemed relaxed, as did Lila, who was sitting next to Egan. A dim orange glow was visible through a window, the only sign of the New England pagan ritual in full swing on the other side of the Park.

"So, you're in?" Egan asked when they had settled in around the table. He had offered each of them drinks when they first entered, but Welp wanted to keep as clear a head as he could, although after imbibing half a dozen beers at the barbeque, the horse was already half out of the barn. Sloe also declined, and Lila requested a root beer. Egan had *tsk tsk*'d them all, then poured himself a glass of wine from a sideboard.

"I need to know exactly what you have in mind before I give an answer. First and foremost, what does this mean for the Park?"

"Not a thing," Egan replied. "Oh, the open field might be cut into a bit, but not much, if at all. I want to make sure there is a buffer between the Stallers and the amusement park and vice versa. But I own the large, wooded parcel on the other side of it. My plan is to use about ten acres for Starlight."

"Starlight?" asked Sloe.

Egan nodded. "Starlight Amusement and Entertainment Center. Seems appropriate." He cleared his throat.

"Twinkle, twinkle, little Sloe…"

Sloe jumped in.

"Riding across the park, look at her go…."

Then together,

"Up above us all she shines. Like a sparkling star, forever mine."

Sloe's mouth was crinkled up in the way she had when she was trying not to cry, and Egan looked like he had gotten smoke in his eyes. He reached out across the table to Sloe and took her hand.

"That was Mama's song for me when I was little," Sloe said thickly.

Egan nodded, wiping the invisible smoke from his eyes.

Welp felt a bit guilty for interrupting, but finally cleared his throat.

"Egan? Amusement Park?"

Egan gave Sloe a smile, then turned to Welp and nodded. "Yep. The full shot, rides, games, and a BMX track and stadium inside of it."

"And an outdoor concert stage," Lila added that.

"Yes, definitely," Egan said, nodding enthusiastically. "That was a great idea you had. It will pull in people that otherwise might not visit for the other parts."

"And you want me to run things?" Welp said dubiously.

Egan nodded agreeably, turning back to him. "Yes. With your expertise with bikes and mechanical things, seems to me it would be a good fit." He looked back at Sloe. "And you've got your mother's head for business, Sloe. The fact that you've been able to keep making a living selling used games and toys says a lot."

Sloe snorted. "Not a good one, I haven't."

"Maybe not, but you've managed it. Not," he added, "that that will be the case with Starlight. I want Welp to be the Chief Operating Officer and you the Chief Financial Officer. If you're willing." He then mentioned salaries for each of them. Somewhere on the order of triple what they collectively made right now.

"For *each* of us?" was Sloe's shocked reaction.

Egan was nodding again. "Commensurate with the responsibilities. But I fully expect Starlight to bring in a hell of a lot more than those salaries, plus operating expenses, once we get rolling. There isn't anything like it in this part of the state. Hell, there isn't a combination amusement park, BMX racetrack, and concert venue in New Hampshire or New England at all."

Sloe asked, "So how do you know anyone will want to come?"

Egan leaned back in his chair and waved his wine glass at them. "What's the line? If you build it, they will come? Besides, leave that to us. We'll take care of the marketing and advertising."

Welp blinked. "Us?" He glanced over at Lila, who had been listening quietly. She had a bemused look on her face.

"Egan asked me if I would be interested in investing in Starlight, now that I am a woman of means. Little means, at least. I've said yes." She seemed to know the next question he would ask and pre-empted it. "No, it doesn't mean I won't be leaving, but it does mean if I do, I'll be coming back."

He nodded at this, but was still in a bit of shock. He wasn't sure if it was the offer for him to help create something like Starlight, or that Egan would even entertain giving away profits. Either way, the Park manager wasn't the man he had been.

Or at least the man we thought he was.

"So, we have a deal, then?" Egan was cocking an eyebrow at Sloe and Welp.

Welp looked at his wife and smiled. She grinned back.

He looked at Egan and asked, "Will there be a merry-go-round or a roller coaster?"

Egan blinked. "Ah...yes, of course. The carousel will be the centerpiece of the amusement grounds, and I'm planning on an old-fashioned wooden coaster. Why?"

Welp ignored Sloe as her eyes narrowed.

He held his hand out and as Egan took it in his own, Welp shook it enthusiastically and said, "Then it's a deal. Let's just hope things don't spin out of control, although I'm sure there will be a lot of ups and downs."

Welp appreciated the groans from Sloe and Lila, but relished even more what he considered the highest form of pun praise from Egan. A blank stare and dead silence.

They all accepted a glass of champagne following the sealing of the Starlight deal. Sloe and Welp excused themselves shortly thereafter, and Lila found herself alone with Egan. She was staring into the slender crystal glass in her hand, still trying to fully wrap her mind around the day's events, when he spoke to her.

"You were right."

The words took a moment to register. He was sitting just a foot or two away, looking over at her.

"Huh? Right about what?"

His lips drew together in a grimace before he said, "About me. How I've treated the Stallers. Most people. Everyone."

She shook her head, disagreeing. "Egan, you paid them for the day. I lit into you without giving you a chance to tell me that, to talk at all. I was angry and upset and worried about the meeting, but I didn't have the right–"

"No," he countered and repeated, "you were right, at least partially. I've resented being stuck here at the Market for a hell of a long time. I can admit to myself that part of how I've acted is because of that." Her face clouded, and he added, "I'm not making excuses, but it is the reality." He took a breath. "And I offered to pay them because I knew what your reaction would be to the closure. I, ah, didn't want to disappoint you."

He had the look of an embarrassed teen again that she found endearing. She felt her cheeks heating up, but smiled, reached out and pushed a lock of his hair off his forehead.

"Well," she said finally, "How can I complain about that? And I understand, I think, about how you've felt about being trapped. I don't agree with some of what you've done, period. But I do understand. We're all where we are because of where we've been."

She raised her glass again.

"But that doesn't mean we have to stay in the same place."

After a moment, he raised his glass as well and the two glasses gave a clear, high note as they touched.

Chapter Twenty

Frank wasn't performing at the barbeque, preferring to just enjoy the evening with his lady. The party had just gotten going and he and Marina were wandering in and out of the small groups of other Park residents clumped together around the field. There were many conversations, and laughs, about the 'gun show' and the visitors, who had taken off shortly after the Stallers cleared out of the field.

As he and Marina approached one group of revelers, Frank was surprised to see Jerry McMurphy, their newly hired 'twat', standing with Marty Florchet and Amanda Fleming. He watched with amusement as Velcro tried to make sweet doggy-love to Jerry's pinstripe pants. Jerry, always proper, was trying, unsuccessfully, to extricate himself from the terrier's grip while simultaneously carrying on a conversation with the women.

Good luck with getting him loose. He isn't called Velcro just because he always stays close to Amanda.

Marty was speaking as he and Marina joined them.

"I swear, when the guy came out to check the camper before they took off and saw Amanda coming up, dangling a shotgun from one hand, I thought he was going to wet himself." She cackled.

"Hmmph. As though I don't know how to handle a gun," Amanda said, acting a little insulted.

"I think it was the cane in your other hand, and you feeling your way along, that almost made his bladder cut loose," Marty replied.

"Am I to understand that you held some sort of gun show at the Park?" Jerry's voice wavered a bit as he increased his shaking. The dog seemed convinced he had found his true love.

"At the Market, technically, but yep," replied Amanda. She took a sip from her plastic cup and held it out toward the lawyer, who, after hesitating, politely took it but simply held it away from himself without drinking.

"I assume all the requisite permits were in place?" Frank knew the attorney was trying to convey a sense of legal seriousness to things, but the musician felt the attempt was totally undermined by the humping dog.

"Jerry, you know Egan is a stickler for the law," Frank joined the conversation. Marina gave a small snort next to him but covered it by putting her own cup up to her mouth. Jerry made no attempt to hide his own derisive sound but didn't pursue the topic further.

"Frank, I thought you would be here somewhere." He removed an envelope from inside his suit pocket. "I have something for you." The envelope he held out was unmarked.

"Jessie?" he ventured.

McMurphy nodded. "It was to be delivered following the previous item. But as you left on your jaunt shortly thereafter,

I decided to wait until you returned rather than leave it at your trailer."

"Much appreciated," Frank said as he held the envelope up. "Doesn't appear to have a treasure map in it."

"It's a letter," the lawyer said rather shortly, shaking his leg once again, as oblivious to Frank's humor as Amanda appeared to be to the dog's amorous adventures.

Frank looked at McMurphy and said, "Right. Thanks." He slid the envelope into his back pocket for later reading. "Going to stick around for the festivities?" Frank noticed Marty had been slowly moving closer to the unmarried middle-aged attorney.

"I don't think—"

Marty grabbed his arm, interrupting whatever he had planned on saying. Someone's stereo was blasting out a country song over at the other end of the field.

"Come on, Jerry. Loosen up and let's show these kids some old-fashioned line stepping." She pulled him toward the sound of the music, ignoring his protestations that he didn't dance. Amanda's cup was still in his hand, with Velcro hanging on to his leg for dear life. About ten feet away, Velcro suddenly dropped to the ground, apparently having reached the maximum distance he would travel from Amanda; he trotted back and took position next to her. Frank would have sworn there was a slight lovelorn look on his furry face as he watched the man being half-dragged across the field. Marina excused herself to Amanda and Frank, saying she was going to go find Sloe.

With only Frank and Amanda remaining, the blind woman cocked her head toward Frank and said, "So, everything went well?"

"Well enough. Tough on Lila, though," he added, mostly to himself. He was thinking about the revelations that flooded his 'adoptee.'

Amanda nodded, seeming to understand his last comment, although Frank didn't think anyone from the camper group had shared the conversation.

But it is the Park, he thought. *Things seem to become common knowledge through some sort of osmosis.*

"Frank."

"Mmmph?"

"I hear you finally came to your senses and got with Marina." It was a statement, not a question.

"Uh...yeah, we are together. Not sure about me coming to my senses, though."

"Hmmph. Well, I just want to say, I'm glad. You've done right by that girl, Lila. Same as you've always done right by people around here. It's about time you did something for yourself."

He was a bit taken aback. He had known Amanda since he first arrived at the Park and knew she had been good friends with Jessie. But he and the old vendor weren't close. Her words touched him.

"Thanks, I–"

"Now don't go screwing it up." Amanda turned and began tapping her stick back and forth as she headed toward the sound of the music, Velcro close by.

Frank closed his mouth. Then he laughed.

It wasn't long before Marina returned but rather than being accompanied by Sloe, it was Egan that walked beside her.

"Frank," Egan said easily. More at ease than Frank remembered seeing him.

"Howdy, Egan."

"Listen, I want to run something by you before I talk to Welp and Sloe about it. Lila is already onboard but—"

"Where is Lila?" Frank asked. "Too tired out from earlier?"

"No, she's going to meet me over at the house shortly. Ran into town to open a bank account to get that check safely squirreled away."

Frank pursed his lips as he nodded. "She's sticking around?"Egan grimaced. "Maybe? She has that trip to Maine she wants to take." He was obviously not happy at the thought, but then added with a chagrined smile. "She did say that since she's a Staller now, she would be back if she does leave. Now, I'd like your opinion about an idea I have..."

A few minutes later, having filled Frank in on his tentative plans, and Frank having agreed that he thought it sounded quite reasonable, Egan took off to track down Sloe and Welp before heading back to his house.

Frank looked at Marina.

"If they go along with it, it's going to be interesting around here. More interesting than usual, I mean."

Marina said, "You know he was looking for your blessing, right?"

"What? No, that wasn't–"

"Frank, don't be dense. Egan knows how much they look up to you and trust you. I'll bet you a back rub he tells them he cleared it with you."

"How the hell would we find that out? Ask them?"

"They will probably mention it. Even if they don't, come on. It's the Park." Considering he had just been thinking along similar lines, he couldn't disagree.

"Huh. Are you reading my mind?" He asked her jokingly.

She raised her head and looked down her nose, reminding him of Wichapi, as she replied in mock seriousness.

"Mighty are the powers of women."

"Indeed," he said. "Come on, since it's apparently a time of miracles, I want to see if Marty actually loosened Jerry up and got him to remove that spike from his ass."

Marty had, and Frank spent a little while watching their boot-scooting, or, in Jerry's case, loafer-scooting, then headed back to his place with Marina. For the moment, they were rotating between their two trailers.

A little while later, as Frank mused over the day's events in bed, Marina skimmed through a nutrition article on her tablet next to him. He had seen the title: *Essential Amino Acids: Master Regulators for Nutrition.* Not what he considered enthralling reading, but each to his, or her, own.

After a few minutes, he turned to her. "Marina?"

"Mmm?" Her eyes didn't leave her reader.

"I'm sorry."

"I forgive you." She reached out and patted him, still scanning her reader.

"You don't even know what I'm apologizing for."

She looked at him, then nodded and put the reader aside. "Ok, shoot."

He took a deep breath. "I've been carrying a lot of baggage around."

She snorted. "You mean that Amtrak car you've been dragging behind you since we met?"

He grimaced. "Yeah. And we've...I've... never talked about it."

She pulled herself up from under the blanket and hugged her legs, watching him. She spoke slowly.

"I know, Frank. I mean, I know there was a kid who died and that you have been blaming yourself all these years. But—"

"Kenny. His name was Kenny. He was a student and..."

Marina didn't speak, just reached over and slid her hand into his, pulling it into her lap.

"And he died because of me. Because I was so wrapped up in myself, my image of myself, that I didn't keep him from doing something stupid. And it killed him."

Unshed tears pooled in his eyes as he told her about Kenny's senseless death, Rhonda Coti, and his alcoholic descent following her call. Throughout, Marina held his hand, her blue eyes soft. When he talked about meeting Jessie and her not-so-subtle ongoing guidance that put him back with the sober and living, they both laughed, tears of sadness and of memories rolling down their faces.

They shared a silence, then she gave his hand a squeeze.

"It's funny. You've kept people at a distance, me included, but not by being a hermit." She gave a small chuckle, but there was a layer of sadness wrapped around it. "You like to say that you don't get involved, but you have to know how many people count on you and what you've done for them. I'm not just talking about Sloe and Welp. Who was it that got me the interview at the hospital when I first moved into the Park? Hell, you even went and got ordained when Mike and Larry couldn't find a local minister to marry them."

She stroked his hand with her free one. "You can't, no one can, protect everyone from their own stupidity. Maybe you were selfish back then, I don't know. I didn't know *that* Frank Pullman. But the Frank Pullman I *do* know is about the least selfish, least self-absorbed, most caring man I've ever met." Not letting him object, she kept talking, her voice quieter than before. "Now God and me, we haven't particularly been on speaking terms in quite a few years. But I have to believe if atonement was needed, and I'm not saying it was, don't you think you've done more than enough?"

He felt his chest tighten as he looked at her, then reached out and brushed a tear from her cheek.

"I love you, Marina."

She sniffed and wiped her eyes. "I know you do." She picked up the tablet and put it on the nightstand. Her hand came up and slid the strap of her nightshirt down her shoulder as she swung her leg over his lap. "But maybe you can show me in a bit more concrete fashion."

He smiled as he slid his hand under her hair, and their bodies came together. The warmth emanating from her mirrored his own, and his head buzzed as he felt himself letting go, the train car carrying the weight of his past uncoupling and rolling away. For the first time, he was able to offer Marina his complete self, not just physically, and he felt a different kind of warmth as they finished together.

It wasn't until a little while later, as they lay next to each other, her leg over his, that he realized the warmth he still felt wasn't just from their joining. It had been so long since he last felt it, he hadn't recognized it at first.

Contentment.

Chapter Twenty-One

Frank was up and making coffee as the first rays of sunlight made their way over the edge of the horizon and worked their way through the trees to his kitchen window. On the counter next to him was an envelope, another letter from Jessie, delivered late last night by their lawyer, Jerry. Considering her last letter from the great beyond had upended his and everyone else's life, he wanted to have some caffeine in his system before opening it.

The coffee maker finally beeped, and he mixed up his light and sweet morning beverage. He chuckled, remembering telling Marina the previous morning that he liked his coffee like he liked his women…and limping for an hour after her foot came down on top of his in response.

The woman in question was still asleep in the bedroom, so Frank tucked the envelope into his shirt pocket and made his way out to sit on the picnic table. He blew on the steaming cup before taking a sip. Feeling he had fulfilled his caffeine requirement well enough, he set the cup down, pulled out the envelope, and opened it. He felt a pang of disappointment when he saw the typed-out pages, having hoped to see Jessie's neat, flowing script.

Frank,

How's it hanging? Better than me, obviously – ha! I'm down to one finger at this point. Jerry brought over a special rig that lets me use my eyes to look at words and letters to transcribe, but it's going to take a while to get this done. Jerry isn't half the ass everyone thinks, although right now he isn't looking very happy.

While I always said I didn't want a funeral or a lot of fuss made, I hope there were at least a few cups raised along with some music when this damn body of mine finally gave out.

One side of his mustache twitched as he remembered the Saturday following her death. More than a few cups had been raised, and more than a few people needed Mike DeTony and his special hangover treatment the following morning. That Saturday was also, to Frank's memory, the only day aside from the gun show the Market hadn't opened. There had been music, although the usual throw-together group had not included him; he hurt too much and after raising a taking part in a few toasts to Jessie's memory, he escaped to his trailer. The old pain-driven thirst had returned. He fought it, helped along by his dead friend's mental chastisements. It had been close, but every time he reached for his truck keys, Jessie's voice had been there, cajoling him . He was still sitting on his couch when the sun came up the next morning and Marina, who at that stage had been simply a friend, entered the trailer silently and went about making a pot of coffee, adding just the right amount of cream and sugar to the mug she handed him, did the multiple days of dishes stacked in the sink, and left, returning shortly with a plate of scones she placed on the dinette. He had observed her shuffling around as though he was were watching a TV show. It wasn't until she turned to leave that he came to himself enough to speak, but before he could, she tossed a container of vitamins to him and left.

He wiped his eyes and continued reading Jessie's letter .

Now don't worry, I'm not going to get sentimental. You would think Jerry forged this if I did. And I won't bother giving you any more guff about you carrying that load of bricks around. Since it's been a while since I headed to wherever the hell I'm going, I figure you either finally put them down or you'll be hauling them with you until you drop, so there's no point.

I want to explain about the Park and leaving you my share. I'm sure you figured out the main reason I did was to protect Sloe. She's a Staller through and through and I know she can't imagine being anywhere else, but she has no desire to run the place any more than I did. She's a smart girl, but you're my insurance that she is taken care of, and no one puts one over on her. You have a nice big cynical streak that I've always appreciated, and I'm counting on that to make sure she's taken care of.

Yes, I could have left my share to Sloe in a trust with Jerry managing it, but there's the other reason for handing it off to you.

Frank, you're as much as Staller as I am at this point. That doesn't mean you have to stay, but this gives you a stake in the place. A bigger stake, I should say, since what you've done for so many of us makes you a stakeholder, by any definition. And before you go arguing with a dead woman, think about it. I talk a good game, but when you sloshed your way to Sun, I was balancing on the head of a pin, between being cut off by Daddy, trying to make enough to feed Sloe, and just keeping my shit together in general. You did right by me, and Ginnie Jean, and a lot of others, even before you dried out. Welp, Mike and Larry – shit, you even took that newbie girl who works at the hospital under your wing.

Stallers take care of each other. That's really what the Park is about. And you've done good, Frank. Even if you spend the rest of your life traipsing around to whatever East Bumfucks festival you find, marching in parades, the Park, and Stallers will be here. And if you let them, they'll take care of you. Like you've taken care of them.

And I lied. You know I've never been one to miss an opportunity, and this is my last chance to give you some advice.

You have as much responsibility for that kid's death as a guy who can't stop a moth from frying itself on a lightbulb. Maybe you could have acted differently, but in the end, you didn't push him into that quarry. He made his own choice, stupid as it was. Shit happens and sometimes we screw up, yes. But if you let yourself get bogged down in the bad choices you might have made, you'll never get around to making good ones.

Get your head out of your ass, would you?

Love ya.

Jessie.

He was just putting the letter down when he heard the screen door on the trailer open and turned to see Marina coming down the steps, mug in hand.

She snuggled up next to him on the table and slid her arm through his.

"And what's my pirate smiling about this morning?"

Chapter Twenty-Two

The crowds were lighter than they had been at the height of summer, and as the time crept toward closing time, they thinned out even more. Lila saw there were fewer vendors, too, limited to Stallers. The seasonal table renters had packed it in following the last big weekend before Labor Day and wouldn't make another appearance until the following spring.

She was sitting off to one side, watching Frank go back and forth with a man about the selling price of a small electric keyboard; she suspected the two would reach an agreement. The man obviously wanted the keyboard and while Frank wouldn't let it go at a loss, Lila knew he was more flexible on prices than most other Stallers. He might not make as much on a single sale as some of the other more bellicose vendors, but he did tend to make more of them overall. It was the 'trust' vibe he put out.

*He certainly got me to trust him. Not that he did some sort of pitch. He just—*A light crunching noise from behind her interrupted her musings, followed by Egan's voice.

"Watching the little people work?" He came around in front of her. Instead of his usual suit, he was wearing an open-collared shirt with a sports jacket. He looked more relaxed than when she first met him as well. She thought it suited him.

She stifled a giggle and said, "Well, as ten percent owner in the Starlight Amusement Park, I wanted to check on the new musical director."

"Hmph. That's assuming the damn thing gets off the ground." Egan started listing out the various problems that had come up over the last few weeks.

"Stop!" Lila laughed, and held up a hand in surrender when it seemed the list would never end. "My head is going to explode! Besides, most of those things have been ironed out, haven't they? Welp's been working non-stop, and Sloe told me this morning that Starlight is on track to open in the spring, same time as the Market."

"Well...yeah. Things seem to be getting straightened out," he admitted reluctantly. At her continued raised eyebrow, he added. "Yes, fine, they're straightened out. Welp and Sloe are on top of things." He seemed annoyed at the admission, then muttered, "But it's all still a pain in the ass."

She patted his hand. "And you're loving every minute of it," Lila said. "Admit it."

He brightened and smiled.

"Damn straight," he said. "Starlight is keeping Sloe and Welp busy, so Willie is handling the end of season business for both Wheely Good Bikes and Sloe's Toy Attic. My niece griped about that, bless her mercenary heart, but I reminded her that it was her decision to personally run the gift shop at Starlight and get everything up and running for it. She'll get a chance to fleece more Tips than you can shake a stuffed pink lion at."

Lila laughed again and Egan joined in. But then he turned serious, and she knew before he spoke what he was going to bring up.

"You have to go?"

She didn't answer immediately. She looked over at Frank, who had completed the dickering with the man about the keyboard. Successfully, apparently, as the customer now had the keyboard tucked under his arm and was counting out bills into Frank's palm. She turned back to Egan.

She held his eyes and said gently, "Yes."

Egan didn't speak, only looked back, and she felt a pang, wishing things were different. But she wanted, needed, answers, and those answers were in Maine. She hoped, at least.

She reached out and took his hand.

"Egan, I have to try to find out about, well, me. And my mother. And maybe even why Mama Elise was killed. Or at least a path toward finding out why."

He nodded, looking disappointed but understanding.

"Lila, I..." Egan trailed off, blushing.

She felt a twisting warmth in her stomach and chastised herself. She knew how he felt about her, even if he hadn't said it outright, and she had similar feelings, but she had so much on her plate. It didn't seem fair to either of them. Besides, she hadn't even kissed him. For all she knew...

"Lila, I had an idea. Might be crazy, but..."

"Crazier than building an amusement park?" She smiled to show she was only teasing, but he blushed again anyway, and she realized how uncomfortable it was for him to share whatever the idea was. Squeezing his hand she said, "I'm sorry, please, go ahead. What's your idea?"

"I, well, I thought that, assuming Starlight turns a profit, and I'm sure it will, we could take a percentage and donate it to that Pine Ridge emergency fund Wichapi mentioned. On an ongoing basis."

Her eyes widened in shock as he continued.

"From everything you've said, it seems like even a little extra could make a real difference, and I think it will be more than a *little* extra." He looked at her, waiting and looking worried that maybe he had overstepped.

She grabbed the lapel of his sports jacket, pulled his head down, and drew his lips to hers.

They broke apart sometime later but stood close, arms around each other. Around Egan's side, she saw Frank studiously polishing a trumpet. He started clearing his table, putting his musical wares in the back of his truck, keeping his eyes trained anywhere except toward them. She stifled a laugh and pulled back.

Egan looked as dazed as she felt, and she giggled as she stroked his cheek.

"Thank you, Egan. It means a lot. More than a lot. And even though I have to go, I will be back. Besides, I told you I'm staying for the Closer, so we have another few days before I leave."

He smiled. "I'll take it." It was his turn to pull her to him.

Frank, who apparently had been waiting until he was certain she and Egan were not going to start another make-out session, walked over.

"Welp asked if we could meet him and Sloe over at Starlight when we finished up." His mustache quirked up. "You two done?"

Egan stepped back, and brushed his sport jacket officiously, causing her to have to stifle another laugh, and said, "Of course."

As they walked toward the hedge opening leading to the in-progress amusement park, Egan asked, "Marina around?"

Frank shook his head. "She got called in to cover a shift at the hospital. She should be back anytime, though. I left her a message to meet us over there."

As they approached the hedge, Lila noticed most of the rest of the Stallers were closing up shop as well, and she nodded to the various vendors she now knew, at least by sight.

They passed through the gap between the Market and adjoining field, the hedge now augmented by an under construction wooden twelve-foot paneled wall that would ultimately separate the market and amusement park. As Lila scanned ahead, she saw men and women wearing construction vests and helmets scattered across the site, working on the final stages of Starlight's construction.

Although Lila visited the site almost every day, she still shook her head at the progress every time.

Which is all Sloe, she thought.

In her role as Chief Financial Officer and de facto business manager, along with being the Starlight project manager, Sloe seemed to be channeling a combination of her mother's negotiating skills and a Marine drill sergeant. Gods help the crew chief that told her that something would cost more than the original estimate or that they wouldn't hit a deadline.

Frank told Egan Sloe should be at the trailer that acted as Starlight project headquarters. Egan nodded and split off from them as they continued toward the performance area where Frank said they would find Welp.

They turned left toward the rear of the site, passing the frame of what Lila knew would be the gift shop, made a detour around the BMX track which, at the moment, was simply a marked off dirt area, and finally arrived at the stage area.

Frank whistled.

Lila ascended the small staircase and took it all in. She had seen it in its early stages, but now that it was almost complete, she was doubly impressed. The stage itself was fifty feet across and thirty feet deep at the center, with the rear portion backstopped by a horseshoe shaped wall, some sections still only the support braces, wider at the ends than the center. The wall would extend around to the sides of the platform when completed and would also curve up and over a large portion of the stage. Along with the partial ceiling, the wall and roof would be laminated onto a thick plaster backing which, according to Frank, would provide acoustics comparable to a large concert hall.

She would take his word for it. Her experience was limited to playing in bars where, more often than not, equipment and musicians were wedged into a corner of the room. She had considered herself lucky if she could even hear herself on the monitors over the sound of the patrons and televisions blaring sports and news.

Welp, who had just emerged from behind the stage, climbed up and headed toward them.

"Welp, that looks phenomenal," Frank said, taking everything in as he turned in a slow circle at the front of the stage. "If the acoustics work the way they're supposed to, it's going to be the best damn venue north of Boston."

"It all better work properly or else the supplier is going to have to deal with the wrath of Sloe," came Welp's reply.

Frank chuckled agreement, and they began discussing the details around the integrated sound and power systems. As Lila wandered back and forth across the stage, she tried to follow the technobabble, but was quickly lost.

She stepped to the edge and jumped to the ground, once again mentally thanking Mike DeTony for his ministrations. Her leg was as good as ever, with not even a twinge.

She looked back to the stage where Frank and Welp were still deep in the arcana of amplification.

"Unless we want to run the risk of blowing a breaker during a set, I think the MGPs need to be rerouted to their own dedicated circuit."

Welp was nodding as Frank's fingers traced a schematic taped to the side of the tall green box mounted on a pole at the edge of the stage. He looked up at Lila, who stared blankly back at him before nodding agreement with whatever it was he was saying.

As one of Starlight's owners and a musician, Lila appreciated Frank and Welp wanting to include her in the discussion, but she was three states outside her comfort zone.

"Guys, I'm going to go check in on Egan and Sloe." Lila said.

Frank nodded absently, and Welp said they would meet her over there shortly and went back to the conversation with Frank using words Lila was half convinced were made up.

She doubled back to the opposite side of the stage and headed toward the front of Starlight. The markers that had been so prevalent a few days ago, showing where various rides would reside, had been mostly replaced with the actual rides themselves, although most were not fully assembled. Up ahead, she could see the trailer with HQ spray painted on the side, nestled near metal scaffolding that reached fifty feet or more into the sky.

As she reached for the trailer door handle, she could hear voices inside.

As she stepped inside, Marina looked over at her from her perch on a desk against the far wall. Sloe turned from looking at a laptop screen, Egan standing next to her. All three turned when she entered and gave her a nod in greeting. Apparently, she had walked in the middle of a conversation as Egan looked back down at Sloe and put his hand on her shoulder.

"It wasn't a criticism, Sloe. You've done better than anyone else could have, including your mother. It's just that every tiny thing seems to cost twice what we expected."

Sloe patted his hand and smiled up at him. "Thanks, Uncle Egan. Sorry if I sounded defensive. It's just so many balls to juggle. It's been making me a bit emotional lately."

Marina looked at Sloe for a moment, but didn't say anything. She slid to the floor from the desk and smiled at Lila.

"Hey you. How does the stage setup look to you?"

Lila noticed the trailer was extremely warm, Sloe's space heater toasting the interior to that of a greenhouse. She quickly discarded Frank's loaned oversized barn jacket onto an empty chair and gave Marina a quick hug.

"Amazing!" She didn't mention essentially running away to escape the technical conversation.

There must have been something in her expression because Marina chuckled and said, "They started talking sound system Klingon, didn't they?"

Lila giggled as Marina gave a sigh and shook her head. "Boys."

As if on cue, the trailer door opened, and Frank and Welp came in.

"Welp, I'm telling you, another five degrees on that back ceiling angle and—"

"Gentlemen!" Marina cut them off.

They looked around at the group.

Frank stepped over and put his arm around Marina as Welp walked to Sloe, smiling.

He said, "Sorry, honey. We were just discussing—."

Sloe said, "All I care about is that things are working to spec. We can make refinements after opening." She looked at her husband and Frank, daring them to tell her there was a problem.

Welp immediately said everything was fine and, after a moment, Frank agreed, muttering they had just been discussing changing the sine wave to improve bass acoustics, but Sloe cut him off.

"Excellent," Sloe said. "That acoustic wall was a bitch. I had to get someone in from Boston to do the design." She echoed Welp's earlier comment. "It damn well better live up to its advertising."

Egan said, "I'm sure it will. Your reputation has undoubtedly made its way across all of New England."

Sloe stuck her tongue out at him. "Oh, come on, Uncle Egan. I'm not that bad."

He snorted. "Then tell me why the coaster crew chief guy kept grabbing his crotch after that last status meeting, checking to see if he still had his family jewels?"

Sloe sniffed in reply.

They all chuckled and Lila looked around at them, feeling the now familiar comfort of being with them. But she knew she couldn't put things off any longer, and the warmth was joined by a heaviness in her chest.

"Guys."

They all looked around at her.

"I'm leaving after the Blowout."

The smiles that had lingered after the exchange between Sloe and Egan disappeared.

Lila noticed neither Frank nor Marina appeared surprised, and guessed Egan had at least told them of the possibility prior to her confirming it with him. Sloe and Welp, however, looked shocked and hurt.

"Lila, what–" Welp started, but Sloe put her hand on his arm and shook her head slightly. He paused and looked back at Lila.

"I...understand. But you know you can..."

Lila felt a lump in her throat and wrapped her arms around him in a bear hug

A hamster hug, she thought with a hiccupping laugh, her face buried against his chest.

"I'll be back, Welp." She stepped back, wiping her eyes, and glanced over at Egan, but immediately skipped to Sloe, not daring to look at the park manager.

Sloe gave a sad smile, but nodded. "I understand. And yes, we are here when you get back. There's always a spare room for a Staller. For you."

Damn it!

She couldn't hold the tears back. They flowed freely down her face, but they weren't just for having to leave. They were for Mama Elise, for having been frozen out by Wichapi over the years, for never feeling she belonged...for twenty years of pain. Her hand was trembling as she reached up to wipe her face and she shook her head, trying to grapple with the rush of thoughts and emotions.

Arms enveloped her, and she didn't need to see to know it was Egan. The feel of him, his scent, was enough. She burrowed against him and allowed herself to keep crying for everything she had never had, along with what she was walking away from.

Finally, she pulled back slightly and looked up at him. His smile was as soft and she sniffed and returned it.

As she looked around, everyone's eyes were glassy, even Frank's. There was sadness and understanding on everyone's faces. But even more than that, was another emotion, something she hadn't really believed she would experience again after Mama Elise.

Love.

Chapter Twenty-Three

It was Frank who spoke first.

"Will you be here for the Closer?"

She gave her face one final wipe with her arm. "Yep. I won't call it a final gig since I hope you don't replace my spot in the Stallers while I'm gone, and I'll leave the next morning." She grinned. "You're stuck with me for a couple of more days."

Frank's mustache twitched and the left side of his mouth came up in what she now thought of as a patented Frank half-smile. He said, "No replacement."

She nodded and looked around at her new family.

From next to her, Egan said, "Speaking of the Closer, Frank, I sent out those invites you asked me to. I'll say again, I really don't think it's necessary, though."

"Egan, if you're serious about wanting to have Starlight be a venue for solid music, this is the best chance we have to do unofficial tryouts for what will fit in and draw a good crowd."

"We're having guest performers for the Closer?" Lila asked. She looked at Egan.

Egan sighed. "Yeah, Frank's idea, obviously. I'm not against it, in theory. And it does make sense. It's just that Oddbow and the Closer have always been just Stallers."

"Why Egan, I didn't know you cared," Frank said. "It wouldn't also have anything to do with having to pay them a stipend to perform, would it?"

There were chuckles at Egan's grimace.

"Fine," he said. "I did say it was a good idea, in general. It's just that the budget is stretched already."

"Leave that to me," Sloe replied. "I'm sure we can squeeze it out."

Welp added, "I can hear the stones complaining already about blood loss."

"Funny." She elbowed him gently. "Now, I'm hungry. How about you treat your wife to a nice bratwurst in town?"

Welp shook his head as he led his wife away, muttering he would swear she was pregnant if he didn't know better. They excused themselves and left the trailer.

The comment about eating reminded Lila of something.

"Frank, are you still going to the Bagel Bonanza in Hilford, Maine, later this week?"

He said, "Yep," and before she could ask the question on her mind, he added, "And I'm happy to head that way a day early, if you're up for traveling together."

She nodded, feeling a sense of relief. She was going, regardless, but it would be nice to have the company at least on the way. "Thanks. But since Welp managed to replace the carburetor on my scooter, we can caravan."

She forced herself not to fidget at his return stern look.

"I'm happy to drop you off wherever you need me to and can come back after the bagel festival. If you need more than a week, no problem. I'm good at finding things to keep myself occupied and can do some sightseeing."

Marina slid her arms through Frank's. "*We* don't mind waiting and doing some sightseeing." Frank looked at her for a moment, then his mustache twitched and he nodded.

Lila realized she had been flanked. She had every intention of coming back to the Market as soon as she finished looking into things in Maine, but had not wanted to involve the Stallers in whatever awaited her there. Apparently, that would not be an option. And being honest with herself, she liked the idea of having a nearby backup if things headed sideways.

"Sure," she replied to the couple.

Marina nodded happily, gripping Frank's arm tighter. They all stepped outside the trailer into the day's dimming light and Marina asked, "You two want to join us for dinner? Frank says I'm incapable of cooking for less than a dozen people and I can't deny it, so plenty to go around."

Egan said, "Thanks but I'll take a rain check. A few things I want to go through this evening."

Lila added, "It would go to waste on me since I gorged on McDonald's for a late lunch today."

Frank made a face at her choice of cuisine and he and Marina said their goodbyes.

She looked at him, feeling awkward, and finally said, "Well, see you in the morning, Egan."

"I'll walk you back to the yurt." He held out his arm and after a moment's hesitation, she slid her arm through his. They walked companionably in silence across the now mostly deserted construction site and back into the Park. Aside from an occasional parental shout for tardy kids, the evening was filled with crickets and katydids performing one of the season's last concerts.

"So." Egan said casually.

"Mmm?" she replied, enjoying the relative tranquility.

"The house has six bedrooms."

"I know. Remember, you gave me the grand tour?"

He stopped. "What I mean is that you don't have to keep sleeping in the yurt."

Since their earlier kiss, well, many kisses, she had been expecting something like this, but hadn't consciously decided what she would say when it came up. Now that it had, she was glad her answer came out smoothly and, more importantly, gently.

"Thank you, Egan. Really, it means a lot. I'm just not comfortable with that right now."

"It's the age difference, isn't it?"

Lila blinked at him. She knew he was just a few years younger than Frank, which meant he had to be somewhere in his early forties. She didn't think he looked it, though, unless he was putting on his officious Park Manager face. Which, she was glad, he rarely did these days.

"Um…no. I hadn't given that any thought, honestly." Her mouth quirked teasingly as she then asked, "But out of curiosity since you mentioned it, how old *are* you?"

He cleared his throat uncomfortably. "Old enough. But if that isn't the problem, what is? I'm offering you a place to live, no strings attached. You would have your own room, your own space. We are business partners, aside from, well, whatever it is we are." He cocked his head. "Or is that the problem? Did I screw myself by offering you partial ownership of Starlight?" He seemed to realize how that sounded and added quickly, "Not that it had anything to do with the offer. I really think you will be good for Starlight. And, well...for me." He looked at her earnestly.

He really looks so cute when he thinks he has messed up.

She shook her head, reassuring him. "No, I know. And no, that's not it. Mind you, living under the same roof and being business partners could pose some unique challenges, but that isn't it either. It's just..." She took a deep breath.

"Remember when you were talking about your father having basically pre-defined what you would be doing? It's like that, I think, in a way. I'm not done yet. I'm still figuring out what comes next."

"You said you were coming back after your trip to Maine." Egan said this softly.

"I am. And I'll be staying here for now. Hell, 'for now' might mean years. Or it could mean weeks." She shrugged. "I don't know what I'll find in Maine." She looked at him, hoping he would understand.

He stared into her eyes for a moment, and she wished she had a blanket to wrap around her. She felt he was peeling away layer upon layer of her being.

After a moment, he nodded. "I get it. I think I do, at least. And all good, Lila. You need your own space. That's understandable. Let's leave it at this. We are business partners. And...and friends. Right?" Again, that earnest look, hoping he hadn't screwed things up, and the warmth from their earlier kissing bubbled to the surface.

Oh Egan, what am I going to do with you?

She was tempted to say it, but didn't want to muddy things anymore than they already were. Instead, she simply replied, "Yes, friends," and smiled.

Chapter Twenty-Four

The Closer was the next day and Lila, along with Frank and Marina, were manning a check-in table set up for the arriving musicians. Lila had never been overly superstitious, but seeing Tuck Williams getting out of the old-fashioned station wagon, she reconsidered the whole demon summoning thing.

"Darlin'!" The small man with the oversized cowboy hat called out as he spotted the group at the table and walked directly toward her, arms outstretched.

Instead of responding, Lila looked over at Frank, who had the good grace to look chagrined.

"Frank—" she started, in almost a growl.

"Sorry, Lila," He motioned at a familiar figure getting out of the paneled van next to the station wagon. "Looks like Lark needs help getting unloaded." If it had been anyone else, she thought, Lila would have described Frank's quick movement away as scurrying.

No, forget that. He is scurrying. Damn coward.

She cut herself off as Tucker Williams got close to the table, arms still out to return an unproffered embrace.

"Tucker Williams, I have no inten—"

"Tuck, honey? You left me just sitting here."

A somewhat petulant, lispy woman's voice emanated from the car Tuck had just vacated.

Whether he heard the voice and ignored it or was so intent on reacquainting and re-accosting Lila that he didn't notice it, Tuck was now within a few feet of Lila, arms still out.

Lila cursed under her breath. "Tuck, don't even *think–*"

"Tucker Williams, you get over here right now and help me out of this car!" The petulance was now something closer to a banshee's cry, and Lila felt her right eye twitch at the grating sound.

Cat's claws on a blackboard it might have been, but the call did get the diminutive man's attention. Tucker stopped cold as though he had stepped into quick-drying cement.

He sighed and turned. "Coming, sweetie pie." There was a slight slump to his walk as he walked back to the car.

For a moment Lila almost felt pity for him. She was reminded of a stray dog she had known as a young girl. It had been the happiest mutt she had ever met, bopping between households, getting a bit of love here, a snack there. A neighbor had decided the dog needed a permanent home, put a collar on it and only allowed it out on a leash for nice, controlled walks around the block.

She watched as he opened the car door, and a dainty hand stretched out from the interior. Tuck grasped the tips of the fingers, and a bare leg appeared below the bottom edge of the door. It was a shapely leg, Lila thought. She wondered about the rest of the package, but didn't have to wait long.

The owner of the leg was attractive enough. Her tiny waist tapered down and out to what Mama Elise had always referred to as "breeder hips." Slightly more politically correct, the woman had what used to be called an hour-glass figure.

Perfectly coifed, her dress gave the impression she was on her way to a cocktail party, complete with heels tall and sharp enough, Lila thought, that they could double as railroad spikes.

"Thank you, Tucker," the woman said primly as she stepped out of the car, looking around as though gauging reactions to her entrance. Seeing most of the men were gaping and more than a few of the women, she seemed satisfied.

"Now who is this that you were so intent on saying hello to you that forgot all about Kirssy?" Her eyes narrowed as she took in Lila, scanning her from top to bottom.

"This is Lila Fortin." Lila was impressed he had finally gotten her last name right. Tuck turned from Kirssy to her. "Lila, this is Kirssy Flowse. My, ah, girlfriend."

The woman playfully batted Tucker's chest. "Now, Tucker, you should introduce me properly." She held out an exquisitely manicured hand, holding it out palm down as she had to Tuck from the car. "I am Tucker's fiancée."

Lila tried to shut down her face but was certain her surprise was evident. She quickly gathered herself and held her hand out. The other woman looked at it for a moment before touching her fingertips to Lila's, then quickly withdrew her hand.

Lila said, "Well, that's wonderful! Congratulations!" Tuck almost winced, and she gave him a big grin. With almost anyone else, she would have felt obliged to give him a hug, but there wasn't any way in hell that was happening.

"Yes, well. Thank you, Lila," was the subdued reply. "Yes, I am one lucky man."

"I'm going to be managing Tucker's career as well." His fiancée reached over and grasped the man's forearm, yanking him to her side.

"How wonderful! I'm sure he will be the most famous metal-grass musician in the country before you can say mandolin."

"Oh no, honey. None of that trash." Lila noticed Tuck was leaning away from his fiancée and the woman's nails dug into the sleeve of his shirt. "No, Tucker will be putting his talents to much better use."

"Oh. I see. Um… exactly what genre will you be focusing on, Tuck?" Lila tried to give the forlorn man an opportunity to speak for himself, but his manager-cum-wife-to-be was not to be deterred.

"Pop!" She was obviously very excited. "It's what sells. Something with catchy lyrics and a beat you can dance to at a club."

Lila thought back to Tuck's original song, Blood on the Banjo, and once again had a twinge of pity. Tuck was a creep, but he was a damn fine musician and passionate about his chosen area. Which was about as far from teenybopper tunes as you could get.

"Well, that should be interesting," she said deadpan, and looked at Tuck again. "I'm sure you'll be successful no matter what you do." He nodded numbly as his new keeper led him back to the car to get his gear.

"Wow," she murmured as she watched Tuck being given detailed instructions on unpacking his car by his fiancée-manager. She turned and saw Frank walking next to Lark and carrying a long, slender canvas bag. She glared in his direction and started toward him at a brisk pace. He saw her headed his way and tried to increase his speed, but was hobbled by the big bag. She quickly caught up to the two men.

"Lark, great to see you. Glad you could make it." And she was. She hadn't gotten a chance to see Lark perform at the Duck Tape Festival and was looking forward to seeing him and his jazz group, Bassjamm, at the Closer.

"Lila! Great to see you, too. I was surprised to get the invite. I understand the Market end of season party has always been a private affair. Good timing for a lot of us, though. After Labor Day, gigs tend to die down for a bit until fall settles in." He looked over at Frank, who had set down the tent, for that was what Lila now saw the canvas bag contained. Frank then started examining the drawstrings on the canvas bag.

"Frank."

He fiddled with the strings some more.

"Frank, it's all good." Lila had decided to let him off the hook. That wasn't her first reaction upon seeing Tucker, but after her chat with him and his wife-to-be, she didn't have the heart to be mad at either Frank or the neutered banjo player.

Frank looked up, his mustache twitching. "Yeah?"

She sighed. "Yeah, really. Tuck is a hell of a musician. I understand why you would want to have him play, putting aside his nineteen fifties, or maybe eighteen fifties, attitudes about women. But...what the hell is the deal with Krissy?"

"Kirssy," Frank corrected her.

"I thought I must have misheard, or that Tuck was stammering."

Frank was still looking at her slightly warily, but apparently decided she was sincere in her forgiveness. One side of his lip curled up as he told her, "Apparently, when she was born, the nurse recording her name was dyslexic, and her mother had her own reading challenges. By the time it was noticed, her mother decided it was a sign her daughter had a unique destiny, so she kept it."

Lila shook her head. "Well, she certainly is unique. But Frank, she said she is going to be his manager, as well as his wife. And no more metal-grass, strictly pop. You know I don't like the guy, as an understatement, but–"

Frank held his hand up to stop her. "I know. Lark called me a few weeks ago. That's the other reason for inviting him. He's an amazing musician and artist. I have something in mind that might help extricate him." He paused. "And I could use your help...if you're open to it." He looked at her.

Lila didn't answer right away. It would be a shame for a talent like Tuck's to be wasted on Brittanygoop but...

"Lila, do you really want to see Tuck spend the rest of his days backing up Kirssy doing Bangles covers?"

"Wait, what? She *sings*?"

Lark joined the conversation. "Some would call it that. She used to pester me to let her do a number at some of the local festivals back home. I let her do it, twice, thinking maybe the initial catastrophe was simply stage fright." He shook his head. "Never again."

That decided her. Whatever her feelings about the banjo player, Frank was right. Tuck was, at the bottom of his misogynist soul, a true artist. It might not be the same as being a Staller, but it did mean something.

"Fine," she said, with some resignation. "I'll help if I can."

"Excellent," Frank replied. He picked up the tent again, and she followed along as he and Lark started toward the designated musician camping area. "Now here's what I'm thinking...."

***

The Closer was shaping up to be the biggest ever held at the Market. Every square inch of dirt and scraggly grass was covered by an eclectic assortment of temporary living quarters, hauled from umpteen regions around the country. Lila had seen Tuck and the ever-present Kirssy a couple of times in passing since they arrived yesterday, and each time that stray dog's face superimposed itself over Tuck's in her mind. As she looked around the field, she saw the expected campers and travel trailers, along with tents of various sizes and configurations. No yurts, she thought, but Frank did seem to have a lock on that market. He really...

Wait.

Over toward the back corner, where the hedge ran up against the new wall separating this part of the field from Starlight, there were poles poking up above the surrounding tin cans. She started walking toward them, squinting.

Probably just some new-age musicians. Back to the Earth and all that. Doesn't mean anything.

As she got closer, she could see fabric wrapping around the upright poles and then an opening in the structure's side, a flap tied back allowing a dim view of the inside.

Son of a bitch.

There was a man sitting in a camp chair a few feet off to the side of the teepee opening. A small fire crackled in front of him, and he was sipping from a mug. He looked up at her approach.

"Hello, Lowanwee."

"Tokalu, when the hell did you get here? And what exactly are you doing here at all?"

"Before sunrise," came the response, no indication given that his presence was out of the ordinary. "And we are here to take part in your Market Closing ceremony. When your Egan Lothe contacted Wichapi, she thought it a good idea as the first step in establishing our alliance."

As was often the case when she dealt with Wichapi, Lila felt like things were tilted five degrees of center. It wasn't a feeling she enjoyed.

"What are you talking about?"

"The Oglala-Staller alliance."

"*What* alliance?" He was talking in circles.

Tokalu shook his head as he stood and stepped to a small table text to the teepee, retrieving an empty mug. He walked to the silver percolator sitting on a flat rock at the edge of the fire and filled the cup, holding it out to her.

She took it.

"Well?"

"You have offered to continue funding the MAAS. I also have no doubt there will be additional connections formed between the Stallers and Pine Ridge, nor does Wichapi.

"Yes." She already had other ideas she had yet to share with Egan or any of the others.

He nodded. "I will admit, I was surprised."

She felt a burning inside. "Why? Because I never knew I was Lakota? Pine Ridge is all I knew. God knows it isn't a place anyone would pick to grow up, but it was my *home*." More softly. "Along with Mama Elise."

He nodded again. "I understand. And while it was unfortunate Wichapi found it necessary to keep your history from you, I will admit I am glad you now know. It is important for anyone to understand where they come from." He seemed to look past her as he spoke, the lines in his face conveying a wistfulness she hadn't ever seen before.

She wondered if there was more to the comment, but this wasn't the time.

"Tokalu, you still haven't explained what you meant by an alliance."

He looked back at her and his face cleared. "You are Lakota, and always will be. But you also have a new family. A new tribe. Wichapi wants to ensure the relationship between the Stallers and Oglala is not one-sided." A hard smile accompanied his next comment. "We have far too much experience with relying on the largesse of others."

"Yeah, that I get. But how does your being here for the Closer even things up?"

"I'm also here as the Council representative to discuss a business deal."

Lila knew 'Council representative' actually meant Wichapi's representative. The old woman ensured her voice was always the controlling one on the Tribal Council.

"What kind of business deal?" She couldn't picture any sort of reciprocal arrangement between Pine Ridge and the Market. Then she felt a coldness in her stomach.

"Wait. There isn't a chance in hell Egan, or Frank for that matter, would agree to go into the feather business. I'll make sure of that, if it comes to it."

Tokalu gave a genuine smile. She hadn't thought he had it in him.

"I have no doubt you would, Lowanwee. Wichapi says you are a strong voice on the Staller Council."

She frowned. "There is no Staller Council."

"As you say," he demurred. "But no, the decision has been made to halt the feather business, as you call it. The business arrangement I mentioned involves the Pine Ridge Market."

"Last I knew, there wasn't a Pine Ridge Market."

"There will be. The whites have long appropriated our culture. We've learned from their lesson, and your Egan Lothe has given us some ideas on how to further our reach, including here at your Market. He has indicated he is going to dedicate a section to sell authentic Lakota items as well as a storefront in Bridgett, with the profits split between the Market and Pine Ridge."

"That's...great?" Lila finally said. She wasn't sure, actually, but on the surface, it did seem to be a win-win for everyone.

"Quite," Tokalu responded.

The back of Lila's brain continued to process the new information as her frontal lobe said, "So, you will be performing at the Closer tonight?"

Shaking his head, Tokalu said, "I am here specifically to discuss the business arrangement with Egan. Matoskah, Wahkan, and Mina have accompanied me to perform at the ceremony."

Lila knew Matosckah and Mina in passing, being a few years younger than them. Wahkan had been in her class through graduation. Even in high school, he had spoken of his plans to become a Council member. He had also been one of the central performers at Pine Ridge celebrations and ceremonies for a few years.

"I'm sure they will do great," not knowing what else to say.

As she sipped the dark coffee, Tokalu seemed content with what he had shared and didn't seem inclined to further the conversation.

She made one last attempt at drawing him out, knowing there were always wheels within wheels when it came to Wichapi's plans and machinations. "Well, please give Wichapi my regards when you return. I'm looking forward to seeing the performance tonight."

The Council member nodded. "As am I," and looked past her at the various performers setting up and organizing their campsites.

She knew she had been dismissed and put down her mug. With a curt nod, she turned and left.

She worked her way through and around the campsites, nodding to those she had seen at the Duck Tape festival, heading for the stage. Most performers had arrived the previous day or evening, but a few latecomers were still trickling in, filling the few remaining empty spots scattered around the field.

Despite Welp's desperate efforts to wire the Starlight stage for the Closer, there were still too many loose ends to be ironed out, so they had opted to hold the show on the rough Market stage. It suited Lila just fine, since that's where things had really started for her. She noticed that a set of metal stairs on wheels had been added center-stage for tonight's performance, which would have come in handy when she first arrived and could barely walk.

Such a long time and a short time ago.

Lila grinned as she saw the doilies fluttering in the evening breeze.

Egan, Frank, and Marina were over at one end of the stage.

Marina was asking Egan, "Any chance my keyboard can be positioned at an angle, stage right? It's how things will be set up at Starlight and I figure it would be good to get used to the new set up relative to the rest of the band and monitors."

"Not a problem," Egan responded. "When Welp had the power feed to Starlight run, he had things upgraded for the Park and Market at the same time. At this point, we could probably power all of Bridgett."

"Almost ready?" Lila asked, stopping between Marina and Egan.

"Yes, I think we are about set," Egan said. "Hopefully, nothing blows up."

"Just lay in a supply of fire extinguishers," Lila said.

"Already did," Egan said, no irony in his response. Then, "Lila, I forgot to mention—"

"That you invited Tokalu and a cadre of Pine Ridge performers for tonight?"

He had the decency to look embarrassed. "Um, yeah. I meant to, but things have been so crazy this last week. I take it you ran into them?""Oh, yes." She tried to keep her voice casual. "I just had a conversation with Tokalu about a 'business deal' he said you and Wichapi have been discussing." She raised an eyebrow.

More embarrassment. "Oh, that. Yes, I think there is money to be made for all involved. Native American crafts have a lot of value in today's market. God bless white guilt, along with the craftsmanship of what your folks at Pine Ridge make."

"But no feathers or anything related." It was a cool, flat statement.

He shook his head vigorously. "Artwork and various pottery. To start at least..." He hesitated. "But you know how much–"

"Egan!"

He held up his hand and finished his statement. "How much money there is in those types of items? I'm not suggesting re-starting that business your family had. But there are legitimate sources for eagle feathers and souvenirs from them."

She took a deep breath before responding. Egan was just being Egan. He had said it himself. He was what he was.

As she was what, and who, she was. "No eagle related stuff."

"Fine," he replied after a moment of trading stares with her. She knew there would be future conversations about the topic.

Thankfully, Marina chimed in. "No worries, Lila. I think Egan likes his body parts right where they are."

That produced a laugh from all of them, Lila included.

Frank pulled out his pocket watch. "A couple of hours until the festivities start. We should probably take a bit of a break before set up."

"Sounds good to me," Marina said.

Frank took her hand and Lila watched them walk toward the Park, glad that Frank had finally figured things out for himself and that the two were together.

Egan looked at Lila. "You good? I really did plan on telling you about Tokalu and the Lakota Nation store."

Lila nodded. "And I like the name," she replied. "Where is the store going to be?""There's a vacant space next to Bridgett Tobacco."

"You think you can cut a good deal for it?"He smirked. "I assume so, since I own the plaza."

She looked at him for a moment, unsure how to respond, so didn't. Instead, she said, "Well, think I'm going to head to Marina's and kick back for a bit." She turned to go.

"Lila."

She turned back. "Yes?"

"Something I want to show you, if you can spare a few minutes."

Hmm.

She raised an eyebrow but said, "Sure."

He waved toward the Park, past the edge of the Market, and they headed that way.

Neither felt the need for forced pleasantries, having spent so much time together of late and they entered the Park area in companionable silence. Egan pulled ahead of her, walking the path toward Frank's place. Lila wondered what he could want to show her there, considering she had spent most of her nights over the last few months in the yurt just outside it. As they came up to the trailer, though, he continued past.

"Well?" he asked.

He had stopped in front of the vacant trailer two down from Frank's. It looked no different from many of the others across the Park. Cream colored with two stripes running around it, an apparent attempt at spiffying up its appearance. The small yard circling the trailer was tidy, a small fall-barren flower patch adding a bit of potential color in season. There was a stone path leading toward a small deck outside the door.

"Well, it's certainly a nice trailer," came Lila's response, not knowing what else to say.

"It's yours," Egan said.

"What?" Lila really wished people would stop saying nonsensical things to her and expecting reasonable responses.

"It's yours," he repeated. "I said I understood you needing your own space. And, well, you're a partner. The least Starlight can do is make sure you have a few rooms and a bath."

"Egan," she said slowly, "I'm leaving, remember? And I told you—"

"Wait. Please. You said you didn't want a room at the house. I understand that. But this is different." He repeated, almost defiantly. "You're a partner. And...well, I thought if you have a place of your own, it, ah, might make it more likely that you would stay around when you come back." He gave one of those panicked looks he did when he thought he had put his foot in his mouth, and quickly added, "Not that you have to stay, obviously. It's yours, whether or not you're here. I mean—"

"Egan." Lila sighed, interrupting him, but not knowing quite what to say. Part of her felt she was being manipulated, but the look on his face was so sincere she couldn't be angry.

Then she noticed an image painted on the trailer siding.

"A sacred hoop?" She walked to it and ran her hand over the circle, intersected by lines crossing in the middle.

"I read it was called a medicine wheel. I thought it might make you feel more at home." He looked at her hesitatingly.

She felt a lump in her throat. "My people call it both. It's used by many plains tribes to represent life and death and how we all have a path between both." She reached out and touched the fluffy object attached to the center of the intersecting lines. "Is this–"

He was quick to reassure her. "Tokalu brought it, per my request. It's genuine, Lila. He swears it's from a real eagle."

Her vision was getting blurry.

"This is...it's very sweet, Egan." She looked at him. "I'm still not sure–"

He shook his head and gripped her hand. In almost a whisper he said, "Look, I said I understand why you won't take a room at the house, but really, the trailer would be a lot more comfortable than Frank's yurt. And it's just sitting here at the moment, since the previous tenant moved out." Then he added quickly, "I didn't kick anyone out. It was that short-timer, Fred Wilkins." She nodded, having met him in passing. "He left last week. The Park makes enough that the rent won't make any sort of difference. It can sit vacant as long as you need to decide what you want to do." He paused and let her hand go. "I just want to..." he trailed off, looking down at the gravel.

She stepped close to him, her hand coming out, just touching his.

"Thank you, Egan. I accept. But I expect a monthly bill."

He looked up. She continued to hold his gaze, waiting for him to take the lead.

He did. Their lips met and his arms came up around her.

He was warm, which matched the growing heat within her. His hand slipped up her back to her head and he ran his fingers into her short dark bob, tugging her hair gently.

"Mrph," she murmured as their kiss continued. She pulled back slightly and gave him a small smile.

"Maybe we should go into my new trailer so you can show me around."

Egan blinked owlishly.

"Um...okay. Yes, of course," he said, clearing his throat. He turned his head to face the trailer. "Well, the kitchen is—"

She grinned and put her hand on his cheek, turning his face back toward hers.

"I was thinking more of checking out the bedroom," she said.

Chapter Twenty-Five

Lila was sure she would be smiling all night after the 'tour' of her new trailer, but didn't care if anyone noticed. Egan had taken great pains afterwards, as they lay together on the former owner's left behind futon, that he had no expectations, was simply happy, ecstatic actually, that she had seen fit to share with him...

She had found it necessary to kiss him, deeply, to shut him up. But she did truly appreciate his words and the honesty behind them. She planned on coming back to the Park and Market after Maine, but what might follow that, she still didn't know.

The current performance was by a reggae group, Island Salt and Pepper, fronted by a guy with a heavy Bahamian accent but backed by a woman and man as white as Lila had thought herself to be until Wichapi's visit. Lila nodded along with the music, but most of her was wondering when the 'Save Tuck' part of tonight's program would start.

"Excuse me, Miss."

It's time.

She turned to see Mike DeTony in a three-piece suit, looking at her as though she were a stranger.

Out of the corner of her eye, she saw Tuck, Kirssy gripping his arm possessively, standing within hearing distance of her and Mike.

"Uh, yes? Can I help you?" She responded in the same polite, formal manner as Mike had, giving no sign she knew him.

He held out his hand. "The name is Lowell Gantry. I'm a booking agent for the Alt Rock bar chain. I'm sure you've heard of us."

"Alt Rock? Of *course* I've heard of you. You are *huge* out west. What are you doing here?" She raised her voice as she spoke and put as much fan-girl enthusiasm into her words as she could manage.

Mike continued, raising his volume as well. He spoke officiously, and she suspected he was doing his best to channel Egan at his most prickish. "I'm a managing partner for the company and our primary talent recruiter. We're expanding our footprint and looking to sign new, upcoming acts. I'm trying to locate Tucker Williams. He and his band performed just a little while ago."

That he had, but not without a blow-up prior to him taking the stage.

An argument had taken place between Frank and Kirssy as Tuck remained silent and simply looked on. Frank had informed Kirssy that Tuck had been hired to perform metal-grass, the music he was known for. Kirssy had countered that Tuck was moving into a new, and more lucrative, area of performing and that was what he would be playing. She had only shut up when Frank told her either Tuck performed his standard repertoire or the offer of the stipend would be rescinded and she and Tuck could head back to Ohio that night.

Tuck's performance had been mesmerizing from his band's first number, a new song called Still of the Night, through to the last, his signature Blood on the Banjo. The Staller crowd had gone wild with cheers and applause as Kirssy looked on, disgust on her face.

Lila had angled herself during Mike's spiel so she could see Tuck and Kirssy. She wasn't sure Tuck was listening as he was still working to replenish himself from a large jug of water, but from the gleam in Kirssy's eyes, she was sure the would-be pop singer had heard every word.

Kirssy smoothed her low-cut flowered dress, fluffed her curls, and approached them.

"Excuse me."

Mike raised one eyebrow. "Yes, can I help you?"

"I'm Tucker Williams' manager. And fiancée. Is there something I can help you with?"Mike's smile had so much charm oozing from it, even Lila felt it. He reached into his jacket and whipped out a business card. "Excellent. Yes, Lowell Gantry, booking agent for Alt Rock."

Kirssy reached out and plucked the card between her long nails, waving it coquettishly. "Yes, so I heard. I'm not familiar with your establishment, Mr. Gantry."

He gave her a toothsome smile. "You will be. We are currently more of a regional presence in the western states, but we recently took on a private equity firm as an investor. With the millions they have poured into Alt Rock, we expect to be nationwide in the next twelve months.""I see," Kirssy said, the gleam in her eyes brightening. "And as part of this expansion, I assume you are looking for quality musicians to perform?"

If Mike's smile got any bigger, Lila thought, his face was going to split wide open.

"Exactly, Miss, ah?"

"Flowse."

"Miss Flowse. Yes, I am. And I believe Mr. Williams is exactly the caliber of performer that would do well working with us." He added, "*Quite* well."

"That sounds very interesting, Mr. Gantry. As it happens, my Tucker is looking to expand his own impact beyond his Ohio roots. Tucker!" She called over her shoulder, sweetly. The performer, oblivious to the conversation regarding his future that was taking place, continued intermittently chugging water and wiping his face with a towel.

When he didn't immediately respond, her sugary sweet tone switched to one more reminiscent of metal scraping across a rock. "*Tucker!*"

Tuck's flinch almost caused his ten-gallon hat to fall off his head. He adjusted it as he responded.

"Yes, honeypot?"

"Get over here. This man wants to hire us."

Mike raised an eyebrow. "Us, Miss Flowse?" he said as Tuck scampered over.

Kirssy fluffed her hair again. "Yes, of course. I am lead singer for Tucker's new group. Tonight was a favor for an old friend, doing some old grassy metal songs. Going forward, Tucker will focus exclusively on a more relevant and current sound. Pop with perhaps some new-age if we can find an appropriate pan-flute player."

Lila choked for a moment, apologizing for a bug having flown into her mouth.

Mike, however, never broke character. "That is a shame, Miss Flowse." He shook his head sadly. "Yes, quite a shame. Our focus, and frankly that of most successful and forward-looking establishments, is the future, not the present or past." Firmly, "And that means cutting-edge music and artists. Like metal-grass."

Kirssy looked like she had just bitten into a lemon.

"I see," she finally said. "Well. That is interesting."

Tuck finally spoke, bursting in excitedly. "See, honeypot, I tried to tell you."

Her stony stare squelched any further comment from him. She returned her attention to the putative agent. "I'm sorry, Mister Gantry. You see, my forte is in vocalizing and speaking to the angst and emotions of the future generations of women. Not," more lemon biting, "the degenerate wailings Tucker has been forced to slum with in the past."

It had taken a lot, but Lila watched as Tuck was finally pushed over the edge. Aside from his ham-handed attempts at seduction, music, *his* music, was the one thing Tuck truly cared about. He pulled himself up straight. "Degenerate wailings?" His voice rose. "Degenerate wailings? You told me I was the finest musician you had ever heard."

Kirssy sloughed off her fiancé's change in demeanor, misreading how big a mistake she had made. "Of course you are, Tucker. And you've been wasting your time with that drivel you've been performing. When I take over—"

"That's what it's all about, isn't it, Kirssy? You. You couldn't get anyone to let you perform, so you figured you'd use your womanly wiles on me to become a star. Isn't that right?"

His tone finally cut through her condescension. She looked at him in shock. Her sticky-sweet smile quickly reappeared as she stroked his arm.

"Tucker, honey, calm down." The tone was one an adult might use with a tantrum throwing three-year-old.

"Calm down, my country ass! It isn't about me. It's about you wanting to be some sort of pop diva! Well, screw that!" His hat hit the ground in front of him as he whipped it off and slammed it down.

A spark of panic was in Kirssy's eyes as she realized the depth of her miscalculation. "Now, Tuck, sweetie, I–"

He shook his head violently. "No, that's it. I was willing to try something different to make you happy. But you're pissing down on everything I've worked on, worked for, all these years. And the only thing you give a shit about is getting your overdone face on some commercial for Maybelline."

That seemed to hit the woman where she lived. Her cheeks turned bright red, and Lila could tell she was about to lay into him.

"Excuse me." Mike-Lowell interjected, projecting slight boredom with the ongoing back and forth.

The two men looked at him, apparently having forgotten he was there.

"You obviously have some things to work out." He pulled out another business card and held it out to Tuck. "Mr. Williams, if you wish to get in touch, you have my information.

Tuck took the card and nodded. "I will, thanks." Turning back to his erstwhile fiancée and manager, he said. "Feel free to take my car. I'll find my own way back to Ohio. See you around."

Kirssy looked like she had been slapped. She pulled back, staring for a moment at him, then patted her hair, turned, and walked down the stage stairs, disappearing down a narrow aisle between the rows of chairs, her dress swirling around her.

As Mike turned to leave, Lila caught the slightest hint of a wink from him.

She and Tuck were alone now.

He was looking down at the card in his hand.

"Tuck, I'm sorry." And she was.

When he looked up at her, she saw something she had yet to see on his face. Embarrassment.

"Thanks." He shook his head. "You know, I should have known better. A classy woman like that, tying into me."

Lila decided to not ponder his definition of classy and said, "You know, you are damn good. What you've done to meld two such different types of music, it's amazing. You should be proud." She added, "Even if the thing with the Alt Rock clubs doesn't work out, you shouldn't give it up."

She just hoped he would forgive Frank when he discovered the ruse.

Will he forgive me? And do I care either way?

She had helped because she hated to see anyone, especially someone with his ability, waste his talent and have their dignity stripped. It was a shame he was such a pig.

Maybe this whole thing will open his eyes and teach him something.

He nodded, paused, then, his old smile returning, said, "You know, now that I'm single again…"

Maybe not.

"Not a chance, Tuck." She gave him a hard stare. "Do you really want to spend the rest of the night in the ER?"

He exploded with a horse laugh and took a step back. He picked his hat up where it still lay in front of him, brushed it off, and set it on his head at a slight angle. "Not a chance! Need to make sure future little Tucks have a chance to make their mark." He winked.

Lila shook her head and found herself laughing along with him.

Damn, he's a piece of work. But when he isn't trying to jump me, I could almost like him.

"Well," he said, "guess I better hit Lark up and see if there's room at anyone's inn."

"How do you feel about yurts?" Lila asked.

He raised an eyebrow, and she explained about her former temporary domicile, which she didn't need now that she had her trailer.

And, she thought wryly, if Frank had a problem with her offering it for Tuck's use, he wouldn't dare complain to her, considering he had sprung Tuck's invitation and asked for her help to extricate the metal-grass musician from Kirssy's clutches to begin with.

"Sounds good to me. Reckon I'll go track Frank down." He touched the brim of his hat and dipped his head slightly. "Ma'am."

All she could picture was a rooster having evaded a farmer's ax as she watched him walk away.

Chapter Twenty-Six

Egan had insisted that Frank and the Stallers take honors as the closing act, which was fine with Lila. As they worked their way through the set, a genre -jumping list of songs that she and Marina finding out what they were about to play as Frank announced the titles to the audience, Frank did his usual swap-outs of instruments. He was, she thought, the most versatile and best musician she had ever worked with.

And one of the best friends she had ever had, not that she had had many.

In truth, she thought as she looked around the stage and down into the crowd, every friend she had was within spitting distance at the moment. Marina behind her keyboard, Welp and Sloe in the front row, and Egan being helpfully unhelpful, trying to give Willie guidance at the control board.

Her eyes lingered on Egan as she did minor adjustments to the guitar in her lap. Her plan to take time to decide what to do about him had been jettisoned after seeing the sacred hoop painting.

She gave herself a moment to enjoy the memory of their time in her trailer.

Her trailer.

She still didn't know what the future held. Nor what would happen with Egan long term. But…time enough, after she made the trip with Frank to Maine.

She saw Harvey a few rows back in the audience, arguing good-naturedly with Forrie about who knew what. A few seats over from him was Amanda with the ever-present Velcro in her arms, who seemed to be almost quivering with excitement at all the activity. Over on the other side of the onlookers, she spotted Mike DeTony and his husband Larry, arms around each other, foreheads together, having a murmured conversation.

So many others. And she knew all of them by name and sight, if not personally. Yet.

She looked back at Egan who, apparently feeling her gaze, glanced up from the soundboard. Instead of quickly looking away as he had generally done in the past, he held her eyes and smiled.

She returned it, then saw Frank coming toward her across the stage, carrying the sax she had used in Ohio. It had a red ribbon tied around it. She laughed and stood on her tiptoes to kiss his cheek as he gave a small bow and handed it to her.

She ran up and down a couple of scales to warm up, her eyes wandering across the small sea of people watching them, feeling relaxed and, while not at total peace, closer to it than she remembered feeling before.

Until her eyes lit upon Tokalu, now standing in front of the stage.

What is he doing here? I figured he would be packing up to go back to Pine Ridge.

His gaze was steady, almost expectant.

She glanced over at Frank, who was waiting for her to give him the nod that she was ready. She pointed her chin down at Tokalu. Frank's eyes narrowed as he looked down at him, then he nodded back to her, and told the crowd it would be just another couple of minutes before they did their final number. He made a show of re-tuning his guitar to give Lila time.

Lila set the sax down on her chair and descended the metal stairs. She stood in front of him, hands on her hips.

"Well?" She knew he wasn't here simply to watch Frank and the Stallers perform.

He said, "You are leaving for Maine after the Closer, Lowanwee." It was a statement, not a question.

Her eyes narrowed. "How do you know that?"

He shrugged, not answering the question, but continued.

"As I said earlier, understanding where one comes from is important. It is part of what informs who we are. But sometimes," he paused, and for the first time in her experience, he seemed unsure of how to continue. Then, "Sometimes, delving into the past can also alter our beliefs. About ourselves, and those who helped us get to where we are." His watery eyes held hers as he spoke.

She blinked, and opened her mouth to respond, but he turned and walked away through the crowd, disappearing into the twilight.

She pondered his words...or were they a warning?... and got back on stage. Frank raised his eyebrows at her in question. She swallowed the lump that had formed in her throat and forced a smile, grabbing her sax and turning to face the audience.

Frank walked back to the center mic, did a quick count to four, and launched into the next song.

Lila had thought Dixie Chicken was a Garth Brooks song, but she later learned it was written by a band called Little Feat. It took a couple of bars for her to get her musical bearings, but then she dove in, her full-throated playing matching Frank and Marina's as the stage and field reverberated with the funky back beat.

When it was over, she wiped her face with the hand towel hanging from her mic stand and nodded a smile at Frank and Marina, then down at Egan at the soundboard still standing with Willy. Dusk had faded and stars blanketed the sky, only slightly obscured by intermittent lights from the Park and two small spotlights on each corner of the stage.

As Frank tapped his mic, Lila felt a stab of disappointment, expecting him to let everyone know the concert was over, although she wasn't sure how much more performing she could handle after the last one.

To her surprise, when the crowd finally quieted, it was neither an announcement that the Closer was over, nor to announce the band was doing an encore.

As Frank led Marina and Lila through the last verse and riffs of Dixie Chicken, he found himself looking more often over at Marina than at the audience. He had been doing a lot of thinking of late, the deep kind he had spent so long avoiding. About himself, the past, and, especially, about the future. A future with the keyboardist at his side. At least if he managed to not screw things up.

He didn't know how many festivals and celebrations across most of the lower forty-eight states he had attended over the years, initially performing solo then, reluctantly, joining other musicians that simply wanted the chance to jam with him. In fields, on temporary stages, in parades, some of which he was ultimately asked to lead. All in memory and in honor of a high schooler who would never get the chance to because of a bizarre accident and a stupid mistake.

But it wasn't Frank's mistake.

He had always known that, somewhere inside. But on top of Kenny's death itself, his own arrogance leading up to the accident had weighed heavily on him. And he would carry guilt for the rest of his life for not taking a harder line at preventing the teen and the other kids from going to the quarry.

It *had* been an accident, though. And Frank shouldn't, couldn't, carry the load of other's decisions and actions anymore. Kenny had been so full of life, wanting to experience it to the hilt. What would he have thought of Frank giving up his own for so long in, as Jessie had called it, self-flagellation?

He would probably keep attending festivals, but hopefully it would be the Stallers going or, at least, Marina, if Lila didn't stick around.

As the last note of Dixie Chicken faded, he wiped his face with the bandana from his back pocket; he saw both Marina and Lila wipe their own faces and grinned.

The Stallers can jam, can't we?

It took a minute and a lot of tapping on the mic to get the crowd to lower their volume enough for him to be sure his voice would carry to everyone.

"Attention. Attention, K-Mart shoppers."

The older Stallers chuckled; the younger ones looked around in confusion at the hoary joke.

"Listen up! The Stallers are done, but the party isn't quite over. We're going to do one last number, and I do mean *we*." He waved across the crowd. This time, the confusion spanned all ages in the audience.

"I'd like to invite the performers from tonight to come back up, as well as anyone else that wants to join in." He waved his hands at the immediate protestations. "Doesn't matter, no experience necessary. A song in your heart is more than enough." He pointed to the side of the stage where Willie was laying out instruments collected from Frank's spare room. "Nothing electric, we're going old school acoustic."

There were mutters from the crowd, and the visiting musicians started making their way forward, led by Lark and Tuck. They were followed by more than a dozen Stallers. Some of the returning performers brought their own instruments with them, some, along with the Park Stallers, grabbed one of the spares from the pile as they all lined up in front of the stage.

Frank saw Forrie Laperse with a pair of maracas and smiled; next to him, Marty Florchet had a flute. Harvey Kettles stepped up next to Marty and pulled a harmonica from his breast pocket and Frank grinned. There was a yapping and more movement in the remaining crowd. Willie was guiding Amanda Fleming through the onlookers as she clutched a banjo, Velcro bouncing back and forth in front of her, his barks clearing the path.

Better watch it, Tuck. I'm not sure about Amanda, but if Velcro plays, you might have a run for your money.

Amanda was the last to join the large group in front of the stage. Frank looked around, nodding with satisfaction, and picked up his acoustic guitar and walked down the stairs. He turned and saw Lila and Marina follow, Lila's sax hanging from her neck on a strap, Marina carrying a pair of cymbals. He cocked an eyebrow at her. To his knowledge, she didn't own cymbals, nor did he. She simply winked at him, and he shook his head, chuckling.

He looked around at the surrounding throng and nodded.

"It's been an interesting season, not that they aren't all interesting." A round of laughter. "But this year, new friends, new paths..." He felt a tightness in his throat as he looked over at Lila, then Marina. "Well, hell, turns out Egan has a heart!" He pointed over at Egan, who had opted to watch the final festivities from the sidelines. Laughter morphed into applause and cheers and, although Frank couldn't tell in the dim light, he was certain Egan's cheeks were red. The Park manager bent his head as various Stallers patted his back.

Frank waved to get everyone's attention again.

"All right, folks, all right. We don't want to overwhelm him. He isn't used to it. Now, I know it's dark out, but Egan has taken care of that." He raised his hand and pointed dramatically toward Willie at the control board. A corridor of pole-mounted electric lanterns came on, lighting a path from the back of the crowd out through the Market.

He ran through some chord progressions, not having planned a song in advance. As was often the case, his fingers, connected directly to his psyche, quickly dropped into a groove and he started repeating the opening refrain of the song he now knew they would play.

'Beginnings' by Chicago was not what anyone would peg as a standard marching song, but this wasn't a standard marching band.

He didn't bother to call out the name of the song. The other musicians would either know it or pick up the tune and the Park Stallers would follow along as best they could.

Facing toward the brightly lit corridor, he started a cadenced walk as players flowed into place behind him and onlookers made an open path ahead of him.

The procession followed the lantern walkway, passing empty Market tables through to the Park, and continued toward the open roadside gate. Tiki torches lined each side of the road as far as he could see, heading off into the night.

He realized he was no longer alone at the front of the phalanx. Marina marched along to his left, her cymbals keeping a light beat to the song. To his right, Lila swayed, wailing away on her sax. He wasn't really surprised, but he raised an eyebrow when he saw Egan on the other side of Lila.

Frank leaned forward to get Egan's attention and winked, receiving a scowl in return.

Definitely not a professional bunch, he thought, wincing slightly as a clarinet hit a sour note, but then laughed, along with Marina and Lila, at the loud *whoops* that followed it.

He made a U-Turn back toward the Sun Market and Trailer Park sign now a quarter mile behind them. The rest of the players jostled to follow, and there was more than one curse as they re-formed behind him. He spun around, marching backwards as he looked at the faces of his neighbors, friends, and family.

He tried to come up with an appropriate description of the assemblage and ongoing performance.

Enthusiastic, messy, slightly off-key, more than a little chaotic...

He smiled.

Good enough.

Lila's journey, to Maine and beyond, continues in an upcoming novel.

And stay tuned for **Brotherly Love**, where familiar faces from **Lost and Found** return alongside a cast of new characters as they uncover old secrets and grapple with life, love, and loss.

ABOUT THE AUTHOR

Michael J. Preston was born in Queens, NY, and spent his formative years in upstate New York. Eschewing normalcy from a very early age, he hitchhiked around the U.S. after high school, playing some of the best street corners and worst bars around, and declaring he would never work for 'The Man'.

Starting at nineteen, he spent the next few decades doing the Man's bidding, albeit reluctantly and with a lot of complaints on both sides about his attitude. These days he can be found shouting at his computer screen, chasing small humans and furry critters around, and working on perfecting the family recipe for red sauce.

He is the author of the previously published horror novel, **Rathcrog**, written under the name Neil T. Jacobs.

www.michaeljamespreston.com